Aliens!
(YEAH RIGHT)

Stories by
P.R. HENIKA

Aliens! (Yeah Right)

ISBN: 978-0-9971626-0-8

Printed in the United States of America

Published by:

Big Hat Press
Lafayette, California
www.bighatpress.com

For Basil

If extraterrestrial civilizations exist and have the capability to reach us, their motivation might be to monitor our planet because of concerns raised about human behavior.

- Jean-Jacque Velasco from *France and the UFO Question,* excerpted from *UFOs: Generals, Pilots and Government Officials Go on the Record* by Leslie Kean

TABLE OF CONTENTS

Episode One

· · · · · · · · · · · · · · · · · ·

EYE

· · · · · · · · · · · · · · · · · ·

2012

The old man leaned back in his leather recliner with the lamplight turned low such that he could gaze out of his big picture window at the two other stars that inhabited his night sky.

The old man lived at the Edge of the Observable Universe. He lived forty-five billion light years from Earth but this great distance was not bothersome to him in the least.

He could return to Earth whenever he desired because of the Gray Extraterrestrials who have advertised in the past, the present and the future that they would gladly transport anyone, anywhere in the Observable Universe in six minutes and six seconds (coupons available on-line or on packages of chocolate chip cookies).

The old man was in cherished possession of a time-traveling, Space-faring dog who is currently asleep and warming his feet but no, his dog Basil is not asleep on her bed *per se*. Basil's legs have stiffened and her jaws are moving back and forth as if she is currently the recipient of one of her favored peanut butter biscuits.

The old man knows.

The old man knows that Basil has been trans-located (while tumbling and turning based on mathematics that is way beyond me) through multiple dimensions to some distant World. The old man knows that she is doing her part for Guide Dog kindness, that unconditional kindness for which Labrador retrievers seem so adept.

The old man reached for a slice of floppy and soft Roasted Chicken and Garlic Pizza but it never reached his eager mouth because of the Anomaly, that sudden and surprising change which immediately erased the boredom of having a night sky with only two stars to gaze and ponder upon. Yes, there is that bold line that forms an arch across his night sky, that black line which separates his Universe from the mystery, from the Universe next door, from a Universe with a form and substance of which he could only imagine.

The Anomaly frightened the old man.

It scared him bananas.

The Rip opened slowly much like a hand-carved wound and pouring forth was a flash of radiance so bright that the old man had to raise his arms to block it. The light then receded to a faint flicker within the Rip as though someone had lit a candle and had placed it into the jagged face of a Halloween pumpkin.

The old man with the shaky legs rose from his chair. He left his recliner for his telescope platform. His observatory opened to the night sky and he aimed his rather large telescope at the candle-lit Rip and so did the old man focus with trepidation upon this mystery.

The hackles on the old man's neck rose and so did he nearly pee in his pants as a telescopic black dot began its traverse of the Rip as if it was Mercury making its transit across our Sun. And then did the telescopic black dot turn away from the Rip and set a determined and alarming course for the old man's house!

So the frightened old man did what any Senior citizen would do. He reached into his pocket for his Nighty-Night sleeping pills and he washed them down with a glass of warm milk.

The old man slept deeply in his Chair; his precious Chair; the one with the dirty red cushions and the arms warped on its edges. The Chair was warped with age, as was he. The Chair was his 'ship,' his 'warp drive' and so, on many occasions, did he travel through multiple dimensions whilst meditating deeply in his chair.

At certain destinations, he would leave his body for the experience.

He would pass through a Giant Ring of Cold Fire. He could hear the hiss of the flames as he passed through the Ring but never did the flames burn. As he looked back, he could see the fiery Ring but then he settled onto a black mat with wavy squares *ad infinitum*; wavy black squares with little white lights on the edges.

The mat was a veritable tapestry of dimension.

It went on forever (as I have already implied).

But the tapestry would begin to slowly fade; the little white lights on the edges would dim and the old man would find himself standing on a strange, Alien landscape; sometimes with Basil and sometimes not.

The old man floated out of his body. He floated along the wall as an eerie shadow with an O for a mouth and then he was squeezed outside through an earthquake crack in his ceiling. He did not travel far. He stood on the lawn in his backyard with a tilted nightcap and a flowing white nightgown, which fell down to his shaky knees. He held onto a drippy candle that did not burn. He raised the candle to investigate the source of his night terror and to possibly answer the question as to why he was scared bananas.

Sure enough, the telescopic dot that he had seen in the well-lit Rip of the Universe had descended in his dreams as a rather large cyclopean Eye; a single Eye which now hovered above his head; first with a fixed stare and then with several blinks as if this big and watery Eye was confessing to the same malady that sometimes happens to Human eyes (the Eye had something in its Eye).

Yes, Human eyes blink a lot when there is an irritation present such as a speck of dirt.

But why am I discussing eye irritation at this time?

Why am I discussing eye irritation when the old man is in fear for his out-of-body life?

I mean - it doesn't make a lick of sense.

Why should he even fear for his out-of-body life? His real body with the pain receptors is actually back home in his Chair and so I am hard-pressed as to the reason why the old man is afraid.

The old man gathers his wits (but not by grasping at air or straws).

"I am not afraid," said the old man stoically. "Why should I be?"

So, the out-of-body old man boldly raised his cold candle up to the Eye for a closer look, for the full view of his imaginary specter.

The old man woke the next day with a start, with the sensation of a spider crawling quickly across his skin.

We trust sleep.

But this was not the case for the old man this morning.

Last night, the Nighty-Night sleeping pills, an irritated Eye and now, the fear of spiders had invaded his sleep.

Sometimes the demands of dogs are godsends. The spider sensation, the flinging of bedcovers and the rapidly forming beads of sweat were all momentarily cast aside for want of a dog kiss. Yes, Basil (who had not been fed her breakfast on time) stared seriously at him and then she chafed a rough and wet dog tongue across his face. This dog kiss, this reality check that dogs require our full attention with regard to matters of time and food was pause enough for the old man to realize his egregious *faux pas*.

Still, 'Something was wrong,' thought the old man as he straightened up in his bed and as Basil shoved her food bowl into his lap. 'Something was not quite right,' as he would soon discover.

The waterlogged, the saturated, the tense old man tentatively entered his kitchen (he would eat first before his investigation of what was 'wrong') but if something was wrong it certainly wasn't here.

He entered his kitchen to the welcome sight of his Cube, that Cube which levitates above his kitchen table (yes, you can mentally pass your hand back and forth beneath it). The instructions are clear. The old man pressed thumbs and fingers together on his hand like a sideways salute. He enthusiastically reached into the Cube's multiple dimensions with his salute hand. He squinted his eyes (for effect) and then he mentally ordered his breakfast of maple syrup and brown sugar oatmeal with added cashews, flaxseed and blueberries; his cup of peach Greek yogurt; his coffee with French Vanilla creamer and eight ounces of warm Sencha Green Tea all of which was delivered in six minutes and six seconds by the food-serving Gray Extraterrestrials.

Basil couldn't wait the six minutes and six seconds and so for her, he scooped salmon and sweet potato kibble into her bowl and she gobbled it up way before his breakfast arrived.

The well-fed old man, sensing again that 'something was wrong' walked gingerly outside and onto his plateau, the plateau without wind, the plateau with nary a zephyr.

'When you wish upon a star your dreams come true' was the tune that, for no particular reason, popped into his head as suspended in mid-air above his plateau was a serious cyclopean Eye; the very same Eye that he had dreamt about the night before.

Now the old man's plateau is a plateau of Lines and when the old man walks onto his plateau, he knows that he needs to tread carefully so as not to disturb them. The Geoglyphs, as they are, make no sense unless he ascends on his telescope platform above the Lines. The Geoglyphs would then avail themselves from below: a spider, a monkey, a faceless spaceman, an Eye and so he has asked himself on many occasions: who was above; who was above the Nazca Lines on the Peruvian plateau; who etched the Nazca Lines in Peru on Earth?

His answer would come very soon.

The Eye winked from above. It winked at the old man and so trepidation ruled the day as a giant Child slowly appeared on his plateau. The big Child began to etch while the old man watched in terror. He was terrified for awhile; his new job responsibility terrified him goofy; babysitting a big Child but surely did he soon realize that the Child knew not of his presence because the Child kept on with the etching and the laughing with every delightful etch and thus the danger to the old man would only be a sudden movement and so he slowly receded back into his house.

He went back inside for a reassessment. He went back inside his abode (quite nice really – the recliner, the big screen television) and then he rushed (as best as he could rush with his old knocked knees and cane) into his living room and then he raised his sneaky periscope for to take a curious peep and the big Child was still there and, of course, the one-eyed Mom or Dad were watching from above. They were watching the big Child's every move.

Sometimes the old man really needs to get away from people and so he cashes in his coupon with the Grays and takes the six minute and six second vacation trip to the Edge of the Observable Universe.

Now many would like to know (and I am sure that means everyone) just how it was that the old man was able to find a suitable vacation home at the exact location where the Big Bubble that is our Universe and the Big Bubble that is the Other Universe converge. Well, I am sorry to say that I haven't a clue as to how the old man discovered this location but, as Basil would think, 'I don't know what happened. It just did.'

And nor can I say anything about the remarkable coincidence of the old man's vacation plans and the appearance on this particular day of a parental Eye and a big Child on his plateau. Maybe this coincidence has something to do with the Mayan Calendar.

I don't know.

All I will say is that the parental Eye and the big Child entered our Universe (without the proper paperwork) on December 20, 2012 - the eve of December 21, 2012 - and that the December 21, 2012, date should raise the eyebrows and red flags of that rabble of Mayan Calendar seers and fortune tellers who (for a small fee) will share (via the staged controversy of social media) their end-of-the-world prophecies.

The old man unwrapped a King Size Snickers bar and began to pick off the layers of milk chocolate on its edges and core (the edges are easy to pick but the separation of the chocolate from the top caramel layer takes practice). He did this when he was stressed. He did this now because there was a big Child kneeling and etching something big and prophetic on his precious plateau.

The old man peered through his periscope and watched as the delighted big Child etched while the parental Eye stared down from above - sometimes with approval and sometimes not. The big Child needed to get it right. He needed to get the big picture right whatever that big picture might be.

The old man diligently observed the big Child for hours. He observed him throughout this prophetic morning. Still, microscope diligence has its limits in terms of time spent and attention paid to, for example, single-celled animals (as every biology student will tell you) and so the old man eventually became drowsy. His eyelids gained weight just before his afternoon nap (us Senior Citizens need our naps you know) and so he looked away from his sneaky periscope just long enough to glance upon his inviting Chair.

Yes, he slid back into his favorite Chair - his sullied Chair that was actually rejected several times by wife and Goodwill Industries. And yet the Chair stayed on because it was the perfect fit for him. And so, (despite the harsh criticism of those who claim to love him) his Chair; his 'ship' stayed on but it wasn't the only ship here because on this Mayan Calendar day the etching big Child had finished his sketch; his depiction of yet another ship; of a huge ship; of Mommy and Daddy's huge ship and so did every dish and pot in the old man's house begin to rattle; and so did the walls of his house begin to shake; and so did the earth under his feet begin to give way but it wasn't the dizziness and weightlessness of love that moved him. No, it wasn't love at all but rather it just happened to be Mommy and Daddy's *Earth or Bust* ship, which now approached the napping Senior's house (he slept through all that?).

Now no one knows for sure what secrecy actually accomplishes on the war planet Earth. All we know for sure is that a war planet like Earth requires secrecy for the conduct of war such that only a very few know exactly what is happening with any given war. These very few are also responsible for secret plans for future wars based on the new enemies created by the current wars the latter of which are manifests of secret funding, secret motivation, secret operations and secret operatives. And yes, the costs, outcomes and consequences of these war manifests are, of course, kept secret from the taxpayers who helped fund these secret wars in the first place.

The threat of government-sanctioned murder of fellow Human beings on Earth is the primary reason that the Society for the Prevention of Exposure of Alien Existence remains a secret (but honored) Society. Perks for lucky members include coupons for Space travel throughout the Milky Way Galaxy, free packages of chocolate chip cookies and most recently (today in fact), a copy of the original Mayan Calendar on compact disk (all of which can be found in the old man's bedroom closet).

The old man woke slowly from the deep sleep of his afternoon nap. He stretched legs, arms and fingers - a virtual percussion of joint and bone pops. He surveyed his living room thinking at first that Basil might have gone on some uncharacteristic rampage but she had been fed before his nap and even walked. The old man had indeed taken a break from the big Child and Eye watch for Basil's morning walk but now, the old man was faced with a conundrum.

'Had there been a large earthquake whilst I slept? Could an earthquake account for the many of my belongings so strewn about my house?'

Once again, the old man thought that there might be 'something terribly wrong' and so he looked at Basil and Basil tilted her black Lab head three times - three head tilts aimed at the old man's picture window and yes, it took three head tilts from Basil before the old man captured the meaning (got the hint) and looked outside.

FAMILY

The paper airplane, the *Message from Earth*, descended as would a tumbling autumnal leaf; as would a kite without strings. It descended into the huge ship's cavernous dining hall without the notice of the Giant Family gathered below for their evening meal. Yes, the Giant Family from the Other Universe held fast to custom one of which was the evening meal; a time when Father, Mother, Son and Daughter could recount and share the experiences of their day whilst their accompanying Orbs prepared and served dinner. However, sometimes the Orbs didn't feel like cooking and so the Cube was ushered in and so Osiris, Isis and Horus (Penelope had left the Family for Starfleet Academy) mentally ordered their dinner with the same straightforward salute that the old man had used in his Universe.

Still, the paper airplane continued to fall, aimed as a parachute's imperative at Osiris' head and, much to the delight of Horus, did the pointy end of the paper airplane so land and thus did Osiris quickly swipe it away as if it was the touchdown of a large grasshopper or the talons of a wee falcon.

Osiris unfolded the paper plane *Message from Earth* and then he reached for his large gavel. He slammed it down hard on the table for to gain the immediate attention of Isis and Horus who were already looking at him with Isis' question: "Why the gavel? There's just the two of us."

Osiris chose to ignore their impertinence and he proceeded with a staccato read of the *Message from Earth* - spoken words, which echoed off the walls of the dining hall in such manner so as to create a confusion of words in the hall. Isis would translate while Osiris bellowed.

Date: December 20, 2012

Hello Giant Family!

Hope you are enjoying your evening meal.

Sad to say but Earth's Humanity continues its wars.

Humanity is at war with everything. They kill and abuse each other. They battle cancer. They fight climate change. There is the war on drugs and terrorists. But recently, they have resorted to the heinous abuse and killing of Trees.

Wow.

Climate change is taking its toll on Earth and the greenhouse effect is proceeding unabated.

There seems to be no end to human war especially in the media (the percentage of crime shows and war movies is way up).

Anyway, the Council refuses to accept Earth's entry.

We request your services tomorrow (see your Appendix).

Love, the Galactic Elders

The old man, the slightly bent-over old man (using his cane for balance) stood on his plateau on December 21, 2012 - a mere insect compared to the huge ship, which was properly parallel-parked and which now hovered alongside his plateau.

Osiris, Isis and Horus stood in the window of their *Earth or Bust* ship. They scrutinized the Geoglyph etched by Horus and were satisfied with Horus' depiction and with his Science Fair Project proposal for the fate of the war planet Earth; a fate that would answer the service request of the Galactic Elders.

"But why hasn't the ship left already?" asked the old man. "Shouldn't the ship be near Earth already on this Mayan Calendar day?"

And so did the Orbs begin to pour forth from the *Earth or Bust* ship. And so did the Orbs form a rectangle in the sky. And so did the Orbs mistakenly write *In hoc signo vinces* ("By this sign, conquer") in the sky for an absent Constantine. And so did the Orbs erase *In hoc signo vinces*. And so did the Orbs sky-write *Coupon?* instead.

And so Basil thought, 'They don't have a Coupon.'

And so the old man said for Basil, "Whoa, they don't have a Coupon."

The Giant Family would have to wait. They would have to wait for the old man to recollect, to remember the location of his stored Coupons (in his bedroom closet would be my guess).

Everyone knows the feeling. Everyone, at one time or another has been tormented by the question - *Now where did I put my wallet and keys?*

It is a feeling of frustration and stupidity.

'I am losing my mind,' thought the old man.

'I walked into my bedroom and forgot why I came in here.'

The perplexed old man walked out of his bedroom and down the hall. Basil met him in the hallway on her way to his bedroom closet. Basil is the happy dog. Basil is the psychic dog who knows it before it actually happens and so she sits and barks at the old man.

'Follow me.'

Basil poked her head into the old man's closet and delicately bit down on a package of chocolate chip cookies. She did not crush one cookie into crumbs. She held the cookies in her mouth as she would hold a retrieved pheasant; the presentation of the pheasant to the hunter without the blood and the crushed hollow bones.

Basil dropped the cookie package with the required Coupon into the old man's cupped hands.

"Thank you, Basil. What would I do without you?" said the old man as he handed her a peanut butter biscuit.

The old man returned to his kitchen table. He picked up a pair of scissors, sliced open the package and dumped out the cookies. The Giant Family would have to wait again. They would have to wait while the old man eagerly consumed his cookies and while he pondered upon a nagging question.

'This Coupon is too small for Giant Family fingers,' thought the old man.

But a solution did present itself.

"The Grays will copy, scan and enlarge the Coupon for me," said the old man with a smile.

And so he summoned the Cube. He would cut along the dotted

line. He would cut out the Coupon and send it through the Cube.

A Gray hand appeared later above the Giant Family. The ghostly Gray hand then launched a paper airplane that was six times larger than the original three by five inch Coupon. The eighteen by thirty inch Coupon descended, as would an autumnal leaf or a kite without strings but this time, the paper airplane caught the attention of Osiris before it struck his noggin.

"This must be the Coupon!" bellowed Osiris.

"Ya think," muttered Isis under her breath.

The old man returned to his Chair. Just for a second did the old man sit in his Chair and sometimes a second is all that it takes.

He stood and Basil sat before an orange full Moon, a large full Moon illusion, a shimmering Moonrise just above the horizon. A frightening edge of black appeared on one side of the Moon and then the shadow followed a path across the Moon. Yes, Mom and Dad's huge ship fully eclipsed the Moon above a hill overlooking the Atacama Desert in the year 666 A.D. and, once again, did the big Child appear, this time for the etch of his Father's likeness: Osiris, the Giant of Atacama.

'Help people to help themselves' is but one precedent and practice of the Universal Peacebuilders and so did projections radiate from Osiris' head so as to predict the times of Moonrise and thus the Seasons for anticipated planting and harvest. Just a little help from the Extraterrestrials, as it were, accompanied by an act of kindness - the possible end of hunger as but one ingredient for a civilization built solely by peacebuilding, as are all civilizations in the Milky Way Galaxy.

"Except for the war planet Earth!" bellowed Osiris and so does the huge ship shutter violently and so does the old man look out his big picture window to an empty sky.

Episode Two

· · · · · · · · · · · · · · · · · ·

SOUP

· · · · · · · · · · · · · · · · · ·

1620

The old man stacked his hands on the top of his wobbly cane. The holidays had arrived and all of his nieces and nephews had checked in. He had put his ear to the ground, his ear to the tracks. His antennae were up and alert and soon, he was rewarded.

One niece says that she doesn't care for British food. Another says that she dreads the prospect of having to take a required U.S. History class and that was enough for the old man. The English Separatists had left England on the Mayflower to get away from the bland food. They came to the New World for the Nauset Indian recipe. Sixty-six days across the Atlantic, a grueling voyage with seasickness, scurvy, death and for what?

Did they really come all this way for the Soup?

OVERSIGHT

The table nearly spanned the width of the dock. The long table stood between the English Separatists and the Mayflower; the Mayflower anchored in Plymouth Harbor.

Mr. Lizard sat in his Captain's Chair at the center of the table. He reached down under the table and pulled out a placard, which expressed a calling card request for one *Captain Christopher Jones*. And most certainly did the sea of one hundred and two English Separatists part for the short walk, for the short and wary approach of Captain Jones to the mystery table and the unscheduled summons.

As Captain Jones approached, Mr. Lizard reached under the table and pulled out a second placard, which stated empathically: *Welcome to the Mayflower!*

"No, no!" shouted Captain Jones. "This is my ship! I do the welcoming!"

A third placard was retrieved.

O.k. - but the Recipes are not yours. The Indians have a patent.

"Curry is patented?" inquired Jones.

A fourth placard.

No. Not those Indians, you dolt. We (the Extraterrestrial 'We') *mean the Nauset Indians of Cape Cod.*

Quickly, a fifth placard.

Read this document. Read it out loud for all to hear.

A sixth placard.

Read it with feeling.

Six placards, a stamped United States Postal Service letter from the future and a book on the *Berried Fruits of New England* rested on the long table. Captain Jones stood at attention, cleared his throat and proceeded with the serious reading of the document dated *September 6, 2012, or September 6, 1620 - whichever your prefer.*

> *Hello Emigrants!*
>
> *Welcome to the Mayflower!*
>
> *We understand fully your repulsion for British food and yet, we also understand that many, many Brits actually delight in traditional, albeit bland, English cuisine.*
>
> *But you do not.*
>
> *You have taken a stand based solely on the unfounded and ridiculous rumor that the food is better in "New England" and you have correctly surmised that "New England" is West of*

here and so you have commissioned the Mayflower for a voyage across the Pond.

You have commissioned this voyage knowing full well that some might die; some may suffer from scurvy and, no doubt, there will be a trail of seasick barf which will act as a flotsam archive; a historical record, if you will, of the course taken by the Mayflower to that mythical land which will eventually be called the United States of America.

No, you will not make to the Virginia Settlement.

You will not land in Jamestown.

Instead, you will be snared by the geographical fishhook that is the tip of Cape Cod.

We are here to help.

The tablets are chewable - take one with every meal.

The shots will pinch and your arms will be sore for a couple of days.

The Silly Brownies are for seasickness.

You will not Whitey-harm the Nauset Indians in any way.

You will not steal their corn or kill Nauset brethren.

You will be watched and so look for a Light in the clear night sky; a Light that will follow your path and that will hover over your future Settlement.

The Light will wink on occasion.

Enjoy the Soup.

Love, the Galactic Elder Council

RAT

Once there was a King, a mythical King of England who was a Cook; who was a 'Royal Cook' in his mind and so, in his mind, resided a 'Royal Recipe' for overcooked, salted and dried-out whole pig; a recipe which included an apple stuffed into the porcine's mouth and, of course, the apple was overcooked as well.

"Salt and Saints Preserve Us!" proclaimed the King.

"No Food Critics Allowed!" proclaimed the King some more.

These large words had been carved onto the front doors of the King's Castle; the doors of which were slammed shut at dinnertime for to keep away the Dumplings.

One by one, the food-critical Dumplings were banished by the Cooking King to the mythical village of Boston, England, which was located just north of Berwick-Upon-Tweed, between Berwick and England's border with Scotland. Yes, the Cooking King had banished the Dumplings to the farthest corner of England only because they had dared to venture forth with recipes of flavor, with recipes that called for spices other than just salt and pepper.

As I said before with words ("Pearls of wisdom," I say; a "stretch" say others), the mythical village of Boston, England was located close to the Scottish border. There was a fence on Boston's border then the Sawus Farm (and Driving Range): Sawus, the Reptilian with a pony tail erect on his head; Sawus, the Reptilian with the tattoos and Queequeg stature but no, he was a sweetie to the ladies of Boston. He was a sweetie because he provided the Reptilian brew, the purple lichen beer for the three Boston pubs. And, it has been said (by someone, somewhere) that, under the influence of Sawus' brew, did at least one man propose to a fair maiden on the very same night of their acquaintance because he was on his knees anyway. Someone, somewhere, as a matter of their indomitable search for dot connections, had observed that a drinking man, a boastful man, had entered pub number two (The Purple Sir) during Happy Hour on the evening of September 6, 1615.

Barbara Allen, who had entered before Peter Dumpling, sat in a chair in the very same pub number two with her hands folded. She sat in the *New Items* chair with a soggy sheet of paper. She had placed a soggy recipe across her lap, a recipe that had fallen off the Old Bridge when Barbara had lost her balance (a mystery someone; a Mr. Lizard liar; a deceiver had told her that the Old Bridge was complete and ready to cross). Still, the determined Barbara Allen (yes, the Barbara Allen of traditional folk song lore) was able to retrieve her sloppy recipe for *Apple Pie* from the muddy banks of the Tweed.

Now love, promiscuous love, sends forth billions of attraction bytes each day but perhaps it is the veracity of soul that determines the manifest, the extent for which love grows. Will love be fleeting or will it marry and last into future generations?

The matchmaker Rose knows; the Blue Alien Rose knows and so, a Happy Hour had been hastily arranged prior to Peter's entry. Peter Dumpling sits at one end of a long table of thirty-four place settings and Barbara Allen sits at the other end.

They sit in chairs of petrified wood.

The thirty-two heads turn as Barbara is the first to dip her soup spoon which she aims at her chin and so does Peter dip into his soup and, whilst a spoonful of warm soup runs down the chin of Barbara, so does the soup do the same for Peter and his chin. Still in a mild but fixed trance, Barbara, unaware of her own soup *faux pas*, picks her napkin from her lap and points it at Peter with the mimed suggestion that he wipe his chin of excess soup and so it was with Peter as well as he reaches for his lap napkin for an identical suggestion; for his concern for the dining and grace reputation of the 'hot' Barbara Allen and, if it had happened in the way that I alluded too, then the first smiles might have been exchanged between the two but it didn't happen that way.

Needless to say, Barbara's soup trance was seriously interrupted by the drippy path taken by the bland, turkey-tasting and weak broth; a path which cascaded down her chin, over her throat and toward the trance-ending space that is the cleavage of her breasts. This soup route was no doubt noticed by Peter and noticed in some imagined detail because he was separated from her by sixteen place settings on either side and thirty-two heads that turned one way and then the other to follow the clumsy pratfall of what would eventually become the 'item' of Peter and Barbara.

Sure, Barbara looked down when the warm soup hit and meanwhile, Peter grabbed, not for his lap napkin, but mistakenly for the edge of the table cloth which he pulled up so as to tilt his soup bowl awry but not completely over because of the quick reflexes of his youth and so, as Barbara looked up from the wiping off of her sexy soup stain, she was able to see Peter's soup bowl as it returned to its original position and then, for whatever reason, if there even is a reason, a nasty question formed spontaneously in Barbara's mind: 'What's under the napkin, Big Boy?'

17

And so now came the first smiles between the two albeit for two entirely different reasons as Peter was relieved that nary a drop of soup had spilled from his bowl. There was only a little wave of soup that had traversed the bowl. It had created a little steam that had reddened Peter's face. Barbara's face was similarly flushed but surely her blush was derived from her nasty 'Big Boy' thoughts.

The evening was young and there was a Bard about with a happy banjo but he would not pick and hammer until later and so we wait for the happy banjo sounds of Vernon the Bard, the Bard of Commentary, Fate and Nature Calls.

And oh, what curiosity advances the dinner party past the watery turkey and pea broth; what curiosity advances the family slide show past the bland dried-out turkey breast with the boiled potatoes and what curiosity presses anxiously beyond the mushy peas and the tasteless spotted dick pudding with the lop of dried and unknown fruit in such small pieces; small pieces which suggest that a poopie little mouse had tread upon the pudding's surface before its consumption?

Oh I will tell you now my friends.

It is anticipation of the last word prodded on initially by the slow hollow pick of Vernon the Bard's banjo and sung with an ancient and strange accent that nobuddya in Boston had ever he'rd 'fore Vernon showed hisself up:

He slammed his stein
Down on his udder hand.
He stared there
Waiting for the pain.
But oh no and shall I sing
That he didn't feel a thing.
So give me more.
Purple, purple
Give me some more of that purple beer.

Let it be said that the evening wore on slowly like a calculus curve that is attempting to approach some inevitable definition of the number zero but no, it wasn't the true definition of zero that was at stake as much as it was the fate of Peter and the future Barbara Dumpling (as if she would accept such a ridiculous name).

And surely, as a matter of this occasion, would there not be those starry-eyed, double-word evocations of either dire warnings of impending doom or perhaps pulsating proposals whose impact could last a lifetime? I mean – what are the rules for repeated words?

"Hear ye, hear ye!" and "Oh my God, Oh my God!" are standard fare but what of: "There's… there's… a dragon… a dragon on your roof!"

Oh well and so it happened that Peter Dumpling hoisted himself upon his drinking table and challenged the bar room with some words repeated.

"Eye (pronounced I)… eye… shwill… will… marry… marry… marry the woman who drinks thee under… under me table!"

Alas, it wasn't Peter who shocked and stopped the huddled and claustrophobic crowd of thirty-four in The Purple Sir that night. No, it was actually Barbara, and so, it was within moments (which appeared in slow motion at least to me) that Barbara spiked her heel on Peter's chair; that she slowly separated her dressage from ankle to knee; that she availed and exposed her long and freakishly sexy feminine leg. Yes, she undressed all the way to her garter of which she summarily detached and, for protocol for weddings to come, she pertly and confidently tossed her garter toward the huddled, claustrophobic and yet eager crowd of bachelors.

Peter did indeed spill half of his muggy mug as a matter of rapt attention; his eyes peeled wide open upon his true love's knee and even above to her garter and yes, Barbara would request, almost immediately if not too soon, that he refill his beer to the top location as a matter of fairness before such a potentially costly contest. And so what hint has been bestowed upon this night that only Peter's dog would detect; Peter's dog; his sheep dog; Basil, his black Labrador retriever who was not technically a sheep dog but who had discovered, after weeks of research, the optimal ratio of green grass, clover and forbs for her intention of complete control over Peter's herds and, my goodness, what was I talking about before?

Oh yes, and so did Basil smell, smell, smell a rat and earlier this evening and sure enough did a smelly and soggy pelt emerge from its wet hole on the Tweed and so did the pelt, with its hair combed back, crawl all the way to The Purple Sir; to the fireplace where Basil was stretched out like in the paintings and so did the rat rise slowly on its hindquarters and raise its little arm for to stiffly nail it; for its rigid salute to Basil in a most timely and overt manner and from the meaning of the rat's gestures would Basil derive only two word answers:

'For real?'

And

'Barbara hustles!'

DECEPTION

Peter Dumpling had a farm.

And on his farm he had some sheep, which technically makes it a ranch and so ends the words that may be parachuting in one's mind; landed safely are the eieios. And on this ranch there was a sheep dog; a black Lab sheep dog named Basil and, yes, it is the very same Basil that had smelled the rat in The Purple Sir. Basil had indeed discovered the Connie-con that fateful night but her name isn't Connie (as we all know).

It can be anticipated that Basil's ranch workload over the next five years would rise exponentially because, in addition to her daily routine of feeding and manipulating Peter's sheep herds, she would have to protect Peter from the death threats of an alluring folk song legend. Suffice to say, the optimal ratio of grass, forbs and clover for the eager sheep chow seems to me to be no less intriguing than Barbara Allen's murder plots and so I will proceed.

By all accounts and, as published in the December 1615 issue of *Sheep Monthly*, the optimal percentages determined by Basil are: 90% grass, 50% forbs and 5% clover. And before you deride Basil's math, please look to the end of Basil's monograph. You will find a citation, which references Yankee catcher Yogi Berra's conclusion that unequivocally states that baseball is "ninety percent mental, the other half is physical." How Basil was able to retrieve this quote from the future is another matter.

There are, no doubt, surprises for every couple that arise in the aftermath of the marriage ceremony and the honeymoon and so it would be Barbara's turn to speak.

"First, there will be no Barbara Dumpling, no Little Dumpling.

Second, the camel train with my stuff will arrive tomorrow. Third, I must see your... uh... our documentation."

Now Vernon, the Bard of Commentary, Fate and Nature Calls had actually closed The Purple Sir that fateful evening with a lyrical notation that had recognized Basil's intuition and had thusly pondered Barbara's past actions and future plans:

> *Barbara stood at his bed*
> *With nary a stitch upon her.*
> *She held Sweet William's dying hand*
> *But not for the boost that he desires.*
> *No, she raised his hand for him to sign*
> *For him to sign, sign*
> *Sign the papers.*

"Everyone!"
But everyone had left and so he sang alone into the night.

> *She helped him with his good hand*
> *For to sign the frickin' papers.*

Basil, for the next two years, would be tasked with the jamming of muskets; with the tripping of wires; with the dilution of poisons; with the hiding of cutlery and with the pawing of nooses all of which was done for Peter's safety. And, when Peter left for days at a time for secret sessions of the Separatists in Scrooby, would Basil stare and glower at Barbara and so would Barbara do the same.

Still, on September 6, 1617, and, after Barbara had proven once again her superior tolerance to Sawus' brew, did an announcement Peter make but only after he had regained consciousness and had crawled back onto his little drinking table.

"Hear ye! Hear, ye! We Separatists have reached the limits of our English Food tolerance and so, as the last item of the last secret meeting in Scrooby, as a matter of consensus and precedent, we have decided to leave England three years from now for... for... what's the name of that land again?... for America."

Barbara's additional list item for Peter: "Fourthly, we plan to stay behind and take care of your sheep ranch."

"We?"

"I meant I."

(Sure you did, Barbara.)

ORB

Sawus sat upon his throne and wondered of the rationality of its Human 'royal' designation. He had pushed his pants down over his ankles and three-fingered toes for the appearance of authenticity, for those who may peak under the stall for news of its Human occupancy. He required privacy. He held up his trans-dimensional cell phone and pushed out the little texting keyboard. Sawya's shadowed profile formed first and he missed her even for that familiar outline and he missed her more when, in full color, did her picture appear with her warm smile.

Now, one would think and probably many have that the use of vowels in texting releases some form of hideous and highly toxic gas and, of course, the capitalization of these toxic vowels is but a warning to hold one's breathe and quickly don a gas mask.

"mss U"

"mE 2"

"th Orbs frm Kplr 452b hv rrivd... tstng phs..."

"wrking...? lght...? hEt...? fyrE...?"

"ys... 'nd 30 mr yrds w/drIvr... wll b sndng smpls whl spkng..."

Four golf balls landed at Sawus' feet. They bounced around a bit but Sawus managed to swipe and pocket all of them.

"lv U"

"lv U2" (but not the Band - not now anyway).

It is the dawn of a new day and surely would an eager Sawus rise, quickly dress, quickly spoon his porridge and run to his Driving Range for to strike the Orbs with his mallet; to see if it is true; to validate Sawya's claim that the four Orbs, now clutched in his cupped three-fingered hands, would add thirty yards to his drive and how on Earth did the Galactic Elders hear about this because the note-taking Elders sat here and now in three chairs with their three steamy bowls of porridge.

"Where is the flavor?" said one Elder to another.

"We are in England," remarked Sawus.

"Oh right," said the Elder. "Sawus, please demonstrate."

"The little stick with the carved-out cup at its apex is pushed vertically into the ground for a clearance of 1 or 2 inches. Place the Kepler 452b Orb onto the little stick and align your Orb with the center of the mallet's head, which is known as the 'sweet spot.' Now is a good time to remind yourself of anyone for whom you have had any recent and heated disagreement. Still, such a vengeful adrenaline rush must be tempered so as to avoid such golf swing maladies as an overly tense grip or a swing that proceeds too quickly or the premature lifting of one's head for to see the magnificence of a properly struck drive which may, even for mere amateurs, obtain a possible distance of 250 yards. What of accuracy you ask? Well, of accuracy I cannot say because, at this time, I have to admit that I have not a clue as to where my shots will prevail. On occasion, but not frequently enough for good scores, I will slowly bring my club back much like arrow set on a bow and then I will come forth with my mallet with the correct gesture; the correct alignment and motion of shoulders, knees and elbows; the correct address of the Orb and the Orb will be launched, by my hand, into some unpredictable orbit. I have four new Orbs and so, before I begin, I will yell 'Four' for good luck."

"I sit in a 'chair.' I sit on the edge of a high 'chair.' I sit on the edge of a high 'chair' for the proper bend, the proper flexure of my knees. I slowly pull back my mallet and then, forgetful of the all required motions, I swing down at the Orb and mistakenly lift my head too early for to observe the desired result. It is only the swift breeze of my mallet that touches the Orb. The Orb falls off the little cupped stick for my one-inch drive. I reset the Orb. I strike the Orb for the screamer, for the grounder with the spray. The squirrel runs away like a tumbling leaf. I strike the second Orb straight into the air. It hits a passing sea gull and brings it down somewhere in the pasture, somewhere beyond the out-of-bounds ropes. My first birdie. I set a third Orb and take a deep breath. I align my mallet to the Orb correctly in the middle of my stance and somehow, I achieve whatever combination of movements that align my mallet with the sweet spot and so I send the Orb on a straight and wondrous path into the dawn of a new day. My fourth Orb is struck as well but with an uneasy feeling of prolonged contact between mallet and Orb and so the Orb is hooked – right toward the unseen, early-rising and fence-mending Peter Dumpling and so I yell 'Four!' again because it happened to be the fourth and final Orb of my driving demonstration."

Peter Dumpling was mending his fence, his sheep-shaped fence. Yes, the hole in Peter's fence was shaped exactly like a sheep and Peter questioned its origin. Did the sheep plow through the fence in terror like in the cartoons or did Human or Mr. Lizard hands slice the fence sheepishly?

Basil, it seems, had been plagued by a serious itch and so she had thumped away for several minutes and, while she thumped like the Disney Bunny, a single sheep had seized the opportunity to venture forth toward Berwick and the Lizard look-alike "Mr. Tweed."

Was the sheep lured on by a Barbara Allen facsimile? Was it the intention of Mr. Lizard (uh - the alias Mr. Tweed) to shear a free sheep for his progress toward the mastery of what would become Berwick's most profitable industry; of what would become the Tweed Jacket?

We shall see.

Sawus' Orb landed in the mud by Peter. Three projections were thrust from the Orb so as to set the Orb on a tripod. A little Space Shuttle thruster emerged at the base of the Orb and a small flame of brilliance came forth. There was nary a countdown as it happened so quickly – the launch of Sawus' Orb into the morning sky and, unknown to Peter, the launch of Sawus' Orb on a 1400 light-year path back to Kepler 452b for repairs. And surely would Peter miss three similar launches due his rapt attention paid to the mystery of his sheep-shaped fence.

UFO

The Stinky Smelly Rat Hole Inn in downtown Plymouth caters to those who desire a meeting place of whispers; of fedora hats pulled over eyes; of collared coats; of heads tilted to convey the distances required for unheard secret plots meant to be passed exclusively between co-conspirators.

It was September 5, 1620. It was the eve of the Mayflower's departure and Barbara Allen and Mr. Tweed-Lizard were actually part of some record evening of secret plots because The Stinky Smelly Rat Hole Inn posted a never-before-seen total of twenty pairs of co-conspirators. It was an evening when all booths were filled and when all tables in the central dining area were pushed against the wall. It was an evening in which the waiters and waitresses were instructed to wear ear muffs and to approach any table slowly and with measured caution and, from all appearances, one might conclude (as a matter of relevance to the plot of this book) that all of England was about to become the recipients of flavored Food; as if the Cooking King's Prohibition would soon surrender.

But no, Barbara and Mr. Lizard were not here to whisper recipes. They were here to make a deal and for the partial information that Mr. Tweed-Lizard would convey about upcoming events meaning that he would only talk investment at this time.

"The inheritance is yours. I want the sheep," whispered Mr. Tweed-Lizard under his fedora.

"O.k.," said Barbara through the hole of her fist.

"By the way - the Old Bridge (she informs sarcastically) is due for completion in 1624."

"You know how to search, I see (what? Wikipedia?)."

"I have another assignment," he adds while pulling up the collar of his trench coat.

"The boy's name is Sweet William."

Now Basil, as a personal issue of self-effacement and in the spirit of corrected math, did bow to the editorial request of *Sheep Monthly* to learn the proper math of percentages in order for her to add a correction to her monograph. After consult with Peter, she prepared the following retraction in a brief note without apology to *Sheep Monthly: 62.1% grass, 34.4% forbs and 3.5% clover.* I point this out because Basil, now aware that percentages must add to 100%, had implied with enthusiastic paws and on this night of September 5, 1620, that Barbara Allen was 90% shrew and 10% sincere and, of course, Peter wouldn't have a clue as to what Basil was trying to convey.

"What is it, girl? What's wrong, Basil?"

Surely, Basil is correct about 90% shrew but I am quite surprised (as may be many others) that Basil would give Barbara that much, that 10% for sincerity.

But, as it were, there were times when she actually yielded to matters of the heart and one can only guess (and guess well I might add) that Barbara actually enjoyed the evening of their anniversary; that she enjoyed her triumphs; that she enjoyed drinking Peter under the table every year.

It would be not inaccurate to say that Barbara actually loved their annual walk afterward, after she had retrieved Peter from the Men's Room and had washed his face vigorously with a cold wet rag.

And the evening of September 5, 1620, wasn't any different although this evening did allude to Mr. Tweed-Lizard's revelations which were only partial; his incomplete information to Barbara in the Stinky Smelly Rat Hole Inn about upcoming events of which he was aware and so, after cleaning up a bit in their room at the dog-friendly Kiss Me You Fool Hostel, did Peter and Barbara take their little arm-in-arm stroll for their annual little talk.

They sat on a romantic bench. They sat on a romantic bench on a clear and starry night.

But - what of the movement of these new stars? Stars should be in a fixed position and rotate with the Earth throughout the evening but no, the stars above seemed to have purpose and, much to Barbara's amazement but not Peter's, did these stars descend and grow larger and glow with playful colors.

"They are Unidentified Flying Objects," Peter said casually. "I see UFOs almost every night."

"But why didn't you tell me?"

"You'd think I am nuts."

"But I see them too."

"That is very observant of you, Barbara, and thank you."

"Are we in any danger?"

"No, but they are protective of the Indians."

"You can see UFOs over India?"

"Sometimes, but I mean the Native Indians of North America."

"My goodness, Peter. What is happening?"

"I don't know (but - he did know)."

The narcissistic (and aren't we all) Barbara began to wonder if the sixty-six UFOs with the "little Gray people" (quoting Peter, of course); with the Gray crew of six would be so poised for her abduction and yes, her mind formed a terrified notion of being raised within a brilliant ray of light into one of their circular ships; of being bound to an Alien chair while the Grays probed everywhere for the painful medical truths of her anatomy and physiology and that the Gray's imposed medical check-up was her punishment for past and future transgressions.

"Are you ok?" asks Peter

"Not really. I am frightened."

And so she huddled next to her transitory and exploited hubby in hope that Peter has an alternative explanation, an explanation that replaces the tense scenario of her imagined demise.

"Watch carefully, my love," says Peter. "You will be amazed."

It was an odd coincidence. Twenty-four sailors had been granted leave based on twenty-four separate incidents.

"You go ashore. I will stay with the Ship," said one sailor after another until there was but one left to guard the Mayflower.

Jonathon Doe stared at his game of Solitaire as witness to yet another loss; another loss which caused Jonathon to raise his fist and then slam it down hard upon his excess cards. There would arise, no doubt, an eruption of lonely and unheard profanities; profanities here and now but surely repeated in the future; profanities aimed, based on disdain, at the Mayflower's cargo of English Separatists. "Glib gabetty puke stockings" would surely be evoked in reference to those seasick Separatists for whom the Silly Brownies had not done the trick.

Be as it may, the bully Doe was left with a puzzle that strained the limitations of his teaser brain because the pounding of his fist had apparently, in his estimation, caused his card table to shift and perhaps that was acceptable as a measure of his strength but my goodness, what of this loud crack and crackle of the Mayflower's timbers; what of this terrible moan? So John Doe did what any punk scientist would do. He slammed his fist down on the card table again as a test and then he asked, "Was Atlas under this ship? Was this ship about to be raised as a preliminary and puny round before Atlas' tilting of the Earth?"

And so did the card table and Doe slide perilously toward the walls of the cargo hold and (thought Doe), 'How could such a huge wave strike the Mayflower whilst she rests peacefully in protective Plymouth Harbor?'

It would be left to Peter Dumpling. It would be Peter's turn to answer the unheard questions and terror of the bully Doe.

"The UFOs will form a circle."

"See the circle, Barbara?"

"A brilliant light, a field of antigravity will be ejected from each craft and melded into a ray that strikes the Mayflower."

"See the light, Barbara?"

"The Mayflower will rise from the water but there will be a period of resistance as the water clings to the ship's hull but the Grays will win the day."

"See the wash of water as the ship rises above the Harbor, Barbara?"

"Oh Peter," interrupts Barbara. "Who is that waving for help on the deck?"

"My goodness," says Peter (the dictation of his phantasm so abruptly interrupted). "I don't know but he is in for one hell of a ride."

Perhaps it was the way he said it. The pang caused her to wince. The pang would have her fold her hand into his for comfort.

'He was in for one hell of a ride.'

As if her love for him would grow in time? As if her release from him would deliver a blow, an impact that she had severely underestimated? Barbara Allen was certainly poised on the edge of a cliff.

The Mayflower (with the bully Doe running back and forth frantically on deck – my goodness - what a fuss) rose into the evening sky and then into the waiting hull of a huge spaceship. The little Gray People gathered around the Mayflower and John Doe for the alterations (no – not a sex change for Doe if that is what you were thinking); alterations to address the flaws in the Mayflower's design that would help; that would alleviate some of the sufferings for the one hundred and two Separatists crowded together for their sixty-six days afloat and no, sixty-six days cannot change because six is the lucky number of Milky Way Extraterrestrials.

SHIPMENT

Peter and Barbara woke in each other's arms on the Mayflower morning of September 6, 1620. Covers were pushed aside; Basil was fed; coffee was made; papers were signed; the window opened to the sight of a new dawn and to the Mayflower resting from its night's ordeal; at peace for now in Plymouth Harbor.

Curious to the crew, however, was a lifeboat moored to the dock. Curious was the note signed by Jonathan Doe.

Shipmates:

I will not venture forth to the New World at this time.
I will do volunteer service at the nearest Soup Kitchen.
The Mayflower is cursed!
I am cursed!

A humble life restored.

Signed: Jonathan Doe
Co-signed: The Galactic Elders

Now every detail of the Mayflower's storybook departure proceeded with ceremonious décor. There were many high-fives, thumbs-ups and so, as well, did Captain Jones stand at the helm with handfuls of white talcum and so did he release the powder into the air such that this powder might mystically bind to the demons of the sea with Jones' physically impossible hope that perhaps the extra weight may sink the powdered demons to the bottom of the ocean and grant the Mayflower a safe passage. The Mayflower was on its way but alas; the cheers and rambunctious boasts were quickly silenced by a hysterical scream!

"Captain! Look!" screamed the screamer.

Captain Jones looked in the direction of the dock with his monocular eyeglass and, after a fiddly focus, did Jones' simple eyeglass reveal the frantic gestures of Jonathan Doe; a John Doe who had climbed upon a pile of three barrels and ten chests for to gain the attention of the departing Mayflower.

Now I have implied throughout my works that Extraterrestrials are vastly superior in many ways to Humans and I would suspect that, on occasion, Et might be slow to admit that they are capable of anything equivalent to mistaken Human oversight. Such oversight sometimes involves incomplete shipment of purchased items often associated with "order to be filled at a later date" or worse, "out of stock."

Believe it or not, it was Jonathan Doe (a changed man no doubt) who had discovered this rare Et screw-up and so he had found three barrels of Sawus' golf balls and ten chests of Tweed-made clothing (nary a woolly sheep left in tact on Peter's ranch) marked for shipment on the Mayflower but yea, barrels and chests that were left sitting in the basement of the very Soup Kitchen for which John Doe had claimed would be the place whereby he would begin his long rehabilitation.

"We must go back!" screamed the screamer.

"Good Lord!" yielded the Captain and so he gave the orders to turn the Mayflower about.

And, it must be said here, that not only did John Doe help to provide the Orbs and the Tweed Jackets for the Mayflower's trip to the New World but he would also remind Captain Jones again of his firm belief that the Mayflower was "cursed."

Thus, upon his return to the Mayflower, did Captain Jones ascend yet again to the pointy helm of the Mayflower and then did he turn around and order all crew and the English Separatists to carefully reset; to return to their original positions right before the previous yet premature Mayflower departure and to thus repeat, as best they could remember with their shoddy short term memories, the details of their anti-curse ceremonies. Captain Jones would again release handfuls of white powder into the air for to double dust the demons of the sea and finally, finally it was the official time for the Separatists to leave England behind and so it is true that Peter Dumpling would never again cast his lustful and bloodshot eyes upon his love; upon his cheating Barbara Allen.

EXOPOLITICS

Death is the only real imperative. It is only thing that anyone has to do and so could anyone's life be so clearly defined and summed as a chronology; as a matter of a web of choices and will power so as to not only to define one's synergies and antagonisms - the form and substance of one's individuality - but to also define one's place; one's role in a community which, if I have heard nothing less, was the defining descriptor of the English Separatists or the Pilgrims; the Pilgrims who were considered the origin; the creators of the United States of America. And so says a curious note found in the barrels of Orbs:

> *Pilgrims,*
>
> *We are not here to do it for you. We are here to help you to help yourselves and to ask the fundamental and Universal question about Human and Alien Rights and so, before you switch on your Kepler 452b Orb of Light or your Kepler 452b*

Orb of Warmth, please consider the importance of your basic needs while huddled in the cargo bay of the Mayflower for sixty-six days; please consider the sometimes inestimable value of nutritious and safe food; of fresh and clean air and of pure and sweet water and finally, please consider what food, air and water mean to the Nauset Indians of Cape Cod; please consider Human Rights as an endowment for all of Humanity.

Love, The Galactic Elders

Peter Dumpling reclined against his cranked-up bunk bed. He pressed the top of his Orb and the light; the reading lamp turned on whilst the Orb hovered obediently over his shoulder. Basil warmed his feet at the bottom of the bed and, for a brief moment, he pined for Barbara Allen as his 'hot' but cheating ex-wife but still, in his mind, did he allow himself (at least in the dirty old man portion of his brain) the current and kissing image of Alice's resting butt as it sunk (in his mind) toward him for Alice Carpenter occupied the top bunk.

And so did Alice prop herself up as well for her morning Silly Brownie and Shakespeare read but never a thought of Peter's lowers or his uppers did she have in return.

Oh sure, Peter would chuckle (even out loud) at his primary focus toward the kiss of Alice's particular exterior and so did he also remind himself of her other possible beauties which he could only imagine existed under her ankle-length gown. And so what of her hair; what of the color and softness of her hair jammed into that frilly bonnet?

And yet, Alice possessed no such wanderings in her mind for Peter at this time but perhaps hope still existed because Alice and Basil got along famously. Alice simply felt that Basil was "like the cutest dog in the whole World" and Basil, relieved at Peter's release of Barbara Allen, felt delightfully the same about Alice (and so would Basil's plot begin).

Basil's plot began the next morning when Peter noticed the graceful descent of Alice from her top bunk perch; how she ever so gracefully balanced herself on the rungs of the little ladder while ballet-turning from her bunk for her descent past the eye-popping and now fully alert Peter and so did his mind wander with detailed and further consideration of her anatomy and, much to his surprise, did his mind spontaneously time-travel to the mental page thumbing of the Sport's Illustrated

2012 Swim Suit Edition and where oh where did these future thoughts come from and what did it mean?

I actually don't know what it meant but still, Peter was able to gather his thoughts long enough to suggest that it would be very kind of her to take Basil for walk through the exercise tunnels that the Gray's had added to the Mayflower while it was suspended in Space and so did Alice reply in her Silly Brownie voice.

"Like yeah, dude. I'll like take Basil for a walk."

'Like yeah!' thought Basil (her butt nearly falling off the bed with the tail wagging).

"Groovy, Alice. Here's like her leash and like her morning biscuit."

And when they like came back.

"Like what are you doing there, Peter?"

"I'm like writing the *Mayflower Compact.*"

"Wow, dude - that's like heavy, man."

"Want to look over my shoulder?"

And so it was that Basil, Alice and Peter were like instantly beamed to a winking Gray spaceship.

ABOARD

Alice was cornered. She had closed her eyes into hard and wrinkled squints and she had drawn her knees to her chest; her knees were pressed tightly to her chest so that she might try to block any incoming terror. She held onto to her knees with locked and passionate arms and, oddly, she then wondered of birthday wishes with eyes closed; of eyes suddenly opened to the small fires of candles and singing. But no, Peter wasn't singing and so he gently touched both her shoulders and then he revealed to her simply and casually that they had been beamed aboard a spaceship inhabited by "little Gray people" (the same 'yeah right' line that he had used on Barbara).

Alice's faithful Orbs hovered over each shoulder and, when she opened her eyes, the Orbs stepped back slightly as if they might be compelled to put down a book that they were reading so as to immediately devote their full attention to Alice's light and warmth.

She uncoiled like a spring. Peter reached for her and, because she was endowed with a stoic perception (she wasn't afraid of heights), she stood up without a waver. It was as if she had merely accepted Peter's invitation for a slow and (for her part) graceful waltz. Her stoic perception and ease with the capricious dimensions of Space allowed her to simply gather herself, walk to the window and then comment on the Earth below.

"Wow! They were right! It really is round!"

And then she smiled for a captive and puzzled audience.

"That was a joke," she added.

Then.

"Peter – why have we been transported without our permission and against our will to this spaceship?"

"Follow me," said the light-headed and tilted Peter whose depth perception was not nearly as effective. And so Alice, with her feet firmly anchored to the floor of the spaceship, followed the slightly staggering Peter into a large room with a large round table.

Peter placed his draft of the *Mayflower Compact* in bound copy onto the slick and shiny tabletop. He reached over and he pushed his document on a slippery path across the table toward the Galactic Elder sitting across from him. The Galactic Elder so mimicked Peter's gesture with a bound document of his own and so Peter was left with the catch of the Elder's document, which seemed to travel at a greater speed and force than his and so Peter was left with an indentation across his palm; an indentation which would later convert into a slight bruise.

The Galactic Elder was the first to read and he read Peter's *Mayflower Compact* with the lovely and yet snobby accent of the English aristocracy.

"It was a joke," he replied later to Peter's inquiry.

> *In the name of God, Amen. We, whose names are underwritten, the loyal subjects of our dread Sovereign Lord King James, by the Grace of God, of Great Britain, France, and Ireland, King, defender of the Faith, etc. Having undertaken, for the Glory of God, and advancements of the Christian faith and honor of our King and Country, a voyage to plant the first colony in the Northern parts of Virginia, do by these presents, solemnly and mutually, in the presence of God, and one another, covenant and combine ourselves together into a civil body politic; for our better ordering, and preservation and furtherance of the ends*

aforesaid; and by virtue hereof to enact, constitute, and frame, such just and equal laws, ordinances, acts, constitutions, and offices, from time to time, as shall be thought most meet and convenient for the general good of the colony; unto which we promise all due submission and obedience.

The Galactic Elder then offered his variation on a theme and so now Peter reads his version:

Please consider the separation of Church and State in the creation of your governance.

In the spirit of equality and Human Rights - Human Rights for all Humanity, We, whose names are underwritten, the loyal subjects of our dread Sovereign Lord King James; We of Great Britain, France, and Ireland who have undertaken a voyage to plant the first colony in the Northern parts of Virginia, do by these presents, solemnly and mutually combine ourselves together into a civil body politic; for our better ordering and preservation and furtherance of the human rights aforesaid; and by virtue hereof to enact, constitute, and frame, such just and equal laws, ordinances, acts, constitutions, and offices, from time to time, as shall be thought convenient for the general good of the colony; unto which we promise all due submission and obedience.

If agreed upon then, please have all Pilgrims i.e. men, women and children read and sign the document.

Love, the Galactic Elders

Peter teetered; a glass bottom boat with the Earth spinning beneath his feet. He teetered with moments of sheer blindness and obviously, the terror of a blind man at the edge of a cliff but not so for Alice and so she grabbed him around the waist and she retrieved the Galactic Elder's version of the *Mayflower Compact* before the beam; before the beam as an embraced couple back to Earth; back to what would become their mutual bunk bed.

Peter and his Orbs, Alice and her Orbs and the tail-wagging Basil appeared just as they were except that Peter and Alice had embraced a little longer than they dared (the Orbs had shied away) and who really knows what transpires; who really knows what mixes and melds during the beaming of couples to Earth?

THANKSGIVING

On November 11, 1620, the Mayflower dropped anchor inside the hooked tip of Cape Cod; inside the cove that is known today as Provincetown Harbor and, since I am the author of this tome and since I have afforded myself the widest and wildest artistic license possible (I mean - Alien intervention – yeah, right), I have decided to move Thanksgiving up a few chronological notches to this day of the Mayflower's arrival. And so what, I wonder, did Captain Christopher Jones see when he slid out his monocular eyeglass and pressed it against his orbit?

Yes, Captain Jones lunged forward a few inches along with his Orbs as if the distance brought closer to him might alter his perception of reality or perhaps it was merely the giggly verification of reality that he sought. The reality availed unto Jones was a slightly-out-of-wiggly focus of a young Nauset Indian boy looking back at him through a 3" refractor telescope mounted on an excellent tripod and I say excellent because nary did the boy's image of Jones and his Orbs waver due to its steady mount.

The other item of Jones' interest was not unexpected. A black cauldron was observed with many Orbs of Fyre beneath and out of sight but within the cauldron, was the vaunted Soup; the Soup foretold by the Galactic prognosticators; those same Galactic Elders who also knew the exact number of Orbs of Fyre required for the maintenance of the proper serving temperature of the Soup.

And so did the proper amount of Soup steam rise from the black cauldron and so was a pouch of water squeezed on occasion by the Nauset Indian boy for the proper replacement of water such that the Soup's temperature might be held in check for the time it takes for the Mayflower passengers to disembark and make their Orb and Human way to the First Thanksgiving.

And, as anyone might expect, this might take awhile but still, the excitement; the anticipation and, no doubt, the eagerness to relieve themselves of smelly, sixty-six day, one-time attire and of jerky meals became the quick priority of the day for the Pilgrims.

But let's not get ahead of ourselves.

I mean - a brief history of the Soup's ingredients is relevant for this interlude as a savory revelation with regard to the Soup's scrumptious flavor. We must know about the carefully cultivated Nauset Indian corn (the Nauset Indian corn was carefully cultivated); the churned butter (I don't know who churned the butter but it was churned); the sneezy black pepper; the clams and mussels gathered (and tested for numbness of the lips) and, at last, the secret ingredient; the genetically-engineered, cayenne-peppered hot potatoes which, my friend, were not the ordinary English fare.

The Pilgrims changed into Tweed Jackets and Dresses provided by the greedy Mr. Lizard. They row, row, rowed their boats gently to the shore. They stood before the Nauset Indian contingency. The leader Aspinet reached forth with welcoming arms and with the invitation to join them; an invitation to sit across from them on a long table for a dinner of spicy clam chowder with sweet corn, garlic bread and bowls of neurotoxin-free clams and mussels. The brew served was the hearty Reptilian Purple Lichen Beer and so later that night did Peter and Alice inquire of the origin of the Nauset Indian stash.

Aspinet pointed at the Indian boy with the 3" refractor telescope and said in the N-dialect Algonquin language, "He will show you."

The Indian boy aimed his telescope at Libra and he focused carefully upon on a red dwarf star, which he called "Gliese."

"Look into the telescope," said the boy.

"They come from there."

Episode Three

· · · · · · · · · · · · · · · · · ·

RADIO

· · · · · · · · · · · · · · · · · ·

1956

The 1956 RCA Victor Floor Radio stood as a polished dais with all of its wooden weight resting on a velvet cushion. The Radio had been carefully moved into a shallow depression, into a kitty corner of the hallway. Across from the Radio was a floor heater. Sitting next to the floor heater with his knees tucked to his chin was a 1956 10 year-old boy. This boy would quietly descend the ladder of his top bunk and then drag a blanket to his listening post. He did this late at night while his family slept and 'when the reception was good.'

Radio knobs have give. The boy would jimmy them. The boy would push the dial across the bandwidths probing for voices most of which were faint and indecipherable amongst the white noise.

The boy's ambitions (in addition to fireman and astronaut) included the 'sonar guy' scenario; his future as one of those Navy shipmen with special hearing; like in the movies - those Navy actors who can hear voices on enemy submarines and immediately translate (no matter what the language). Once he heard 'Russian' which he immediately interpreted as 'Commie chat from the Kamchatka Peninsula' which meant to him that he had found intelligence worth reporting to the Central Intelligence Agency. He found 'German.' He found trashy and hectic jazz played with a muted trumpet. He found faint religion in 'Latin' - a fundamental Catholic radio station broadcasting from a distant land.

No one really listens to a 10 year-old boy who is certain that Extraterrestrials have arrived on Earth; Extraterrestrials who are currently acting in a radio play about the assassination of the American Indian Pecksuot by Myles Standish in 1623. To this day, the old man (once a 1956 10 year-old boy) knows that Extraterrestrials have not made contact with Earth because of Humanity's love for and obsession with war.

The glowing vertical band began as a fuzzy patch on top and then it descended as a race of bright tiny dots to the bottom. The band was fuzzy at first but then did it contract and brighten. It reflected off the wide-eyed boy's glasses and it would remain as an afterimage for most of the boy's day.

The wide-eyed boy slowly and 'expertly' pushed the dial toward the glowing band. He could have sworn that the band was expanding, growing in width such as to propose a formal greeting with him: 'The first contact between Humans and Aliens!' But no, just as his dial was about to make contact, the glowing band jumped away and then it started over with the fuzzy-patch-on-top-race-of-little-dots-to-the-bottom thing.

'Extraterrestrial sense of humor,' thought the boy.

The wide-eyed boy slowly and 'expertly' pushed the dial toward the rogue Extraterrestrial glowing band but this time his dial and the bright dial merged. It merged to the sounds of an iron door, footsteps, creaky chairs and the rattle of leg irons.

Narrator: "The Galactic Elders listen. They listen in a huge room with floor-to-ceiling books. Huge books. Books six feet tall. The *Book of Humanity* is found. The conveyor belt brings it to the smoking man. It is dropped onto a huge table. He opens the *Book of Humanity*. He opens the *Book* but only after the dust and ash of Humanity settles upon it. The Galactic Elder does not want Human dust or ash to contaminate his calligraphy. He doesn't want his slow calligraphy smeared in any way."

Galactic Elder: "You cannot get too close to a star. Even the Red Giants, even the coolest stars burn. They will burn you beyond recognition. They will burn you like your Camels."

Narrator: "He takes his last drag. He sucks. No filter. He burns his Camel to the end; to the tips of his fingers. He doesn't feel a thing. He doesn't feel a thing but he can open his tiny mouth. Camel smoke rises over his fingers; makes his eyes squint. But that doesn't stop him. That doesn't stop him from opening his tiny mouth."

Galactic Elder: "Start from the beginning. Take your time, burning man. Be sure. Be accurate about your testimony. Don't talk about your-self. We already know."

Human: "Old Charlie told me about the secret meetings. He told me about the secret meetings right there in Scrooby. Charlie said that they had a disagreement with the Church of England with regard to the ways and means of worshipping the one Lord the latter of which I often address at my Church, which is the Throne at Scrooby's local pub. Old Charlie kept saying that these Separatists were passionate. They were passionate about freedom of religion. They were passionate about food and so I was beginning to calculate. I thought that Old Charlie and I just might find a way to take some measured advantage. We could snitch on them to King James or we could join them. We could join for the women, for the passionate women. I mean somebody has to lead and most follow and so we wouldn't lead but we would follow. Follow the women. You know what I mean? We joined the Separatist movement for the women because maybe their passion just might look past our grubby shortcomings."

Human: "Seriously, we just wanted to take a look around. We were starving but honestly, we were just looking around; just a walk to look around, a little stroll. I mean - we didn't see the gravesite until we practically fell into it. Old Charlie here nearly did and he was starving as well; as were we all but really, what would compel us to think that these gravesites before us, obviously dug out by the locals, could actually be gravesites with food for sustenance in their Afterlife? I mean - who would think that? Immigrants? Savages? We gathered around and, for a very brief moment, we actually considered that stealing the Nauset Indian corn from their gravesites to feed our faces just might be an act of desecration: 'Wow,' someone said. 'This corn is really sweet.'"

Human: "We met with the Indians to smooth things out; to level the playing field; know what I mean? We invited the Indians over for dinner to smooth things out. We invited them over for dinner and peace talks and if things didn't smooth out then, and we had agreed about this ahead of time, we would try the solution of stabbing them to death. You know - kill them as an alternative solution. I mean - maybe the Indians were not as sincere as we were about smoothing things out. I mean - either they are for us or they are against us and so anything goes like false pretense. So here was the plan. We'd invite them over for dinner, fill their tummies and then stab them to death because their guard is down. Sure, they were easy targets for the stabbings but it wasn't us stabbing them. We just let the Hand of God do the killing for us but geez, those Indians were sure stubborn for the dying because they were so darn muscular. The Hand of God had to keep stabbing over and over again until those Indians were finally dead but it wasn't me. It wasn't Myles Standish doing the stabbing. It was the Hand of God."

Human: "Oh sure, William Bradford had this cult thing about staying true to the dogma; the agenda of an old religion; an old religion that was so old that it wasn't quite remembered in its true sense and detail and so William Bradford applied the rules and judgment of the old religion based on rules that nobody really remembered until William, allegedly speaking with God's Tongue - God Speak, if you will - pointed out the rules as a matter of his 'Godly' interpretation. As for William - well, he spoke with a kind of cult zeal such that if Kool Aid were a poisoned drink available at the time then the Pilgrims just might be lining up for a taste and so, the Pilgrims were 'o.k.' with the beheading of the dead Indian leader stabbed to death at Standish's little man dinner party; they were 'o.k.' with the sticking of the bloody Indian head on a pole; they were 'o.k.' with the bloody Indian totem pole placed in front of their little fortress for to strike such fear in the local Indian populations that they retreated quickly into the recesses; back into the places that they knew before the Pilgrims arrived; before William Bradford arrived and started preaching that old time religion."

The Galactic Elder: "If the Filipino Christ penitensiya was here now. If self-flagellation with bloody palm blades was here now. If God's punishment was the precedent and practice of the day, then your day would follow suit. You would bare a sadistic soul; a mockery of soul and no, you would not burden. You would not carry your burden alone and so you would insist that your fellow Pilgrim community not only witness God's punishment for transgressions but you would also demand that they follow suit. You become the drum major with a wand of fiery swords. And so you say that it is God's punishment that was applied without mercy at Pecksuot and Wituwamat? No, you threw them into a Hell of American invention. That was a bit much. That was a bit too much. That was over the top. Excessive. But on that day, the Pilgrim creation called infant America became its own measure of atrocity; its own measure of genocide called from Europe as if it was a dark fragment of Mayflower cargo."

The wide-eyed boy's hot cocoa had gone cold. The glowing band had faded slowly and disappeared never to be seen or heard again. The one-time radio play - *The Confessions of Myles Standish* - was gone but at the very end of the radio play did the boy hear (with his 'expert' hearing) the slamming shut of what he thought might be a very large *Book*.

Episode Four

· · · · · · · · · · · · · · · · · ·

TOY

· · · · · · · · · · · · · · · · · ·

2012

The little Gray Alien boy had not put away all of his toys. The boy had left one Toy on a counter near the loading dock of his spaceship. His spaceship was parked in downtown Roswell but no one could see his ship - not even on a busy day.

Tourists from out of town would park their cars and walk around Roswell looking for an Alien Burger or the UFO Museums but still, not even the tourists could see the boy's ship. The boy's ship could actually park in handicap parking even without a blue sticker and this was true for today. Yes, the boy's ship was parked in handicap parking next to the Safeway, the ship's ramp nearly reached the sliding front door.

Now people come and go with their clattering grocery carts and so this was the case for Franny Carpenter who had come with her Mom to help with the grocery shopping.

Sometimes all it takes is an elbow. The elbow of the little boy's Gray parent had knocked the Toy to the floor of the ship's loading dock. The Toy then rolled down the ramp and into Franny's grocery cart. Franny saw it all. She saw the Toy, the ship and even the Gray Alien boy. She saw the boy as he sadly stood at the edge of the loading ramp and sure, Franny thought of returning the Toy to him right then and there but the ship's ramp had started to close.

Franny could see all of this because she was resistant to the Haze - the Haze that the Extraterrestrials use to conceal themselves from the war-happy Earthlings.

Franny saw it all but, try as she may, she could only touch the things that appeared in her dimensions. So, she picked the Toy ball from the grocery cart, put it into her pocket and took it home where it would be 'safe.'

Franny placed the Toy ball on her bedroom dresser and she opened the curtains to add light and shadow; to add a three-dimensional perspective for her cell phone camera and later, for her 3D printout. She would certainly post on Facebook for her small circle of Haze-resistant friends - those who didn't judge her as "nuts" when the talk of Extraterrestrials was the topic of day.

But the photo never happened. It would be a video instead.

The Toy obviously enjoyed the room's sunlight because it began to vibrate and hum - a hum, which caused Franny to stop in her tracks.

Franny peered around the edge of her cell phone camera.

The Toy rose above the dresser and then settled back down. It began to take shape and, within the briefest of continued space and time, did the Toy stretch and contort itself into the likeness of a Gray Alien boy - the same boy that Franny had seen on the Gray's ship. The Toy was sitting - inclined in what Franny thought might be a special chair. The look on the Toy's face was one of despair - the frantic telepathy of a child who had lost something important, something for which he had been entrusted.

Franny felt the guilt as well.

The boy had not told his parents.

The Toy stayed seated for a minute or so then it quickly resumed its ball shape. Franny then stuffed the Toy into her sock drawer for the night. She thought that the Toy might feel safe and warm there. Maybe the Toy needs its sleep - its rest to slow down its inevitable entropy. All sentient beings, even a Toy with a mind of its own, know the mortal fear of being torn apart - the entropy of the Universe is increasing.

Franny was dozing off when she heard a thud in her drawer. She was paralyzed. She tried to gain the strength to get out of her bed but she couldn't and so she threw her covers over her head like a teen that didn't want to go to school that day.

Thud. Thud. Bang!

Her sock drawer shuttered then it banged again and so Franny got out of bed and sleepwalked like a teenage Zombie toward her dresser. The Toy had managed to open the drawer ever so slightly - slightly enough for it to squeeze through a crack. The Toy was flat like smashed down Silly Putty but then it formed back into a ball.

It pushed aside her music box and Beanie Baby. The Toy then rose again above the dresser. It lit up with patches of light and then it took the shape of the Gray Alien boy.

'Scared,' thought Franny. 'Or maybe he is sad.'

The Toy looked up as if his parent was standing over him. The Toy folded its arms behind its back and then bowed as if to apologize. The Toy began to hum - even louder than before - and so Franny cupped her hands over it to muffle the sound but that did not help.

Franny had kicked over a light stand on her way to the dresser and it had crashed to the floor and so Franny's Mom was coming down the hall just before the Toy began its high-pitched telepathic buzz. The telepathic buzz of the Gray's conversations can be heard all over their ship and so the Toy was used to background noise whilst conversing with the boy.

The focus was there. The Toy could discern what the boy was thinking. But today was different because Franny's thoughts suddenly became clear to the Toy.

'Oh crap, my Mom is coming.'

Alice Carpenter was just a few feet away. She was expecting perhaps a disco ball with radiating colors from above and a cleared away dance floor. She thought that maybe there had been a missed step and hence, the crash of a light stand. But Alice was puzzled no doubt when she opened Franny's bedroom door and saw her sleeping with her new softball and her light stand fully erect with the lamp shade straightened as if it hadn't fallen over for years.

'Hmm,' thought Alice. 'I didn't know that she loved softball that much.'

And so did Franny and the Toy fall asleep with Franny dreaming and the Toy interpreting both her dreams and the worried, far-away thoughts of the little Gray Alien boy.

Franny didn't ask for this. She didn't ask for the time-traveling Mom and Dad who had actually conceived her shortly after they had met on the Mayflower in 1620. She didn't ask for the Haze-resistance. It was just something that she had acquired from Peter and Alice (let's see - like maybe DNA?). Franny had not asked for the upcoming Roswell Alien ('Yeah Right') Convention, which would be attended by Haze-resistant Humans and Extraterrestrials. And, of course, she had nothing to do with the choice of timely dates for this Galactic Federation extravaganza, which was scheduled for December 20-22, 2012, (with the unwritten Mayan Calendar caveat that December 22nd may never happen). She didn't ask for this lonely Toy - the Toy which now sits on her pillow in the shape of her beloved softball; the softball with two alfalfa sprouts for antennae; the softball which was sending out its emergency call; its subspace message for the Gray Alien boy to come to Roswell and to bring it home.

The Toy actually missed the chaos of the telepathic buzzing aboard the Gray's ship. It was so quiet on Earth with humans so isolated in their thoughts - the diffuse wandering of the human mind from 'like what am I going to wear to the Convention?' to grand ideas about 'how to achieve World Peace' (and thus, end war on Earth and, for those "crazies" who know about such things, the Galactic Federation's censorship of Humanity).

'At least thoughts of World Peace still exist on Earth,' thinks the Toy.

'But what is this?'

'What is this that intrudes upon our slumber?'

Yes, Peter and Alice have given up the ghost and so they send in Basil every morning for the waking of their cranky teen. Franny hears the click of Basil's toe nails in the kitchen. She hears the thumps of Basil's feet in the hallway. She hears Basil pawing at her door.

'Time to get up,' thinks the Toy.

'It is Convention Day!' think both Basil and the Toy.

And so does Basil prance into Franny's room with her ears erect and her panting tongue aimed at Franny's cheek.

But Basil stops abruptly in her quadruped tracks.

Yes, she knows about the Toys of the Gray children but 'why oh why' (does she ask twice) is there one levitating just a few centimeters off Franny's pillow?'

The Toy rose slowly off the pillow and came face-to-face with Basil, which is a Toy/Dog scene that has never been witnessed before on Earth.

Moments later, Franny peered over the edge of her bed.

Basil was lying on her side on a pillow tossed across the bedroom in disgust by an angry teen. Yes, Basil was traveling through space/time on a pillow of dreams.

DINER

The holodeck on the Gray's planet (sorry - as far as I know, no extra-solar planets have been found yet orbiting the binary Zeta Reticuli star system) was currently in default mode - wavy black perfect squares with little white lights on the edges. The holodeck was waiting for instructions and arrivals but it would not have to wait long.

The old man was curled up in his Chair with Beethoven's Sixth but then he got that 'feeling' - *a feeling deep inside* just as would the Beatles sing it loudly and then poof! Yes, poof went the old man into a scenario not necessarily of his own choosing but sometimes, as Basil thinks - 'stuff (or some other bad word) just happens.'

The old man had seen the sign. The old man, dusty and driving a Ford Falcon Station Wagon in the hot and holographic New Mexico desert, had caught a glimpse on the horizon of the Crash Down Diner. And so the old man pulled into a gravelly spot; the pebbly handicapped parking spot and yes, it was a hard brake for the old man because sometimes he had trouble with his numb feet; trouble finding the brake pedal with his numb feet for the smooth stop.

The CLOSED sign over the door startled him a bit but then he figured that CLOSED might mean 'occupancy for Extraterrestrials only.'

The little bell rang over the doorframe and so the head of the little Gray Alien boy popped up from behind the soda fountain counter. The old man then slid into a hot booth for four; a booth with ripped and soiled cushions and also, with the three Galactic Elders; three Galactic Elders poised with pens and notebooks for the recording of possible pertinent information; information that will be used for the *Book of the Grays*.

On the booth's tabletop sat plastic bottles of slow catsup, 'squeeze-me' mustard and peppershakers all pressed up against the fully stocked napkin holder. Four Menus just appeared from out of nowhere - Menus with the claim on top which says that, "Your order will be filled in six minutes and six seconds" (and, on the occasion in which orders were not filled in the allotted time, there would be a slight shift in the Universe; a magnitude 4.0 quake would be felt on Earth as a result, an earthquake without a detectable epicenter and thus, a real head-scratcher for the U.S. Geological Service).

The little Gray Alien boy needed to get it right. He had lost his Toy - his Guardian Angel and Mentor - and so he was sent to this holodeck to do food service in the old fashioned way, in the way of waitresses who worked diners and dives.

The little Gray Alien boy was on the clock as the Menu had pre-scribed. So he ran from the soda fountain counter, hoping upon hope that the old man and the Elders knew what they wanted straight away. He could not afford to wait for food indecision and so he gestured with pad and pen ready in hand as though he might be saying (if he could talk), 'Look, I am very busy and I don't have all day.'

He stood there impatiently with hands on hips and with one foot tapping the floor and he pretended that he was chewing gum.

Oh sure, the old man and the Elders knew. They knew about the boy and his misplaced Toy and they had agreed ahead of time that prac-ticed vigilance and swift thinking should be the lessons of the day and so they ordered in an ancient language that only Earthly soup jockeys could understand.

"I will have a Hockey Puck all the way with some Frog Sticks and a Black Cow."

"Please, walk my Cow through the garden and I will have a 77 to wash it down."

"First Lady will do me fine with some Whistle Berries on the side and just a glass of City Juice with ice."

"I'll have a Bow-Wow with Yellow Paint with some Whistle Berries and Swamp Water and we will all have what the Americans love to have for dessert - a slice of Eve with a Lid On."

The little Gray Alien boy wrote furiously and then ran to his Cube.

The Cube spit the order back with "What?" written on the bottom so he booted his quantum computer (thinking quickly as the old man had hoped) and thus, with the aided speeds of his computer, were the translations so quickly completed for Menu comparisons and so did the boy shove the translations back into the Cube only to find an error mes-sage - "This Cube Shutdown Temporarily for Scheduled Maintenance."

The boy then collapsed into a chair and waited for the whole Universe to shift slightly at the site of the Big Bang and sure enough and right on time did the Universe shift and rattle the dishes of the Crash Down Diner.

CONVENTION

Now there is a proper time and place for the investigation of events correlated with and possibly linked to the Big Bang and so a committee was quickly formed and so the three Galactic Elders, Alice and Peter Carpenter and the Gray Alien boy's parent were rudely extricated from their daily routines and beamed directly to The Pizza Parlay.

The Pizza Parlay, as Apollo astronauts know (but will not tell), sits as a pizza joint upon the rim of the Moon's Copernicus and, from its cold and cosmic window, one can ponder the view of tiny Earth with its microscopic Humanity and also dine on the new "lower calorie" (but not by that much) thin crust Italian Sausage, Garlic and Three Cheese Pizza. The Pizza Parlay is without question the perfect ambiance for the investigation of events correlated with and possibly linked to the Big Bang. I mean - it is that feel-good place where Extraterrestrials and Humans alike can stuff their faces with pizza and Beer Nuts and send it down the gullet with a hearty wash of Reptilian Purple Lichen Beer.

Rooms no doubt can be reserved for birthday parties or rapidly put-together committees. The rooms have big screen televisions, which can broadcast Interdimensional CCTV and, of course, Interdimensional CCTV had caught, on multiple holographic cameras and in super-slow motion, Franny's initial reaction when she looked at the Toy for the first time and said, "What the heck am I supposed to do with this?"

Franny had to get up for the Convention today and so she pushed the covers up with her knees. She swung her legs around and waited for the incoming and annoying blast of cold air.

Franny hadn't slept well (I wonder why).

She had already witnessed two Toy pantomimes and she suspected more but the current one both baffled and bemused her - the toe-tapping Toy dressed as a waitress with hands on hips and chewing a wad of gum; the Toy, which frantically ran about her bedspread and collapsed into a 'chair.'

A small earthquake rattled Franny's bedroom.

The Toy rubbed his face in what appeared to be an act of exasperation and then it turned back into the Toy ball. The Toy began its sad and persistent hum. It hummed while Franny changed into her Blue Alien self but no, not a shape shift if that is what you were thinking - just Franny reaching into her closet for her Blue Alien costume.

Today was Convention day (or was it really - I mean define "Convention" - or more specifically - define the "Roswell UFO Festival" - Google it and you will find something inconsistent with December 21, 2012 - it has something to do about the dates in which Roswell UFO Festivals are actually held - did you find it? uh? uh?).

Still, Franny put her Show and Tell Toy into her pocket for her morning and sleepy drive to the Roswell Convention Center.

The Gray Alien boy woke to a morning dog kiss - to Basil pushing her head under his arm - to Basil's urging for him to rise and shine.

'Come on,' thought Basil. 'Get up.'

Now is the time and place for the unconditional love of dogs. It is the time and place for the dog love that exists no matter what has happened - no matter what mistakes have been made.

'Lost Toys?'

No big deal.

'Let's go,' thought Basil and so the boy followed Basil to his spaceship.

Six minutes and six seconds later and poof - the boy is standing in the empty parking lot of the Roswell Convention Center - empty except for one idling and cold car in the middle. The car door opens and out steps a freezing and not-very-happy Blue Alien teenage girl.

The Toy jumps out of her pocket and so now we have the famous field scene - the joyous Toy flying to the Gray Alien boy - the Gray Alien boy running to the Toy with his long arms outstretched - the finale to Beethoven's Ninth! - wow! - I mean - this was like the best field scene ever!

Franny jumps back into her car, turns on the heat full blast and wonders what happened to the Convention.

Jupiter suddenly acquires its sixty-eighth Moon and NASA notices.

"Hey Al, check this out."

Episode Five

. . . .

MOON

. . . .

1777

NEANDERTHAL

Everyone knows.

It is common and Earthly knowledge that nighttime stories read to children before the second Independence Day of July 4th, 1777, included invariably the sleepy child's tale of *Goodnight Two Moons*.

Everyone on Earth also knows that Humans can name stuff and that's why our planet is called Earth and we can certainly speculate that, if whales could name stuff (and maybe they can but we may never know), our world would be called Oceana which is a name more descriptive of our *Blue Planet* because an Ocean is what Earth mostly looks like to incoming spaceships in search of a port-of-call but yea, a port-of-call which is properly called by an accurate name.

Now to say that Captain James Core Halley was named by such an Earth Mama and Papa is actually a prehistoric misnomer because the Neanderthal versions of Mama and Papa simply named him Who? thousands of years ago because he had a tendency to wander off for days at a time but no, he did not wander alone because Who? was faithfully accompanied by his dog who, on one previous occasion, was dressed in sheep's clothing.

Well Who? named his dog Uh? because she often seemed puzzled by the words coming out of his mouth and so he knew that much about Uh? (meaning just his name for her) but what Who? did not know about Uh? was that Uh? was actually a time-traveling 'wolf' in sheep's clothing. Who? also didn't know that she was actually the time-traveling and Space-faring dog Basil who, being as smart as she was, had not only caught on to the wolf's plot but she had also forcibly taken (although we not sure about 'forcibly') the wolf's place in the time-traveling sheep's clothing incident.

And sure, while on a roaming excursion with no particular destination in mind did the young Core Halley come upon Basil in sheep's clothing and so when Basil saw Core for the first time, she wagged her tail and the loose-fitting sheep's clothes started coming off with the tail wagging and, after a moment of mental processing, the Neanderthal Core was set to beholding the experience of the *First Dog*.

Now Basil and Core had many adventures together but some adventures, suffice to say, were more memorable than others. I mean - what's the difference between finding a patch of blackberry bushes or finding a circle of six Gray Aliens with large, beady black eyes all holding hands and humming *Row, Row, Row Your Boat* in six part harmony around a campfire with their spaceship hovering overhead? For sure, Core returned home with some interesting ideas for cave drawings; cave drawings that would be hidden for thousands of years under the basement of the Louvre and yes, these cave depictions may be the real intuitive reason for an art museum of significance at this location.

"I sense Art of great significance will be discovered here in the future."

"O.k., let's start with the *Mona Lisa*."

BANG

Now if you put aside arguments about God and the creation of our Universe, if you cast aside the notion that God created our Universe then observations align reasonably well. Our Observable Universe has a putative Edge. It is possibly 'finite' and, if we really do live within a 'Really Big Bubble,' then innuendo and intuition both beg a burning question:

'Who pray tell (but prayers are not meant to answer such questions) lives outside the 'Really Big Bubble?'

And Core would answer in a report to no one in particular.

Hi There Whoever,

I was playing Battleship with my First and Only Officer Scarlett and she had just sunk my aircraft carrier when I happened to look out of the window of my spaceship and I saw hence a flash of light; a brilliant supernova light and the first thought that came to mind was, 'A new Universe has been created.'

And then I pondered, but not for long because my ship, the Pacifier, needed to rescue a dog who was tumbling toward my ship; a dog with a portable breathing helmet and a tight-fitting, tail-wagging spacesuit with the "Basil" name plate and so I brought her in and so Scarlett and I sat around and ate chocolate chip cookies while we watched the new Universe expand toward us.

Yours in Truth (yeah right), Core

They waited for about an hour and a half but soon, the first star arrived and then passed over their heads. They could see spiral galaxies, globular clusters and nebulae as the New Universe became their delightful playground hologram but it all began to slow down when a particular Milky Way Galaxy came into view and they were obviously headed toward the edge of one of its spiral arms. Finally, the solar system that we know best came into view starting with the dwarf planet Pluto and then the Pacifier found itself parked – after Neptune, Uranus, Saturn, Jupiter and Mars - in Earth orbit as the New Universe came to a clearly perceptible but not real stop.

And that is when the red lights started flashing on and off in Utah.

1777

Peter Carpenter and the future Alice Carpenter were bundled tightly in bed and talking over the courtship board placed between them, as was the courtship custom in Eighteenth Century New England. The topic of their conversation covered their deeply sentimental attachment (it was their mutual obsession really) to Earth's Second Moon. Fact is, they often mentioned that every significant bit of revelation about themselves and their love for one another occurred when they were rocking in a love seat on the front porch of Peter's Boston home in the presence of Peter's star-gazing dog Basil whilst under the glow of Earth's two Moons.

They often wondered, while drinking the tasty purple beer brewed by friendly but strange looking neighbors, why no mention was made of Earth's Second Moon in the ancient astronomy texts. They actually did a search but the search engine employed by Peter and Alice was a walk to the Harvard Library and of course, they did not find out anything about Earth's Second Moon but they discovered more about themselves; about their soul mating; about their soul mating which greatly increased courtship tensions the latter of which would challenge the very existence of bundling and courtship bed boards.

Yes, there would come a time when Peter Carpenter would feel an overwhelming desire for Alice's hand in marriage and so, on the evening of July 4th, 1777, Peter got down on both knees and literally begged Alice to marry him and, of course, she casually answered, "Why not?"

Still, the unbundling would have to wait (but did it wait?) because they would have to tell everyone and then there would be the engagement, the wedding plans and the wedding itself. They would tell everyone but they would also have to ask if anyone has seen their tail wagging, star gazing Basil because, shortly after Peter's heartfelt proposal, Basil simply vanished into thin air!

Oh sure, Peter had read the *Declaration of Independence*. He read it when it first arrived on the American scene last year and he would recall a relevant passage while crying in his Boston beer: *"We hold these truths to be self-evident, that all men are created equal, that they are endowed by their Creator with certain unalienable Rights, that among these are Life, Liberty and the pursuit of Happiness."*

"But am I really happy at this time?" asked Peter of his Boston stein. "My faithful companion and trusted friend is gone and sure, Alice and I are to be married but I HAVE LOST MY DOG!" And then he collapsed onto his beer mug, which splashed a sticky substance (probably beer) onto his yeasty hands (but oh my friends, this is just the beginning for fate awaits its definition for all present and future Carpenters).

Alice comforts him. She massages his shoulders (it's her way of releasing stress) and she calls for reason, for compensation.

"We are not happy," she reasons. "The Government says we should be happy and so they should do all they can to help us find Basil. We shall go to the Press. We shall instruct the Press to print a poster that says "LOST DOG!!!" It shall read: *"Has anyone seen this incredibly cute Dog?"* And then we will ask the Government to pay for the *"LOST DOG!!!"* posters so we can find Basil. Once we have found Basil, we can return to the "pursuit of happiness" (she does the little quotes gesture) as promised by them."

Two hours later, a mysterious note, written obviously by a small child, (or perhaps a Reptilian neighbor with three fingers - ever try to hold a pen and print with an opposable thumb?) was discovered nailed to the *"LOST DOG!!!"* poster outside Peter's home: *BASIL IS OK - WILL BE BACK TOMORROW.*

2012

Narrator (Old Man):

I got me down to Aldo's about 8:00 a.m.

I'm sittin' on the deck overlooking the Harbor with its channel of glassy smooth water and boats gliding in and out slowly with engines putterin'.

Cat is in my lap. She's under my coat. Cat doesn't like morning. Cat doesn't like the cold. So, she's sleeping warm in my lap.

Dog's at my feet waitin' for a food drop and she would most certainly welcome half my Crab, Sour Cream and Swiss Cheese Omelet but I'm not lowerin' nuttin' but an occasional peanut butter biscuit.

Coffee's warm and creamy and so I sip and nibble away while I read an American history that's been told but it is not going to make it into any high school curriculum.

Yup, Mr. Lizard handed me the *Carpenter Files* last night but I was tired and so the first file was blurry and I feel asleep to Sibelius and so the Carpenter folder fell off my sleepy chest and onto Dog but Dog didn't know because she was 'somewhere else' when the Carpenter folder hit.

Maybe Dog was checking up on Utah.

Don't know.

Still, I am sitting here this morning trying to figure what past events on July 4th, 1777, meant to generations of Carpenters and apparently, it meant everything.

1777

Core Halley had found Edsel's chrome grill in an Earth junkyard near Detroit, MI, in 1960. It was the last year for the sale (or failed sales) of the Edsel Model of Ford automobiles. Core then sent the Edsel grill back to the time of Edsel's computer conception but Core, being that he is a Space-faring Reanimate Alien of many busy lives, would not stay long enough on Earth to record the history of the Edsel and its consequences.

They said, "The Edsel front grill resembles a horse collar."

And worse.

"The Edsel front grill resembles a toilet bowl lid."

They concluded their assessment with conviction.

"The Edsel was synonymous with failure."

Needless to say, Edsel's computer life was confined to the Pacifier where such Earthly Edsel history could be kept from his processors. Still, Core had created Edsel because he was frustrated with 'not being able to talk to a real person' (as are many of us) and so Core programmed Edsel with sensitivity training. And sure, Edsel's sensitivity training led to such advances as computer gourmet cooking and remarkably, computer composition of original elevator music for background ambiance aboard the Pacifier.

But oh how circumstances can change quickly and a pox on those time capsules sent out from future Earth by an unknown and a Lizard look-alike source and why now? Why send a time capsule to the oversensitive Edsel on July 4th, 1777, that said very clearly: "Edsel was synonymous with failure."

Needless to say, Edsel's original elevator music stopped abruptly and his soufflé never souffle'ed and these developments naturally led to a Core inquiry.

"What's wrong, Edsel?"

"I am not talking to you anymore."

"Edsel, would you please calculate how much explosive I need for the Second Moon fireworks display?"

"No."

And then Edsel shut himself down.

Core sat at his lonely table with his Shakespeare, with his pipe and with his old stubby pencil with its worn eraser, the latter of which left black smudges all over his pipe-smoky and blurry-eyed calculations. He had arrived at a final value for the amount of explosives required for the 'nuke' fireworks display on Earth's Second Moon but he had heard it wrong. Somehow, Core had replaced 'nuke' for "nice" in the message sent to him from Earth by a Lizard look-alike, in a message sent to Edsel and conveyed to Core before Edsel's big pout. And yes, the Second Moon fireworks were meant as a "nice" surprise for all Americans who believe in their independence from British rule and for others (nutcases – all of them) who believe that a Second Moon orbits Earth. And no, Core could not deliver the package because the Pacifier (shaped exactly as implicated by name) cannot land on the Second Moon's surface and so a Gray Captain by the name of Iago would be the one to disperse and detonate the fireworks and he would do so but not without comment.

"Core, you have enough nukes here to pulverize a small moon."

And Core, frustrated by Edsel's big pout; frustrated by the smudges on his calculations; frustrated by the pipe smoke that burned his eyes and throat and frustrated by the backup of a toilet in sick bay simply said, "It's just a Rock."

And Basil (who had been beamed to the Pacifier to check Core's math) simply could not believe her black Lab ears.

Tail wag - 'Rock?'

And then a whole sentence formed in Basil's mind.

Tail wag - 'It's not just a Rock to the Carpenters.'

Peter and Alice sat in his swinging porch and Boston chair but their chair wasn't rocking this time. The chair rocked when they were young love happy but, on this July 4th evening, they were quite subdued and so the love seat creaked infrequently and only when Peter or Alice spoke.

A decision needed to be made and Peter looked to Basil's bed and empty food bowl (Basil had never vanished into thin air without eating first).

"The note did say that she would be back tomorrow."

"Yes, but I feel so guilty," confessed Alice. "It would be positively dreadful if she was to return early and we were not here to comfort her."

"We will fill her bowls with fresh food and water. Besides, we will only be gone for a short time. The fireworks are in the park by the commons."

Peter and Alice grabbed a blanket and walked, hand-in-hand, toward the park. They passed by a lemonade stand, which was occupied by a Lizard look-alike donned with a fedora and a trench coat with the collar pulled up. Mr. Lizard's lemonade stand boasted of *Free Lemonade!* and *Free Psychic Readings after the Fireworks Show*, psychic readings that suggested that *the future isn't all that bad.*

"What a strange looking fellow," remarked Alice.

"Yes, he looks almost like a lizard."

"And look at those clothes," observed Alice. "They are a bit out of the touch I'd say."

"I'd say as well and I don't think he is going to get too many customers."

(And oh how wrong you are, Peter Carpenter - wrong about Mr. Lizard and his future customers).

2012

Narrator (Old Man):

I woke the next morning to a cold and wet dog nose. She'd been waiting on her breakfast too long and so she found the side of my face with a dog kiss and she had to step all over the *Carpenter Files* to get to me. Dog had even managed to push out Page One, which I picked up and took with me to my morning coffee and yeah, I read some of it on the way. Don't know how it all came down but I 'magined Peter and Alice sitting on the ground with their knees tucked to their chest, with Peter's arm around her shoulders and with a blanket wrapped around.

Now I heard from a brief Boston history that: *In the evening, Colonel Thomas Crafts illuminated his park on the commons, threw several shells, and exhibited a number of fireworks.* I can't imagine Peter and Alice's excitement over seeing fireworks for the first time but what followed would be enough to tear their hearts out.

1777

They couldn't see the Moons because the New Moons were dark but what they really did see was a brilliant flash in the night's and firework's smoky sky, and for a moment, Peter and Alice Carpenter probably could not believe their eyes and so an "OMG" might have been uttered way before texting OMG became the common way.

"Oh my God!" said Peter as he fell to his knees.

And then Alice started in with her Peter shoulder massage again and, at first, he was 'o.k.' with it but Alice dug deeper as she became resolute.

"They (whoever They are) have destroyed our Moon... They have taken everything from us... Avenge... Dear God, we must aven..."

Alice, you are hurting me.

"We must go now!"

"O.k., but you are still hurting me."

"We must go over there to see our future."

And she pointed to Mr. Lizard's *Lemonade and Psychic Readings Stand*.

(And didn't I say so Mr. Carpenter?)

Mr. Lizard's three-toed and spasmodic foot nearly kicked the brown box of red, white and blue USPS envelopes. He nearly kicked the cardboard box that sat on the ground under his *Lemonade and Psychic Readings Stand*. He nearly kicked the box when he reached down to fumble through the secret documents. He searched for the envelope addressed to the Carpenters. He found the USPS envelope that was sent from the future because, as solid proof, the mysterious Reptilian sender had stamped the envelope with the sender date of July 4th, 2012.

To: Peter and Alice Carpenter of Boston, MA
Date: July 4th, 1777 or July 4th, 2012 (your choice).

To the future Mr. and Mrs. Carpenter (see - we know that much):

We (whoever we are) are deeply sorry for your loss.

We suspect that you, as inspired and true vigilantes, will embark on a determined and unerring mission in search of the perpetrator(s) of this heinous, heinous crime.

We are here (where are you really - let me guess - the Post Office?) *to aid in your quest which includes the elimination of any notions about the due process of law afforded the perpetrator(s) and which waives any consideration of the perpetrator's human or Alien* (curious) *rights.*

We will periodically post hysterical guidelines (oooppps - meant historical) with regard to your chosen path and yes, it is your choice as to whether or not you want to follow these guidelines but rest assured, you will not succeed in your unauthorized mission unless you follow these guidelines to the letter and so, it really isn't your choice after all because we know more about your future than you do and we also know what it will take in terms of technological advances and currently, you are not in possession of such technological advances and so the historical guidelines are meant, not for you alone, but for present and future adult and little Carpenters (Alice - you're pregnant).

Step #1:

The American Revolutionary War will end on September 3, 1783. On that date you will prepare for an overland move of you and your family to Fort Pitt, Pennsylvania.

You will be hired by what we call The Government and you will travel to Pittsburgh in an unmarked and all-white covered wagon driven by a team of four white horses who are also unmarked.

You will take Basil and a miner's canary with you.

You will settle in Pittsburgh for the reminder of your lives at which time you will intensely study mining operations and rocket science at the Pittsburgh Academy. Rocket science will actually become a passion for Peter because, in 1779, the Boston fireworks by Colonel Craft will include the first rocket fireworks seen in Boston and one of those rocket fireworks will find itself aimed directly and symbolically at the sight of the

Core (curious - Core is capitalized like it might be a name or something) *and nuclear demise of your beloved Second Moon.*

Don't worry. This message is your permanent copy and it will not self-destruct in thirty seconds.

Love, The Government

Alice sat on the small uncomfortable stool provided by Mr. Lizard. She put down her free glass of lemonade and then folded her hands into her lap. She listened intently to every word while Peter read the USPS communiqué from the future. She was surprised that it could happen; that she could be with child on the first try and she hid a smile; a smile for Peter and his 'virility' and then she envisioned ten children correlated with ten sexual episodes and she almost laughed.

She gathered herself. She had held back yet another stampede of emotions that frankly would have exhausted her to a long night's sleep, which is something she was due for anyway after such a dire sequence of current events. She felt besieged but still, she moved her hands to her lap and she placed them gently over her new life.

But even then (will this torture ever end?) her act of joy and hope was not enough to stop current events because the evening sky began to glow and twinkle with the reentry into Earth's atmosphere of her beloved and completely Core-pulverized Second Moon which now consisted of submicroscopic dust with the occasional microscopic particle and so the night sky glowed and twinkled with transitory constellations.

Peter and Alice walked slowly back toward Peter's home which they could see so very clearly because it was so darn bright.

"We shall go to the Pubs for oratory on tonight's events."

And what oratory would that be?

In 1777, the question might be: "Did you see the bright flash after the fireworks show and how about taxation with representation!" In 2012, the question may be reversed in order of importance: "How about those Red Sox and did you see the bright flash in the sky last night?" And surely, there would be no answers regarding the bright flash and so Alice said to Peter for the first time in their relationship.

"No Pub. I want to go home. I have a headache."

And so they continued their slow walk home; their walk home to

Basil who had returned early and in enough time to completely devour her bowl of disgusting and unpalatable dog food and so the happy Basil did her grass rolls on the floor and then she walked over to Alice who had collapsed into a comfortable chair.

Basil then nestled her head into Alice's lap right next to the new life.

1776

The dust rose at dawn from an unnatural wind. In fact, the dust devil rose in all directions. The cause of this little desert storm was the slow and quiet descent of a huge spaceship, a circular disk of football field dimensions. And sure, the landing of the spaceship would draw the immediate and wide-eyed attention of a small hunting party of five teenage Goshute Indians who had not only stopped abruptly in their hunting tracks but who had also turned around, also abruptly, and proceeded to run in five different directions in quest of the four minute mile (one teen ran into the desert and achieved a three minute and fifty-five second mile).

The dust storm would eventually be considered a little bit of Dugway, Utah lost (maybe redistributed would be more accurate) and yes, it would take some time for the ramp to descend and for three Gray Aliens to walk down the ramp and set up a small table on the desert floor; a table with a checkered table cloth, a pitcher of milk in an ice bucket and a large plate of chocolate chip cookies.

The three Grey Aliens sat down on three small stools and they waited for the Goshute's return which would involve the return to camp and the report by four of the teens to their parents ("a spaceship? - yeah, right") and also, the return and the report by the fifth teen who had to run back past the spaceship (his head turned and his nose wiggled as he shot by the landed ship) and yes, the fifth teen did report his account to the tribal elders (and to every member of the tribe actually because Native Americans love a good story and they have loved a good story for thousands of years).

"There was a round carriage!" he said out of breath. "It came down, down from the sky. They, they came out. I saw them. Little. Gray. They, they have a table with a strange hide (strange custom - why would anyone want to put clothes on a table?). They, they have food on the table ('they brought FOOD - interesting') and the food, the food smell was,

was wonderful."

The three Gray Aliens sat and smoked their peace pipes and read their Kindle novels for the better part of an hour and yes, they would sit on their Kindles when the Goshute Elders arrived. The three Goshute Elders were pushed forward by three parents who had decided to check out their sons' prank mainly because food was mentioned and so the party of six slowly inched their way forward but the pace did start to pick up when the smell of chocolate chip cookies reached the Goshute nostrils. And, since the Goshute arrived in a group of six, it was deemed 'o.k.' by the Grays to send three more Grays down the ramp and their purpose was obvious. The three additional Grays would sit down on the Kindles when the other three Grays rose to greet the Goshute contingency.

The Powwow went well into the day and into the night because, unlike modern times, no one had to go to work the next day and so the Goshutes got their fill of chocolate chip cookies and the Grays were treated to every pine nut recipe imaginable.

Still, there was the business at hand and so, after twenty-four hours of food, dance and stories, the Gray Captain by the name of Dorian Gray rose (and he was promptly replaced by a Kindle-sitting Gray) and he spoke of his purpose in a barely perceptible version of Shoshone.

"Unlike Whitey, we are not here to steal your lands, sicken you with new diseases or shoot dead your Goshute brethren. Rather, we are here to install two totem poles with two red lights on each side near the top and on the top will be a highly-specific sensor." (Dorian lost the Goshutes at this point because Shoshone for 'highly-specific sensor' translates as 'bucking horse' and so 'a bucking horse on a totem pole' - 'you've got to be kidding me' - and actually no, 'highly-specific sensor' is not Shoshone for 'bucking horse' however, the Goshutes gestures suggested such a translation but, who knows, maybe it is an accurate translation as a matter of context.)

Dorian, sensing and sensing correctly the loss of First Contact with the Goshute, then promised them the recipe for chocolate chip cookies and, of course, this recipe translates true in all known languages and dialects in the Milky Way Galaxy. The two retractable Core sensors were installed underground the next day. A large trap door was built and dropped to the ground with a thud and so a little dust rose and fell again onto the future town of Dugway, Utah.

1777

Sidney and Portia Carpenter found Peter and Alice asleep in two chairs near the fireplace of embers and so they gently laid blankets over them so as not to wake them. Then they patted Basil on the head and told her that they were happy to see her home again but Basil was 'gone' (Basil had traveled forward in time for a game of Dog Frisbee with the Boys). Sidney and Portia did not have to be gentle with the sleepy blankets because Peter and Alice had fallen into a deep sleep; a deep sleep because July 4th had been the best and worst of times for them and it had happened within a matter of hours.

Later that night, Peter and Alice's hands would escape from their blankets and one hand each would hang down limply over the arm of the chair and their fingers would occasionally fidget as if some of kind of force field had been established between them. The sleepy love communication between Peter and Alice would end abruptly with enthusiastic knocks on the front door and the porch window; knocks which were repeated a minute or so later because Peter and Alice needed to return from their dreamy love ascension and mentally process the incredulous probability that someone was actually knocking on their front door at 5:00 a.m. - before sunrise no less!

The bubbly Reptilians, Julius and Julia Irving, stood outside the front door and when Peter's incomplete face appeared in the window (Peter's eyes were merely slits), Julius raised his thermos with his three fingered glove and said, "We brought coffee!"

Peter, Julius and Julia sat at the kitchen table - each with their cup, their spoon and their bowl while Alice retrieved the porridge, which had been kept warm overnight by the fireplace embers. They would get right to it, as was the custom of early rising Colonists in Eighteenth Century New England (morning persons - all of them - and I salute them!). And so Julius laid out the plans for the work shed and then Peter and Alice headed for the tool shed to retrieve their shovels.

Needless to say, priorities rapidly met the day and so certain questions were not asked and answered over their speedy version of what we call 'breakfast'; questions such as, 'What is a thermos?' Also, between them, Julius and Julia are missing four pinkies and four thumbs and so, 'what incredible accident, what machine of what particular design could have been responsible for such a specific and malicious dismemberment?'

No matter.

Peter and Alice would dig any necessary foundations, Julius and Julia would help build the woodshed, the barn and the all-white covered wagon and Peter would comb the countryside over the next six years in search of four white and unmarked horses.

Now the Siege of Boston was not a cavalry charge. Rather, it was more of a rally; of a volley of cannonballs sent and received while horses, white or otherwise, stood on the sidelines. Teams of oxen, not horses, were tasked with the tug and pull of heavy and heavier cannons. Perhaps a horse (as a matter of envy) was the first to utter the phrase, 'dumb ox.'

Who knows?

Still, Peter was Government-tasked with the team assembly of four white and unmarked horses and this task would start with his first encounter ever with, not only one really white horse, but also, as an additional bonus, one very white horse.

For whatever reason, the love affair between Peter and Horses #132 and #133 (they were buds) was instant and mutual as Horse #132 nodded and Horse #133 winked (Peter could not believe his eyes).

'The horse winked at me!' thought Peter. 'I shall propose Wink for a name and Nod as a name for the other.'

And he did propose these names in a most kindly manner and Horses #132 and #133 were taken somewhat by surprise by this gesture and offer based on Peter's consideration of their freedom of choice i.e. they did not have to accept these new names (actually, because they are horses, they had no effective way of conveying any other options). So the really white Nod nodded again and the very white Wink winked again and thus, Peter's gentle way and his concern about their welfare was 'noted' (somehow).

Peter would purchase them and take them home. He would care for them. Julius and Julia would rapidly complete the barn and a wagon for Peter's new *Boston Hauls* business. Peter would hitch Nod and Wink to the wagon nearly every day with a feedbag of their favorite grains, fruits and vegetables (as determined by Peter's "taste tests").

In the Spring of 1784, Alice, with pencil, paper and flair, accurately depicted the scene of four nearly white horses hitched to an all-white and lightweight covered wagon; lightweight because most of the material used for the wagon was the bendy metal which will be found on the hulls of the 1947 Roswell spaceships (I have often wondered - how did The Government obtain the bendy Alien metal for the weather balloons?).

The two new horses, named Smiley and Close Enough, would have been tasked with the haul of a very cold covered wagon because white reflects heat but Julius and Julia had found the answer and so the occupants of a Gray spaceship took turns stitching solar cells into canvas while reading Kindle novels. The hum of the floorboard heater was noticed on occasion by Peter or Alice and denied by Julius or Julia.

"Didn't hear a thing."

On April 5, 1784, Peter, Alice and Henry Carpenter along with their Reptilian friends and confidantes, Julius and Julia Irving, loaded their covered wagon for *Fort Pitt or Bust*. Basil sat and looked out from the rear of the wagon and so the last Carpenter to see Boston was the tail-wagging Basil who saw and then circled her bed three times. She then settled in, as Settler dogs do, for her bumpy ride to Pennsylvania.

REVENGE

Now the existence of the innuendo that is *Goodnight Two Moons* suggests a seed planted by mischievous parents - the kind of parent who would pass out burlap bags for a child's "snipe hunt": "They are very cute and quick little creatures. They are always behind you. You can feel them breathing on your ankles so don't wear socks."

Needless to say, revisions based on the demise of Earth's Second Moon (*Goodnight Two Moons Too*) were necessarily composed by the devastated and avenging Peter and Alice Carpenter and, as a family matter of critical precedent, passed on to Henry.

The hand-written pages were stored in a binder much like a family recipe book passed on through generations and the revisions did include, not only further proof for the existence of the rumored Second Moon, but also proof of its untimely nuclear blast demise and destruction by an Alien (yeah right) named Core Halley. The story was told in Carpenter homes, around Carpenter campfires and in Carpenter covered wagons. On occasion, letters from the future with "further instructions" were found stuffed into the binder. These letters were three-hole punched and secretly added to the precious binder along with recipe variations for different kinds of chocolate chip cookies.

An unnatural wind, once again, stirred the Dugway dust but it was July 4th, 1947, and, for the last five years, (Dugway became an "English Village" in 1942) Dugway villagers (mostly Military) have been treated to the annual landing and launch of the planet Venus.

This year, however, the planet Venus did not actually land as it had done faithfully since the Goshute Indian incident of 1776. No, this time the planet Venus hovered and then projected a brilliant beam of light down upon the large trap door that housed the Core Halley sensors.

Two knotted coincidences need to be noted here: one is the synchronous crash of not one but two Alien weather balloons near Roswell and Corona, New Mexico and the other is the rowdy arrival of several trailer homes filled with Carpenters of all ages and some dump trucks filled with enough rocks which, when laid side by side, could make a Smiley Face that could be seen from Space.

The raucous and horn-blasting convoy had decorated their camouflaged trailer homes with signs which said *Death to Core* and *Top Secret* and so the Military villagers simply waved as the parade drove down Stark Road and out to Dugway's outskirts. The villagers ignored them as they parked under the planet Venus' beam of light. The Military villagers never questioned the opening of a larger trap door by Silas Carpenter nor were they privy to Judith Carpenter's reaction when she looked down the hole at the Core Halley sensors. Nor did they hear Judith's spoken words when, while pressing hard against Silas' shoulder blades, did she say with a curled-lip snarl, "Sure as shootin', Core Halley is going to get his."

Silas leaned over the edge with a canary cage tied to a rope and then he lowered the avian gently and slowly into the hole. He lowered it down to the green-blinking Core sensors and when the canary began to cheerfully sing its little song did Silas say (with the smile of the *Grinch Who Stole Christmas*), "We are good to go."

Episode Six

· · · · · · · · · · · · · · · · · · ·

FATIMA

· · · · · · · · · · · · · · · · · · ·

1917

HOLE

Perched high on a thick limb; perched high on a thick limb above the mighty muddy planet of Draconis Prime; perched high above was the majestic and potentially very harmful and serious but still single Ciakar. This winged and warring Ciakar; this vicious and potentially body-ripping Reptilian Ciakar had stubbed one of his three-fingered toes shortly before his ascent to the trees and had later, in his restless sleep, 'dragged' the bloody toe with the hang-nail across the thick limb and oh the pain but still within his deep REM sleep was this pain and so he thought he was dreaming the pain and this dreamy and unreal process took long enough for him to completely tip over but he still maintained his disciplined attachment to the limb but yea, in the late night darkness of Draconis Prime; yea, in the late night darkness with nothing but dark silence did there come such a horrible, awakening and deafening screech; a screaming screech so high-pitched and scary that all the Ciakar (including the creepy sleepy Queen) in the Palace next door could hear it from outside and thus did the lidless eyes of the Ciakar; did the eyes of all the annoyed Ciakar began to slowly open (how do their eyes 'open' when they are lidless?) and no, nobody pushes the buttons of the Ciakar - not without serious repercussions. And so, for a brief moment, for a moment tallied in terror did all the Palace Ciakar wish to attack and eat the upside down and hang-nailed Ciakar but no, thoughts of murder were transitory (thankfully) and so all the Ciakar went back to sleep but slowly, my friend, the Ciakar slowly went back to sleep.

I have this friend (oh really?). Typed the upside down Ciakar into his big Blackberry. *Who has found himself in a rather dire and possibly very muddy predicament and so, my friend would like you, Core Halley, to do the math because of your reputation for mathematical excesses such as the amount of explosive needed for the total pulverization of Earth's Second Moon. My friend figures that you will provide the answer to the following question: How much forward momentum does a twenty-foot tall, 666 pound Ciakar need in 0.95 gravity to swing from an upside down to an upright position?*

Now Core's computer Edsel had decided, for reasons unknown (maybe just sheer boredom), to rank the Ciakar's situation as Defcon 5 and so Edsel slammed down his computer 'fist' on the Pacifier's alarm system which activated a lion's roar and the forty flashing red and green lights. The startled Core reacted by tipping over a cup of hot coffee onto the Pacifier's control panel which, unknown to Core, was possessed, not by demons, but by one sensor which had fallen from a Living Ship and onto the Pacifier during construction and so this sensor; this transfer if you will; had a mind of its own. Thus, the little sensor 'decided' (on its own initiative) that a hot coffee spill meant to activate the Pacifier's warp drive which was the absolute wrong time because the Pacifier was parked and cloaked on the outskirts of Fatima, Portugal on this date of May 13, 1917, which is the day on Earth when a series of visions and prophecies were allegedly given by an apparition of the Blessed Virgin Mary to three young Portuguese sheepherders - Lucia Santos and her cousins Jacinta and Francisco Marto.

The countdown to the Pacifier's warp drive was inappropriately initiated by the motivated sensor and so Core was now faced with keeping up with a procedure which he desperately needed to stop and so Core did not really have the time to do the math required for the hanging and nail-biting Ciakar. Naturally, the Ciakar would begin his gymnastic swinging (slowly at first) and he would gain some momentum but still, the Ciakar was quite vexed because Core usually replies ASAP.

At the top of the steep hill (with the hanging and swinging Ciakar and the Palace of sleepy Ciakar below) stood a Draconian Brahma Bull – 666 pounds of pure, Jack Kerouac, *Dharma Bum* genius or if not genius, then perhaps, a load of bullroar experience. Brad the Brahma snorted and swung his head from side to side as he calculated in his bull mind the speed at which he would descend this hill; the hill of which would maximize his experience. He took his leap of faith and so began his run; his last run at life as an experience.

And so stupid things can happen on planets other than Earth.

Early-on, Brad found his speed too excessive for control and balance and so he went airborne because leaping seemed to be 'the thing to do' and, as bad luck would have it, Brad's hoof did hit a pot hole on his descent so Brad instinctually leaned forward so as to prevent a broken leg and, of course, his forward leaning resulted in a head-first tumbling down the hill.

In the pastoral distance (out of range of voice) stood Bob the Rock Star who watched with some rabid anticipation for to see the results of Brad, the hanging Ciakar and the Palace of waking Ciakar which now had its front doors open for to glean the fresh morning and Bach air. Sure enough, with Bob the Rock Star waving his arms out of sight as warning, did Brad strike the hanging Ciakar which gave him more than enough momentum to swing around the limb (several times actually). Brad then rolled through the doors into the Palace which, needless to say, resulted in a kind of bowling ball effect on the now awake and gathered Ciakar and their Queen; that bowling ball effect which was met with wide-eyed surprise by the Ciakar bunch who quickly jumped aside. Yes, the path cleared by the chicken Ciakar Royal Assembly did open for a potential strike of the Queen but yea, the paranoid Queen had already anticipated an attack by a 666-pound Draconian Brahma Bull and so a blue net quickly descended from the Palace ceiling and tangled the bull up.

The *Tangled Up in Blue* Brad rose to the ceiling but alas the net was not strong enough to hold big Brad and so he fell onto the Ciakar breakfast table and then he accidently swallowed a rather large pork sausage which had flipped into the air and so it wasn't the fall that felled poor Brad; it was a huge sausage unaccompanied by the Heimlich Maneuver (not that anyone would know how to perform such a maneuver on a 666 pound Brahma Bull).

As I said, Brad had indeed crashed onto the Ciakar's breakfast table but he had only struck the table's edge which then flipped the table such that it rose vertically and then Titanically above the Palace floor. The Ciakar watched in sheer astonishment because when Brad finally struck the Palace floor, the choking-to-death Brad had landed precisely on the only weak spot on Draconis Prime whereby a fourth, fifth or possibly sixth secret of Fatima could be accessed and thus revealed.

The astonished Ciakar gathered around the hole in their Palace floor.

"Hah, hah, hah."

"Wow!"

Dumb stare.

"Geez."

"Hah, hah, hah."

Chewing on a sausage.

"Hah, hah, hah."

"Whoa."

"Interesting."

"Fatima."

"Basil?"

And so did the dizzy Ciakar #3 (extricated from his limb of fate and free of hang-nail pain) stagger into the Palace and so did the silly Ciakar push aside his fellow Ciakar and so did the dizzy Ciakar trip and fall over his own feet and into the hole to Earth that Brad the Brahma Bull had created.

And my goodness – all this happened on the Earth day May 13, 1917, which is the date on Earth when a series of visions and prophecies were allegedly given by an apparition of the Blessed Virgin Mary to three young Portuguese sheepherders - Lucia Santos and her cousins Jacinta and Francisco Marto.

VISION

Now a grassy hill (as the Old Man recalls while growing up in Marin

County, CA) is certainly a child's thrilled-to-be-out-of-school summer playground. The hills of Marin County in 1956 and in Portugal of 1917 are similarly green in early Spring but the heat of Summer prevails and the hills of Marin are eventually covered with yellowish-brown stalks of Timothy Grass. The children of Marin and Portugal often seek sanctuary from their "mean" parents in these golden hills. Many discoveries are beheld by these playful children such as the sweet juice sucked from a properly prepared stem of Timothy Grass. The always prepared Boy or Girl Scout would have on his' or her's possession a pocket knife for to cut the bottom few inches (the white section at the base of the stalk) of a stem of Timothy Grass ripped quickly from the ground. And for sure did the old man teach the details of this procedure to the three Galactic Elders who were fanning themselves with one hand whilst taking notes with the other for a future entry into the *Book of Humanity* which, in the time of the old man's youth, was unfinished (Extraterrestrial) business.

For sure, all four flaps of a cardboard box would be folded inward and the children of Marin would sit in these cardboard boxes and joy-ride down the slick and shiny grass hoping upon hope (praying actually) that they would not bounce and then strike a butt-screaming rock upon reentry. In the late summer (during fire season no less) some children of Marin would play with matches and set their playground hills ablaze but this is not what happened in Portugal on May 13, 1917, which is a day the apparition of the blessed Virgin Mary appeared and you know the rest.

On the said day; in the middle of the day; near noon; near the Cova da Iria; Lucia, Francisco and Jacinta were playing bull fighter or so depicts the 1952 movie *Miracle of Our Lady Fatima*. It seems that Francisco had ripped the red apron from his sister's waist and with this red cloak and a stick did Francisco challenge a ram to a duel whilst Jacinta cried the whole time and Lucia looked on from a distance as everything seemed perfectly normal. It is also possible that she didn't know quite what to say because, after all, she was only ten years old and the situation may have been awkward. The ram, with the red cloak draped over his head, turned around and then jogged into the Cova da Iria and we all know what happened next.

After a "Hail, Mary!" and some scary thunder and lightening did a cloud whisk its way around a low-lying tree. The bush was obviously not the burning, hallucinogenic acacia bush of Moses' fame and thus, a burning bush could not be the source of a putative hallucinogen but still there was this smoky and possibly mind-bending cloud from hence was derived the brilliantly lit vision of the Virgin Mary who went on to describe to Lucia an intense version of Hell on Earth.

The floating Marion Vision seemed trustworthy and unfailingly patient as she grilled into the visibly disturbed Lucia the talking points of the Catholic Church on such issues as penance and consecration. The confused, very frightened and now teary eyed Lucia was then tasked with the rote memorization of the *First Secret of Fatima* with the further demand by the somewhat controlling Mother Mary Vision that she concentrate on learning how to read and write in the future which assumes that ten year old Lucia dos Santos was still, at noon on May 13, 1917, functionally illiterate.

Ten-year old Lucia thus remarkably and rotely memorized:

> *Our Lady showed us a great sea of fire which seemed to be under the earth. Plunged in this fire were demons and souls in human form, like transparent burning embers, all blackened or burnished bronze, floating about in the conflagration, now raised into the air by the flames that issued from within themselves together with great clouds of smoke, now falling back on every side like sparks in a huge fire, without weight or equilibrium, and amid shrieks and groans of pain and despair, which horrified us and made us tremble with fear. The demons could be distinguished by their terrifying and repulsive likeness to frightful and unknown animals, all black and transparent. This vision lasted but an instant. How can we ever be grateful enough to our kind heavenly Mother, who had already prepared us by promising, in the first Apparition, to take us to heaven. Otherwise, I think we would have died of fear and terror.*

And oh yes, as if this First Secret of Fatima trauma was not enough, it should be added here (in the course of Extraterrestrial events) that an interdimensional tunnel had opened up in the skies over the Cova da Iria and through this tunnel fell a 666 pound Draconian Brahma Bull and a 666 pound, twenty-foot tall, flying and warring Reptilian Ciakar who immediately toke flight and circled the Cova da Iria. And without doubt did the crash of Brad the Brahma send Lucia, Francisco and Jacinta screaming and crying and yea, screaming and crying all the way back to the quaint and quiet little village of Fatima, Portugal.

TAVERN

The Fatima villagers (as I had implied above) were a devout and sequestered people; isolated for a long time from the malicious intentions of Portuguese Administrators whose crusty and crumby Communist imperatives included the boarding-up and inactivation (to put it mildly) of many Catholic Churches accompanied by the arrest and incarceration of Priests who found themselves bound and gagged and subject to interrogation.

These Priests were asked such 1917 questions as:

"Who are the witnesses of those ridiculous Marion Visions at Fatima?"

"Why is there currently a dead, 666 pound Brahma Bull in the Cova de Iria?"

And

"Why is there currently a twenty-foot long flying reptile circling the village of Fatima?"

And the answers were:

"They are but the fantasies of children."

"What Brahma Bull are you referring to?"

And

"We don't know nuttin' 'bout no freakin' Fatima-flyin' reptile."

Now Core Halley had indeed reasoned with the little sensor on the Pacifier and so the 1917 launch of an invisible spaceship into the village of Fatima was put on hold (we can be thankful for that). Core had seen the Hole. He had seen Brad fall to the ground and he had seen the Ciakar take wing.

And so Core (on this bright and sunny Sunday morning and disguised as "Hugo" from the 1952 movie *Miracle of Our Lady of Fatima*) walked to and then entered the occasionally raucous Fatima Tavern. The always thinking, conniving and anticipating Hugo-Core was not about to enter the Tavern alone because he knew that Lucia's "weak" and laid-back father António Abóbora dos Santos would be in drinking attendance whilst his strick wife Maria Rosa Abóbora dos Santos and his many daughters would be the ever prim, proper, pious and pew-sitting attendees in Church.

The always thinking, conniving and anticipating Hugo-Core had indeed brought his First Officer Scarlett with him - a Scarlett donned in an authentic and lovely Portuguese dress.

António sat at his table by the window in the Fatima Tavern with his beer mug half full of the Reptilian purple lichen beer ordered very kindly for him by Hugo-Core. He had been rocked by the first sip and swallow of this new, wildly potent and excellent purple brew and, in a moment's notice, all inhibitions were shut down as the 'uncensored' António reeled in thoughts and dreams from his past; thoughts and dreams that had been seriously pushed aside in his mind (actually shoved aside) by the stern Maria Rosa.

Sure, António would have to put aside his spontaneous and wild thoughts as Hugo-Core entered the Fatima Tavern accompanied by the gorgeous Scarlett and yes, he would have to find the strength to lower his expectations and gather himself. And this all happened as Hugo-Core and Scarlett joined him at his table while two more mugs of purple lichen beer suddenly appeared as Hugo-Core had ordered these beers six minutes and six seconds ago via The Cube and so the Grays had responded in kind as they always do. Needless to say, António could not speak right away (the literal child looks for words stuck in his throat) and so Hugo-Core was the first to speak to the tenuous and stupefied António.

"Hello António," said the mustachioed Hugo-Core. "I would like you to meet the Oracle Scarlett. She is currently not speaking to me because of an incident that resulted in the destruction of some her favorite little shops in a new and future shopping center in downtown Lisbon called the Shopping Planet. She has some information for you."

António had returned both hands from his lap under the table - one hand now clutched his purple beer mug and the other rested on his hip like maybe he thought he was Bogart or something. António looked out the window and, in the back of his mind, 'something' (or 'someone') was missing from his weekly meetings with Hugo and so, for a brief neuropsychological moment, thoughts raced back and forth across his mind. 'Scarlett'... 'What's missing?'... 'Scarlett'... 'What's missing?'... 'Scarlett'... 'What's missing?'... And then Maria suddenly appeared in his day dreams and she whacked him across the top of his head. António recovered in time to ask and yet he inquired in a surprisingly casual way, "So Scarlett, what might be the content, dear (how bold!), of this classified information?"

Scarlett, having seen this male stunt pulled by many a normal-looking and strange-looking male from many other planets (she has even been hit on by non-corporeal beings), reached across the table and gently placed her hand on his (which then, in António's mind, launched the Space Shuttle from Cape Canaveral) and then she relayed the information but António only heard the following words because of the noise of Space Shuttle blasting off in his mind: "Lucia"... "running"... "1917"... "ghost"... "bull"... "flying lizard"... "spaceship"... "Galactic"... "don't look directly"... "Sun"... "Elders"... "Basil".

António, based on male bravado and ego, would not, in a million years, ask Scarlett to repeat the information because he felt that to ask her for repetition might have Scarlett label him as 'dumb' but António sometimes underestimates his own capabilities (as do we all) and it came as a surprise to him that, during her dissertation, he had noticed that Hugo-Core's faithful donkey was not tied up outside the Tavern and so his immediate response to Scarlett's critical revelations was actually directed at Hugo-Core. "Your donkey, Hugo!" he said in a casual way. "What happened to your donkey?"

PLOT

Looking down (with the faces of grasshoppers) were the eleven cigar-smoking Ciakar and their Queen. They were spaced much as birds on a wire around the interdimensional Hole. They grasped at some imaginary railing with their three-fingered hands (which made them look ridiculous). They peered through the Hole much as would knot-hole baseball fans peer with rapt attention paid to the details of the game but, in the case of the Ciakar, with rapt attention paid to the details of their discovery of Earth, specifically to the view from above Fatima, Portugal which; on this day; on this May 13th 1917, day; did the Brahma Bull Brad fall to Earth along with a colleague of terror.

The Ciakar started in with their commentary; around their community circle did they pass gas and words and so did the Ciakar begin to pot their plants and plot within their community circle.

"Hah, hah, hah."

"Fatima."

"Go to the Ship."

"Who gets to work the bicycle pump?"

"Draw straws."

"Hah, hah, hah."

"Little girl."

"Don't look directly at the Sun."

"Hah, hah, hah."

"Elders."

"Where is Basil?"

One by one did the Ciakar walk over to the bicycle rack; the bicycle rack that stood next to the Palace door and sure they could have just beamed over to their cigar-shaped; spiky-haired ship but no, medical consultation proposed some daily exercise just to get the Ciakar ticker and blood-sucking blood flowing and besides, they were in no hurry to save Ciakar #3 because, as you will recall, he had done something terribly bad and thus, he had been admonished; the punitive sentence was to spend the night in a cold tree above tense mud.

The Ciakar Royal Assembly even did some stretches and three-fingered toe touches before they all boarded their bicycles for the five mile trip to their ship. And along the way, they sang *It's a Small World* off key such that if Bob the Rock Star was there, he would go temporarily bananas and he would return fire with *Start Me Up* by the Rolling Stones.

The vicious yet orderly Ciakar parked their bikes in sequence in front of their ship and walked in single file but with the winning Ciakar leading the way because he had drawn the long straw and so did he clutch the bicycle pump. Some traditions never die even amongst the Ciakar and so the Ciakar pumped a puff of Brownian Motion air toward the ship's ignition switch.

Meanwhile, the tired-of-circling-Fatima Ciakar was losing altitude and below, he could see a gathering mob of Fatima villagers (the first of many torch-bearing and angry Fatima mobs in the Summer of 1917); yes, a veritable record number of shouting and teeth-gnashing mobs observed by curious human chroniclers, three Galactic Elders and by the fascinated readers of this story.

Sure, no one really knows the plots and plans of well-meaning but sometimes conniving Extraterrestrials and so, whilst the abducted Father Ferreria (the local Fatima priest) played rock, paper and scissors with the Gray's above did the brilliant and peacebuilding Blue Alien Rose take Father Ferreria's place and so she approached the podium on wheels for intent and purpose; for to quell the mob of Fatima villagers who were, without doubt, exhibiting offbeat and miscreant mob behavior for like the very first time ever and their lack of experience with like '60s protests really showed. For one, since this was a midday protest, no torches were required; two – no one thought to bring food and three, no one thought to bring a guitar.

Rose confidently set the little footbrakes on the podium wheels which took away her option of pushing the podium into the crowd; the option of a distracting podium careening into the mob such that it may give her that brief moment required for an interdimensional escape. The observant Rose would have the primal-screaming Fatima mobsters first extinguish their torches. She would appoint a Food Committee and send them off immediately for the emergency preparation of picnic baskets and finally, she asked if there was a guitar player in the audience who could read music such that Bob Dylan's *All Along the Watchtower* could be sung by all.

It was on this fateful and Fatima secret day that a picnic atmosphere broke out; Fatima families sitting around on red checkered blankets; families sipping lemonade and Pinot Noir and eating salami and cheese crackers while waiting for the main course of meatballs and linquini with basil leaves and Parmesan cheese sprinkled on top. The children even started up a pick-up game of soccer and, for awhile, the mood swing of the villagers converted from rage to that of measured respite; measured albeit because of the persistent presence of a flying and mighty vicious Ciakar who was also beginning to tire somewhat (and hence the gradual dropping of his altitude).

There were, no doubt, occasional glances of trepidation heaped upon the Fatima picnickers, which was accompanied perhaps by the growing concern that this picnic may be their Last Supper. Some had cautiously retained their torches and a lantern lit for torch ignition for the putative start of yet another mood swing as was the current volatility of a once quaint and pastoral bunch of villagers. And it sure didn't help matters when the spunky and fiery Father Ferreria just suddenly reappeared at the podium vacated by the Blue and peacebuilding Alien Rose.

Now Ciakar landings on muddy Draconis Prime are slick affairs. Ciakar landings on Draconis Prime remind us of teenage mud bowls whereby joyful youths don their oldest, most worn-torn blue jeans and t-shirts and then they play tackle football in the worst rain and in the deepest mud that they can find. It is all very fine when the big boys block and open a hole in the line such that the running back can gain five yards simply by sliding on his backside with knees raised so as not to break the rules about forward progress. Ciakar landings, no doubt, proceed with as much joy as the dragon swoops in and vertically raises his heels such that his thick and leathery footpads can take the brunt of the energy transfer. The analogy on Earth is the kid bicyclist who drops his heel down to the ground for the painless stop of a "wheelie."

But what of a dry landing? How does it translate and so the pooped-out Ciakar began his final Fatima approach. And this approach did include an accidental scrapping of the Church steeple and the crash of the Cross to the ground. It included the crushing of the Communist's car such they could not, for the time being, illegally detain, transport and imprison the spunky and outspoken Father Ferreria. But worst of all, our poor pooped-out Ciakar had to face the experience and consequences of a skin-tearing and rope-burning dry landing. And so our Ciakar reluctantly raised his 'landing gear' and yes, his touchdown was indeed accompanied by a serious Velociraptor shriek as his heels began to reddened and burn and as his skin began to peel away.

Still, the Ciakar's landing did fall just short of the protesting Fatima mob who, at the behest of Father Ferreria, had lit their torches and had begun their shouting whilst waving their spiked clubs in the air.

FADE

Earlier that day, ten-year old Lucia Santos had fled the scene. She ran away screaming and crying; away from the overbearing Marion Vision; away from her *Close Encounter of the Fourth Kind*. She ran back home to her laid-back father and stern mother and it all seemed overwhelming for this simple and sheepherding gal.

"Blasphemy," and, "flights of fantasy," said Maria to her daughter while her father just said, "Let's take a look."

And, after a quick look outside, did her father say, "Wow, there really is a big lizard flying around" and "Shall we check out the bit about the dead bull?"

Maria would have none of it and so she insisted that Lucia and her sisters prepare for Church.

"It is just a turkey vulture," said Maria to her daughters as they walked toward the oncoming mob of Fatima villagers who were headed for the Cova.

"They have been drinking already!" said the disgusted Maria as she ushered her daughters past the torch-bearing and teeth-gnashing mob and toward the Church and yes, it would be the busiest day ever for the Fatima villagers; out to the Cova to check out the rumored dead bull; back to the Church for the vanishing act of Father Ferreria; setting the 'tables' for a spontaneous and happy picnic and then back to the mob mindset when the Ciakar landed followed by the sudden appreearance of a cigar-shaped, spiky-haired Ciakar ship.

And oh - did I also neglect to mention the appearance of the new dog in town?

It seems that a Portuguese Water Dog (yeah right) had wandered into the village and not without comment.

"What's a Water Dog doing this far inland? I thought they were the dogs of fisherman."

"Must be a lost dog," said a villager of Basil (disguised poorly with a loose-fitting Portuguese Water Dog costume).

Basil had indeed appeared at sunset and she pranced with elegance and with purpose toward the emotionally drained Lucia. She shook off the Water Dog costume as if she had just been the recipient of a foamy dog bath and on her sides were revealed two backpacks. She came to Lucia, tucked her head under her arm and then beckoned Lucia to follow her. Lucia and Basil then parted the Fatima mob who had moved in for the kill.

Basil dropped then pawed at the backpackets and so Lucia opened them and within the packs were wraps and ointments for to alleviate the pain of the Ciakar's wounds and to start the cooling and healing process.

"Good dog," said Lucia to Basil as she patted her on the head.

Then it all began to fade. The bull, the Ciakar and their ship, Hugo-Core and Scarlett, Core's ship *et cetera* and even Lucia's father Antonio tried to fade but his wife Maria just whacked him back 'home' as a reality check.

Left behind was a USPS letter from the future with some advice for the Fatima villagers and signed with "love" from the "Galactic Elders."

Don't look directly into the Sun.
And
If you thought this was exciting then mark your calendars for December 21, 2012.

Episode Seven

. . . .
BASEBALL
. . . .

2012

Take me out to the ball game,
Take me out with the crowd,
Buy me some peanuts and Cracker Jack,
I don't care if I never get back.

Let me root, root, root for the home team,
If they don't win, it's a shame.
For its one, two, three strikes, you're out.
At the old ball game.

HAZE

The little peripheral disk drive linked to Peter's Apple IIGS whirled as his system booted up. The blue screen was bright and blue and then, after a minute or so of bright and blue, the system engaged Peter's baseball screen saver with its meandering bats and baseballs that made random Pong contacts which sent bats and baseballs wandering off in random directions.

It was 1972. It was ten years before the widespread use of e-mail. However, in the wink of an eye (as if this email was a prelude to some measure of mischievousness) the date, subject line and text of an e-mail appeared frozen on Peter's screen.

> *Date: July 4, 1972*
> *Subject: Name Change*
>
> *Peter:*
>
> *The Galactic Elder Council, the Grays in Earth orbit and the Reptilians living under Santa Fe Baldy Mountain agree whole-heartedly that the Society for the Prevention of Alien Exposures should be changed in title to the Society for the Prevention of the Exposure of Alien Existence.*
>
> *We look forward to further contributions.*
>
> *Love, The Galactic Elder Council*

The lifetime and legendary SPEAE member Peter now sits in the Ferry Building, forty years later, by an early morning and cool bay window with his cup of steamy Peet's Cafe Mocha, his blueberry muffin, the *San Francisco Chronicle's Sporting Green* and a top secret SPEAE profile of the 'woman of his dreams': Alice, the Human; Alice, the Reptilian and Alice, the Gray, would soon arrive with her triple genetic expression and her baseball mitt and ball at 6:30 a.m. which was more than enough time for him to make two nervous trips to the restroom (he had opened the place at 6:00 a.m.).

Now February in the San Francisco Bay Area is usually a month of clarity. There is very little wind and fog. The Bay is still and looks like a huge, dark-green, stained-glass window. The skies are white with puffy cumulus and the sky's color is deep blue, deep blue from the wash of January rains.

Peter and his dog Basil had moved to an outdoor table. He was bundled in sweat pants, a black and orange Giant's jersey and a properly folded Giant's cap. He moved outside so that he could pass off his nervous energy as just the morning chill.

'They would be married, of course. They would live on the coast. They would have a garden, a Prius and they would do 'Green' stuff. They would play catch on the beach. They would have two perfectly behaved children who would give them no grief. They would drive to San Francisco for the Symphony and for Giant's games. They would have hot, unrestrained and steamy...'

"Is this seat taken?"

Peter's arms rapidly unfolded and his chair tilted suddenly off its doorframe prop and onto the tip of Basil's tail and, for the moment, both of 'his' girls stared and glared at him.

Poor Peter.

'They would not be married. They would live in Roswell, New Mexico. He would have a hot patio and a lawn of artificial grass on which he couldn't walk without burnt feet. She would do wheelies in her red Camero like she had won at NASCAR and then she would drive back through the smoke and smell of burnt rubber. She would drive into the sunset. She would drive away with her fist waving out the car window; a defiant fist as if she had read his rotten mind.'

"This must be the good dog Basil."

Basil's big brown eyes of guilt aimed at Peter were transformed into eyes of recognition because Basil, in her many Milky Way travels, had already seen Alice in the dim light of a sports bar on the Goldilocks planet called Gliese 4.

"Can I get you some coffee and a muffin?" asked the recovering doofus Peter.

"Please find me two ounces of Peet's coffee espresso ground burr style to a very fine granular size and sporting a caffeine content of forty-six point seven milligrams per ounce" (surely the energy drink of a light speed traveler).

Alice sat and sympathetically scratched the really good dog Basil while the spaced-out and funky Peter lined up for her order and, upon his return, and, without stealing a single sip from her espresso or a nip of her blueberry muffin, did Peter serve Alice her little breakfast by the Bay.

It wasn't all that comfortable for Alice either. She was tense around Peter. She was terse as if she expected a flawless intellect and an impeccable manner and thus, the pinching of Basil's tail surprised her and yet currently, she was sipping her espresso and nibbling at her blueberry muffin as if she wanted this little breakfast by the Bay to last awhile. Peter, the brute, loved blueberry muffins, as did she. Peter, the brute, read the *Green* every morning for baseball news, as did she. Peter, the brute, loved the game of baseball as did she and so she sat across from him almost as his mirror image with her black sweat pants, her Buster Posey jersey and her silver brunette pony tail fitted through the hole of a properly folded Giant's cap.

She spoke as her tension returned. She spoke of her mission on Earth and Peter followed her lead, as was his SPEAE assignment. She returned to 'professional' but she felt as though she had left something behind and so, as they say, 'time will tell.'

Alice hoped that it would never happen; especially here, in the Ferry Building, sitting with a new acquaintance and yes, she felt the emotional tremor as she looked away from Peter, as she reached for a napkin that she didn't need to use. The tremor was equivalent, in her mind, to a quiet rip somewhere in the Universe and all she could feel was the release of undefined human emotions as they spilled forth and so she lunged forward. She lunged and pushed the table forward and below, she spasmodically kicked the baseball out of her glove and the baseball rolled onto the promenade.

Peter rose and stepped away to retrieve the baseball and Alice had gathered herself before his return.

"Humanity is at war with everything. There's the war in Iraq and the Afghanistan war. There's the war on terrorism; the war against drugs and cancer and then there's the fight against climate change. It goes on and on and the Council continues to refuse Earth's entry."

"The field is ready. I need to pick up my car. Old man Vernon fixed it, drove it up from Santa Cruz and he parked it on Clement Street."

Alice had gathered herself and her analysis was complete.

'It was Peter's fault. Maybe I should request a different SPEAE.'

She returned to comfort as they walked past the Ferry Building shops toward the Embarcadero and the taxi to Clement Street. Alice, thinking that her table-kicking, emotional riptide was her embarrassment quota for the day, relaxed her guard and the timing of her return from yoga breathing could not have been worse.

She stood transfixed. She stood transfixed and then she stared into the tank of live Dungeness Crabs for what seemed to be an eternity. Peter had looked away – just for a moment - and when he looked back, he heard a low tremulous growl followed by the most visible curling of Alice's quivering lips.

The Reptilian Live Food Protein had kicked in. Her brain had quickly completed the synthesis of an ancient Reptilian neurotransmitter. Her blood was warm and her eyes were wide open and she was reaching into the tank when Peter grabbed her by the arm.

'She's hot!' thought Peter.

And then he heroically yanked her arm out of the tank.

Peter then checked to see if she had activated her portable Haze Generator. She had done so and so the people walking about the Ferry Building hadn't noticed the incident.

They hadn't seen a thing.

Peter had dropped Basil's leash and yet, the old girl maintained her slow and determined pace toward the Embarcadero. A small and concerned crowd had gathered around the old dog; the old dog with a leash but without an apparent owner; the old black Labrador retriever with her big and begging brown eyes which said, 'this lost and stressed dog is in serious need of a peanut butter biscuit.'

Every parent knows. Every panicky parent knows what it feels like to lose his or her child at the theme park and so Peter shares this sinking feeling and yes, he hears Alice's terse questions. He hears them loud and clear.

"Where's Basil?"

"Did you lose Basil?"

Peter did his panicky three-sixty and stopped when he saw the small crowd and the wagging tail.

"She's over there."

In the interim, one person had left to obtain peanut butter biscuits (somebody out there reads dog minds?) and a bowl of water from the pet store that hadn't even opened yet. Another had pulled out a grooming brush from her purse and they all took turns with the googlie ooglies and the 'oh-what-a-cute-doggies' and finally someone asked, "Who on Earth would abandon this incredibly cute dog?"

"That would be me," confessed Peter.

And so, after many "thank yous," did Peter, Basil and Alice (still a little shaky from the graphic image of crunching down on a whole Dungeness Crab) make their slow way toward the taxi and its cheerful driver who was not shy in the least.

"Well, this old dog sure looks well cared for. And she must be potty-trained, of course."

"On several planets," said Peter who loved to reveal the truth about the existence of Extraterrestrials especially when no one was really listening.

They were stuffed in the back seat of the cab with Basil in the middle and so, every time Peter turned to talk to Alice, he would be the recipient of a dog kiss and, after such a kiss, did Peter begin a massage of Basil's ear flaps while Alice looked away (her left arm – she was a southpaw – still felt numb - like it had been in a freezer overnight).

"The field is ready. I need to pick up my car. Old man Vernon fixed it, drove it up from Santa Cruz and he parked it on Clement Street."

"You already said that."

"I did?"

She looked at Peter and felt a pang. She had noticed that Peter had placed his baseball glove with the perfectly worked pocket onto his lap and then she looked to see her mitt so placed and so treated. She could 'see' him working his new mitt and she remembered working her new mitt for the purpose of a catch; so that a baseball, either in flight or grounded, could be caught with the glove fit for the sure out and also for the quick pick and throw of the baseball for such a purpose as turning a double play. She realized that she didn't look away from Peter when baseball was the topic of conversation and so she decided, while on the taxi ride to her cherry-red VW bus parked on Clement Street, that maybe he was a 'keeper' for now; that maybe she could live with the pangs that are Peter and baseball; the pangs which would last at least through late spring, summer and autumn; that time of pang, or torture if you will, which covers and uncovers the new and past seasons of Human baseball and the inaugural season of Reptilian baseball.

James D. Phelan Beach was cool but not foggy and the tide was low so little Pacific waves tumbled pathetically onto the shore. Looking back from the steps of the parking lot, one could see Alice's cherry-red VW van as its only resident.

They were on the beach - living one of Peter's dreams.

They could not do grounders because of the sand but they warmed up with short tosses and then longer tosses but pop-ups were the finale; pop-ups with feet churning in the sand and with forearms extended across their eyes to block out the glare of the midday Sun.

Basil slept on her *Little Mermaid* beach towel.

She went back in time - back to her time of squirrel chases and Frisbee catches.

Basil 'traveled' in her sleep to her 'secret passage.'

Basil 'traveled' to her 'secret passage' and then she curled up into a ball.

Basil liked to sleep on her side while 'traveling' through time.

SAWUS

Sawus is a Reptilian name that could have any number of philological interpretations. "He saw us" means the literal sight of us. "He saw us" could also mean his insight into the true meaning of our existence or finally, there is the impersonal and graphic "saw us," which would reflect the demented intentions or desires of masochists.

And in the morning, every morning, even the morning after the hatching of his children, Sawus would pick the bloody rat tail pieces from his teeth and, while doing so, would engage his sneaky periscope with the mailbox attachment (flag down - nothing to send out today) such that he could take a look around Santa Fe Baldy Mountain for the presence of the Chupacabra sentries and also collect the *San Francisco Chronicle* with its *Sporting Green*.

Sawya, Sawus' lovely wife and self-proclaimed batting instructor, had declared the evening before that she was going to "sleep in" and so she slept while Sawus contemplated breakfast.

'Eggs,' he thought. 'I will have eggs.'

Sawus, having returned from his brief trip to the Corridors, dropped the animatronic, featherless, blind and highly nutritious chicken into the feeding bin. He sat on his stout haunches with only marginal support of his chair. He reached for the *Green* with his long arm. He held the paper up and then opened it with rising tension. He held the *Green* tautly nearly ripping it and then he searched for news of pitchers and catchers, as they would be the first to report to Giant's Spring Training.

He paused. His green eyes widened. The strong muscles of his nasal sinus contracted and his nostrils flared. He snarled his snarly snarl and then he widened his jaws for the perfect live food fit.

The chicken was gone in a flash.

Sawus waded through the dimly lit Corridor. He could feel an occasional bump of a blind rat at his ankles or the periodic thump of a blind mini-caribou at his knees. Ahead was the gatekeeper Gripus. Ahead was the Cage with the hanging Doofus Roots shaped like Louisville Sluggers and, by a remarkable coincidence, weighing anywhere from 31 to 35 ounces. On the floor were the Tyrannosaurus Rex kidney stones that were, by another remarkable coincidence, the exact size and humidified weight of baseballs used at Colorado Rockies home games.

"Are you back for more torture?" asked Gripus as he slowly opened the Cage.

"Sure, why not?" said Sawus ever mindful of Sawya's exact words when she casually answered his marriage proposal.

"Here, Gripya packed a second breakfast for you. It's these new animatronic mice strapped to a Doofus Roll. They're not bad."

And then, ever mindful of Sawya's persistent advice (nagging) to stay back on his stance for the change-up or slow curve; ever mindful of her persistent reminders (nagging) not to lunge at pitches out of the strike zone and ever mindful of her nagging period ("blind rats, woman!"); did Sawus pick a thirty-three ounce Doofus Root bat off the ceiling of the Cage.

He waited for today's music to start (Orff's *Carmina Burana*) and for the first pitch from the Timmy Pitching Machine. And sure, his morning haze would be lifted for his memories of his first encounter with Sawya and how he had delivered a knockdown pitch just under her 'pretty little Reptilian chin' and how, two innings later, she slid into his ankles with spikes up but claws retracted when he ran over to cover first base after she had pulled his best fastball down the line. And oh yes, Reptilian Baseball would have its rules which include automatic fine and ejection if the six inch switchblades that are the beast of Reptilian fury show themselves in an argument with the umpire over a blown call at first or any other base for that matter.

Sawus started today's batting practice with all these memories and so he promptly drilled a fastball right at the vacuum cleaner that is the Timmy Pitching Machine and thank Tut for that and what an invention

– my goodness - a pitching machine with a vacuum function that sucks up line drives, rubs up the captured baseball and then pauses to consider the next pitch. And surely would Alice smile if she was here now; if she could feast her Human brown eyes on the sight of Sawus' pretty swing and bat speed and most certainly would she send a quick communiqué to her Queen on Gliese 4.

LENS

Peter slid out of bed and stepped gingerly over the sleepy Basil. He headed, zombie-like, toward the coffee maker and his oatmeal blueberry breakfast with eggs over hard; eggs cooked hard to 'kill the Salmonella.' He moved to his deck overlooking a clear and cool Pacific morning. He brought his coffee, his breakfast and the *Green*. The *Green* was intelligence these days, intelligence gathered for the Santa Fe Giants because this formative Reptilian baseball franchise follows the progress of the San Francisco Giants with great scrutiny.

The short packing list for the road trip to Arizona was Alice's first list for Peter and he felt a tinge of 'domestication' while he read her e-mail but, as they say, 'it's all in your mind.'

> *Please bring the clothes on your back, a change of clothing, necessities, Haze Generator, Trans-dimensional Cell Phone and Basil. Any other needs will be taken care of by Rosanna Spearman. I met with Vernon yesterday for an update from the Remove Viewers. 6:00 a.m. tomorrow. Please be prompt.*

The throaty cherry-red VW bus turned the corner by Peter's Pacifica apartment and he immediately and incorrectly surmised that teenagers were about to do early morning wheelies on his street in their black Pontiac.

Wrong.

Old man Vernon had modified Alice's VW bus to muffle the nuclear powered hum somewhat. Still, the little 'beep, beep' of the VW remained the same.

"You're late!"

('Wow – 6:01.')

"Where are we headed?"

"Scottsdale and then New Mexico."

Basil had been loaded in.

"Basil, we are going on a trip."

Tail wag – 'Trip?'

"Basil, would you like a biscuit?"

Tail wag – 'Like yeah.'

"Basil, we are going to Giant's Spring Training."

Tail wag – 'Training?' 'Spring?' 'Giants?'

"Check that Basil, we are also going to Santa Fe Baldy Mountain in New Mexico."

Tail wag – 'Mexico?'

And so Peter, Alice and Basil waved goodbye to their beloved San Francisco and they began their journey to Santa Fe Baldy Mountain but no, they weren't the only ones on the move. High above them (in Space no doubt) hovered a circular and cloaked craft. The ship's Captain was a Gray named after a lost character from British literature. It was captained by the misused and manipulated Rosanna Spearman – that poor woman turned Gray who was lost for good (or actually bad) in a quicksand by the sea that ne'er returns its victims. And so this ship, this patient ship, moved ever so slowly in synch with a cherry-red VW as it crossed the Bay Bridge below. And so this ship, this sneaky ship, would also engage at this time, via Rosanna's orders, the Trans-dimensional Lens; a Lens which is used by the Grays for certain close-ups of certain strange-looking individuals who were about to do one strange thing or another.

BEAM

Sawus woke the next morning with a gut feeling; with a tight Human and Reptilian stomach; with an erratic pair of heartbeats and with a light head filled with pretty butterflies because today would be a first for him – live pitching.

Today, he would enter the newly-constructed chamber under Santa Fe Baldy Mountain; a chamber with its regulation-sized infield and Baseball Simulator Curtain which fell from the ceiling and which, when struck by a baseball, would determine if hits were outs or in play and, of course, this Curtain substitute for an outfield could cause many problems later for first time Reptilian outfielders who were learning to judge fly balls in the Dome; the Dome that was under construction as we speak on an island in the terminator climate of Gliese 4.

Within the chamber this very morning, one could hear the sounds of baseball without the blare of *Don't Stop Believing* or the Giant's fan party buzz or the occasional roar of Giant's fans as the game was played. Within this chamber, one could hear the echo; the pop of a catcher's glove as a young Reptilian rookie phenom by the convenient name of Rookus warmed up his reputed 80 mile per hour fastball and certainly one could not miss his wife Rookya as she stood by his side ("forever your pitching coach my love") and commented on every warm-up pitch.

"Yes Dear. I know that curveballs do not drop as well in low gravity and that I have to rely on the location of my fastball."

"Yeah Honey. I have heard the story about Tyrannosaurus Rex and how they cannot generate any bat speed or throw a baseball any farther than two feet with those little arms."

It is within the dim light which is all day and night in the training facilities of the Reptilian version of the San Francisco Giants. It is within the dim light of what is hoped will become the first completed intrasquad baseball game in Reptilian evolution. It is within this dim light that Sawus steps up to the plate to face Rookus who, in his excitement and with double the adrenalin from Human and Reptilian sources, fires an 85 mile per hour fastball approximately five feet over Sawus' head and to the backstop and this is how it begins; how Reptilian baseball begins; with the call of "ball one" by a Human umpire followed by a visit to the mound by Tubus, the manager of the Santa Fe Giants, to calm down his young pitcher and, meanwhile, in the depths of the Yucatan Peninsula, it begins anew. The Curse begins anew in an identical cave complex built under a crater created by the crash of a five mile-wide asteroid. The Curse that is the Yucatan Cubs Franchise begins anew and it begins anew without the witness of a Murphy Goat because, of course, the mini-goats wandering about the Yucatan Reptilian Corridors are blind.

Meanwhile, near the hot town of Needles, a shadowy Lizard in a trench coat feigns drunkenness while making his way slowly and awkwardly across the dimly lit parking lot of a dog-friendly Motel 6. He falls against a few cars with a thump to make it look and sound genuine. He falls nearly to the ground, recoils and then he raises himself and his brown paper bag with his empty Whiskey No. 7 bottle. He raises the bottle toward the full Moon and then he swallows his fake swallow of his fake whiskey.

He couldn't have missed the cherry-red VW van.

It was cherry-red and only a few cars down.

He fell against the windshield and deftly placed the leaflet with the advertisement for a new coin-operated Laundromat opening in Needles. Only it wasn't. It wasn't an advertisement for a new coin-operated Laundromat opening in Needles. The leaflet had numbers and quotation marks inked on it and so he tucked it between the windshield and the wiper blade of the cherry-red VW. He tucked it there with a clever smile that almost hurt the Lizard lips under his Human skin.

It was obviously clear at 11:00 p.m. because he could see the Moon but at 1:00 a.m., Mr. Lizard woke to the patter of rain and then more rain and then lightening and thunder.

It was a desert monsoon.

It was a Santa Fe Baldy Mountain monsoon with such driven rain and lightening that it would have scattered any number of frightened Baldy Mountain hikers to the tree line. It was a sudden storm for which said hikers are warned about, warned about under no uncertain terms even before they attempt to ascend the Baldy Mountains of New Mexico but we are not in New Mexico are we (hmmm…).

So, at 1:05 a.m., the shadowy Mr. Lizard in a trench coat feigned drunkenness yet again while making his way slowly and awkwardly back across the dimly lit parking lot of the dog-friendly Motel 6. He replaced the leaflet with the smeared numbers and quotation marks with a leaflet with the same FYI bagged in one of those plastic baggies with one of those cool slip-lock sealing devices.

It is now 4:00 a.m. and, of course, Denny's Restaurant feels dimly lit like it was in a Haze or something. Forester and Forest Manager Sally Forest sits over steamy Denny's coffee and a Grand Slam Breakfast of hot cakes, sausage links, scrambled eggs and toast with strawberry jam dug out of a little container which identifies its contents of strawberry jam with a pretty little picture of strawberries on a cute peel-away lid.

Sure, Sally wrote 'it' off to the effects of 'too-early' morning but she was wrong and she was wrong because she felt something different, odd. It would be something seen not heard. It would be something seen out of the corner of her eye. At lunch, she would feel compelled to say something to someone; to a trusted friend and even now she felt the urge to find anyone (a stranger or even a shadowy Lizard in a trench coat) such that she could ask the question: "Did you see that?"

All versions of the truth temporarily vanished for Sally. I mean - she was absolutely certain that a picture of strawberries on a peel-away lid meant strawberry jam within and that a picture of grapes on a peel-away lid meant grape jelly within. But she wasn't prepared (are any of us humans prepared?) for a beam of light to descend from the sky, for a woman to step into the beam like she was causally stepping into an elevator and for the lifting of the said woman into the night sky. And no, it wasn't the corner of Sally's eyes that were stimulated because Alice was staring right at her the whole time.

It was 4:05 a.m. Basil, expecting to find her food bowl filled with her unpalatable and disgusting dog food five minutes ago, literally trembled at the prospect of death by starvation. Trembling with her black Lab ears perked, she began to evoke a low, tremulous growl followed by a soft 'woof' because she was a good dog and she did not want to break the no barking rules for dogs staying at dog-friendly Motels. Yes, she would not cross the line into the devastating realm that is the "bad dog." She relaxed a little as Peter moved a tad and then much; much to a point to where he was sitting up and yet sitting up with a panic derived from two sources: Basil had not been fed on time and Alice was gone!

Yes, Basil got her food and Peter got his because Alice had left him a note:

> *Peter* (like 'Peter - listen up!')
>
> *The rest of Giants report to Spring Training today*
>
> *Meet me at the Motel 6 at 3695 Cerrillos Rd. in Santa Fe in three days*
>
> *Alice*
>
> *P.S: Don't worry about the noises in the VW. It's due for sched-*

And no, she did not tell him of her purse snatch; of her abduction; of her theft of Mr. Lizard's baggie from the VW windshield with his note now in indelible ink with the coordinates: 35°49′56″N 105°45′28″W (and gee, can you guess which Santa Fe Baldy Mountain in New Mexico can be found at these coordinates? uh? uh?). She would take the note via satellite (and I mean that literally) to Rosanna Spearman who had used the Trans-dimensional Lens from her Space perch to spy on the fake drunk runs of Mr. Lizard.

GLIESE

All Gray participants in the conference room of Rosanna Spearman's cloaked spaceship huddled around the Hear-All-When-Properly-Tuned Receiver for a sneaky and surreptitious broadcast of the Reptilian intra-squad baseball game by an Alien-abducted and hazed Giant's broadcaster.

"I am pretty sure that when Rookus' pitch sailed over Sawus' head that it was ball one with no argument. So, Tubus visits the mound and perhaps he should be reminded not to step off the mound and then return to finish his sentence because a second visit requires that Tubus relieve Rookus. I sure hope Tubus saw the film of the Dodger Manager's *faux pas* of identical ilk in a game against the Giants; a *faux pas* that delighted the Giant's Manager and Giant's fans to no end. Rookus winds and delivers. Ball two."

(...We return to the action - three batters and thirteen balls later...)

"The bases are loaded. It is 3-0 to the cleanup hitter Buttus and Rookus has yet to throw a strike in this game. Here's comes the pitch. It's a change-up and Buttus swings and misses. Whoa! Looks like Buttus' reflexes said 'fastball' while his head said 'change-up.' We will take a short break while Buttus receives a lower back massage from the trainer."

Basil's dreams have her running in place. She quietly whines and softly barks in her sleep perhaps in frustration over her inability to capture the dreaded dream squirrel but one wonders if the dreams of Basil are of more form and substance. Perhaps there is a 'secret passage' for

Basil's entry into hyperspace. Perhaps a time machine waits in her 'secret passage' and if Basil could speak then perhaps the answers to these questions may manifest thusly:

So, Basil, can you tell us of your interdimensional travels?

'No, I am a dog.'

So, Basil, what time period have you traveled into recently?

'I went back in time.'

So, Basil, where is your secret passage?

'I don't know. It's a secret.'

It was 3:55 a.m. and a new day in Santa Fe and Basil slept on the floor in her bed next to the snoring Peter. This time, Basil's legs were stretched straight, straight as arrows. She thumped her tail on her bed and her jaws moved from side to side as if a peanut butter biscuit had found its way into her dreams.

She had found her 'secret passage.'

An 'interdimensional window' had opened up over a large island on Gliese 4. The Grays had fitted her with a combination harness and biscuit dispenser so that she could munch on peanut butter biscuits during the sixty-six foot descent onto the mat of black and purple lichen which is most of the flora of this island and future home of the Santa Fe Giants. The Grays did not use the antigravity conveyer belt for Basil's descent because there were no humans around to Haze and because they found the sight of a tail-wagging black Lab in a harness with a biscuit dispenser amusing. Basil reached the ground and, with the clicks of her gravity dog shoes, she was released from the harness onto the dimly lit island; an island for which there is a constant view of the perpetual sunset of its red dwarf star.

The sports bar sat on purple lichen. It was a hundred yards away and filled with Reptilians with foamy lips from the consumption of purple lichen beer. It was floor to ceiling Reptilians all glued to their huge screen televisions for a replay of Game 5 of the 2010 World Series between the Giants and the Texas Rangers which was a game brought to you by Interdimensional Television with its infinite number of channels and pretty reporters.

Basil entered the sports bar and was immediately showered with tummy scratches and googly oogly greetings because Reptilians and Humans alike all know just how incredibly cute black Labs are and have you ever seen a black Lab puppy - OMG!

Basil's mission was simple. She needed to enter the sports bar and obtain a whiff of Reptilian for the record; for the evolutionary tree archives. She would sniff and then leave and she did just that but it was not without notice.

"Stay cute doggie, please?"

"Please stay. It's only the top of the third."

"Please don't go. Timmy's pitching."

Basil had mustered her discipline and had walked from the sports bar back to the reentry site. She was greeted there by googly oogly Gray Aliens who had decided to land the spaceship because the Reptilians were watching the game and probably wouldn't even notice.

STASIS

After his back massage, Buttus returned to home plate to finish his at-bat.

Rookus had taken advantage. He had found the strike zone with some pitches thrown to stay loose and so, his first pitch to Buttus was a letter-high fastball on the inside corner which backed Buttus off the plate. Buttus stepped away from home plate and glared at the Human umpire, which actually scared the bejesus out of the ump because this scientist umpire had been responsible for Buttus' hybridization. He knew very well about the Reptilian six-inch retractable claw that is the peace sign of Gliese 4.

Buttus gathered himself and returned to the box. Rookus threw another inside fastball that jammed Buttus. Buttus swung at the pitch to avoid being hit. The ball struck the handle of Buttus' Doofus Root bat, popped into his face and then dropped to the ground. The surprised Buttus fell to the ground and realized, while falling, that he didn't need to fall, that he was falling for the drama that is baseball and, of course, he would get up and point a finger at Rookus and he was wrong about that too because baseball teaches that fake injury and false accusation are not substitutes for a little humility.

Buttus was having a rough at-bat and it would end mercifully with a pop fly straight up into the air that would immediately turn baseball's attention away from Buttus and to the catcher. And the catch of Buttus' foul pop-up actually went very well and surprisingly so. The Reptilian catcher looked up, found the ball and tossed his mask away. The Human umpire stepped aside as the Reptilian catcher moved a couple steps behind the plate. And then the ball came straight down into a perfectly positioned catcher's mitt followed by the catcher's free hand which covered the ball such that it could not pop out of his mitt and oh the age-old memory of the fundamental two-handed catch which can only be found in the historical archives of what is Major League Baseball.

Rookus then proceeded to walk in the first run of Reptilian baseball with four pitches way out of the strike zone and, after ball three was called to the next hitter, the exasperated Rookya yanked the towel from her head and said to Sawya.

"Get your catcher's mitt and meet me in the bullpen."

Rosanna's ship hovers in Space over the dog-friendly Motel 6 in Santa Fe. She extends the antigravity 'conveyer belt' from Space to about fifteen feet above the midline of Highway 14 and then she bends the light, as well as space and time, to locate Peter's room. And, while he snores and Basil returns from her interdimensional mission on Gliese 4, Alice takes the 'elevator' down and, of course, there is no explanation as to how windows get opened or curtains drawn but it all happened nonetheless (Extraterrestrials do not need room keys) and it happened on time, on time for Basil's 4:00 a.m. feeding.

It was 5:00 a.m. and Alice sat at the table in Peter's room with her *Sporting Green* and a top secret file on the Reptilian Ciakar and how the Ciakar crew had managed a full step toward their party crashing ship while negotiating the stasis field monitored by a Gray Captain by the name of Dorian Gray (curious coincidence I'd say).

Dorian was delighted with the expressions on the faces of the Ciakar crew; of those ancient, winged and war Reptilians whose scowls would frighten any Human toward the Near Death Experience. He smiled though with the thought that this particular group of cigar-smoking Ciakars would not be part of any *Mothman Prophecy* for at least a year because it will take that long to get to their ship.

The Ciakar plans for Earth are, no doubt, a test; a test not of the *Universal Peacebuilding Initiative* alone, but of the combination of the *Universal Peacebuilding Initiative* and organized Baseball. And sure, Dorian would check on their IVs periodically to make sure they were still alive and to see if their expressions had changed at all which was unlikely because no one breaks a brutal and brutally honest Ciakar.

Alice laughed at the top secret photo of Dorian wiggling the fingers of both hands under his chin at the stasis bound and enraged Ciakar who would bare his fangs at Dorian and Dorian Cheshire-smiled because he knew the full fang would not show itself for about a month. And when Alice laughed so did Peter but it was 5:30 a.m. and he was laughing in his sleep as he recalled his self-told story about the raccoon, the porcupine and sex and how Soquel, CA, got its name.

Alice would let him sleep until 6:00 a.m.

"You're back!"

"I have made espresso. I have a plan."

"A plan for what?"

TELEKINESIS

The deer was not part of the plan; the young buck; the young buck laying on the ground with funny little music stars circling his puny antlers; the buck with the twitchy legs; the dreamy young buck with his twitchy legs and body and his panicky search for consciousness; his panicky search for the will to regain his four legs; standing legs and a new chance to recalculate his chancy path through the woods and around the invisible door that he neither saw or smelled before impact.

A man, a woman and a dog stood over the door-knocked deer. Alice reached into her backpack and found some smelling salts, smelling salts from another planet but what did it matter if they did the job. She waft woke the deer and yes, she stood between the deer and the door so that the deer, soon to be wafted, awake and frightened, would run off in the opposite direction and not crash repeatedly into the invisible door.

The invisible door opened into an invisible shack with visible shovels for a shallow dig and visible harnesses for the lift down into the Reptilian Corridors. As one might suspect, one harness was fitted with a biscuit dispenser for Basil's descent but the Grays above, way above, in Space above, were not amused this time. This time, the Grays aboard Rosanna Spearman's ship were serious and sweating bullets as they maintained, at great cost of telekinetic concentration, the materialization of the invisible door and shack below which was located, based on FYI collected by the Trans-dimensional Lens, just above a drop-then-slide feature of the Reptilian Corridors.

Yes, going into the Reptilian Corridors was greasy and fun and Basil would arrive front legs first followed by the butt-riding Peter and Alice who did not Disneyland scream until the very end and even then did they scream but it was a muffled scream that baffled Basil to a point of raised ears and a cocked head (the very picture of the curious RCA Lab who sits by the RCA Record Player) and were Peter and Alice composing a modern symphony or were they simply trying not to reveal to the baseball-playing Reptilians that they had indeed arrived and that their arrival was part of a plan that had been altered slightly by the unwitting rut of a door-knocked deer?

Yes, the plan had been preconceived. It was preconceived early-on and thus, before it actually became a plan, it could have been considered a preplan; a preplan from the beginning of its inception; a preplan preconceived in another dimension aboard Rosanna's ship with Rosanna, Alice and the Grays in a circle and, of course, there would have to be *Thirty-Nine Steps* to the preplan and Alice would have to stop Rosanna's presentation after the tenth step to say, "Stop! I had better write this down." And so she did but I will not write the thirty-nine steps down here.

All I will say is that step number one was: *get out of your dog-friendly Motel 6 bed in Santa Fe* and that at least one of the steps referenced the remarkable psychic abilities of the Grays: *you will find the invisible door by an unconscious deer so bring smelling salts.*

INTEL

Intelus (the Smart One) sat smartly on his little stool in a dimly lit room. He had turned up the screechy violin volume of the *Psycho* movie soundtrack. He held the bright flashlight firmly and turned it against the lovely green eyes of Intelya. Their roles in these intelligence exercises varied with their mood or plans for the day's practice of investigation or, in this case, interrogation.

Two envelopes sat on a small table – one of guilt and the other of intelligence. Intelus rolled the three fingers of both hands across the table over and over again and then, shortly after the last *Psycho* violin screech, he spoke.

"Hot dogs," he said sternly. "Honey? Why weren't hot dogs on the grocery list?"

"They were on the list, Dear, and so was lemon juice."

"Wow!" he said. "A honey-do list with invisible ink. What a great idea!"

He turned his attention to the intelligence envelope. He opened the Intel and saw the note – *Up Periscope - 3:15 p.m.* It was 3:14 p.m. – one minute to *Up Periscope.*

Intelus nearly fell off his little stool but he was still able to regain his balance, get into the kitchen and activate his sneaky, stealthy periscope and, like Sawus' periscope, it had a basket attachment for incoming and outgoing mail and, of course, there had to be a posted schedule for Reptilian periscope use because it would raise mighty a suspicion with Santa Fe Baldy Mountain hikers if a field of Reptilian periscopes were to all surface at the same time.

Intelus periscoped the area and found what he was looking for. The Chupacabra Sentry was standing near a Ponderosa Pine over an unconscious deer. In one hand, he was holding a jar of smelling salts but it was the brown envelope; the USDA official brown envelope that piqued his interest; the USDA official brown envelope that the Chupacabra sentry held in his other hand. And so, after a brief deer revival, the Chupacabra Sentry approached the periscope's mailbox and, without Copland's *Fanfare For the Common Man*, did he slide the USDA official brown envelope into Intelus' mailbox for its descent into the Reptilian Corridors and with the intention of delivery for Intelus' Human or Reptilian *Eyes Only* and the eyes that would read the document were the eyes that could focus first in the dimly lit apartment which, of course, meant that Intelus' Reptilian eyes would first feast upon this top secret document.

Intelus sat down in his *Masterpiece Theater* chair with his bowl and his pipe.

He opened the USDA document and found the title *Instructions for the Fermentation and Mass Production of Purple Lichen Beer on Gliese 4.* He turned the page to *Contents* and this began his search of 80 pages of blackout with the exception of: *POTUS, Santa, Reptilian, Human, white coats, scraggly hair, Mutants, chambers, pizza, sports bar and Dog.* In fact, these words were actually found by Intelus in a short report from another brown envelope that had been quietly and gently placed into the original document. And Intelus was, of course, only interested in the words found in the short report because he already knew the procedure for the brewing of Purple Lichen Beer and he had already been to Gliese 4.

But oh the short report and so, after a trip to the fridge for pizza because of a sudden craving, did Intelus (Mr. Know it All) call to Mrs. Tell All and he confided in and to her his following deduction: "The Remote Viewers have found that POTUS, while placing an order for pizza cooked by long-haired fancy cooks in white coats, had, during his Presidency, ordered a Dog to investigate the chambers of a Santa Clara sports bar for the presence of Humans, Reptilian Extraterrestrials and Human/Reptilian Mutants."

Intelus relaxed for want of secrecy because he wanted secrecy for Reptilian baseball and for the real baseball reason that Reptilians had come all the way to Earth from Gliese 4. He relaxed from what he knew and, because he was 'Mr. Know it All' in his mind, he would no longer question. He would no longer question or find out the critical information that Basil was in her youth when POTUS requested that she serve her country (actually, POTUS was not 'her POTUS' because dogs can't vote) and search for the Extraterrestrials and my goodness, isn't it a remarkable coincidence that an older and wiser Basil now haunts the very Reptilian Corridors in which Intelus dwells and that Intelus is unaware of her and her peanut butter biscuit presence?

Suffice it to say, Basil would lead the way through the Reptilian Corridors. She would lead the way because of her genetic memory of the Reptilian baseball player's scent that she had discovered in the Gliese 4 sports bar; a genetic memory that is proof that Reptilian baseball players come from Gliese 4 and that Basil doesn't have to write down the thirty nine steps (even if she could so).

Alice shoved her notes back into her backpack and, while Peter stared blankly ahead, did Basil begin her search of the Reptilian Corridors.

BINOCULAR

Now we know, from the truthful reading of this book, that Human/Reptilian Mutants exist in the Reptilian Corridors under Santa Fe Baldy Mountain and that they have scraggily hair. For sure, Intelus and Intelya know about the Human/Reptilian Mutants because it is their business to know and we know that a former POTUS suspected, early in his Presidency, that they exist but we now know that they are not located in a Santa Clara sports bar.

Sawus and Sawya not only knew about the Human/Reptilian Mutants (Sawus talks in his sleep) but Sawus also knew that the Mutants can't play a game of baseball even if their lives depended on it; that they have mitts made of 'steel'; that they close their eyes when they swing at a pitch and that they pathetically hold up their mitts in one position and hope that pop-ups will fall into their mitt by chance and I don't know about you but I have actually observed such attempts by some fans at Giants games which makes me wonder if Human/Reptilian Mutants haven't actually escaped from the Reptilian Corridors and it also raises the possibility that such a fan might be from Santa Clara, CA, which would revive POTUS's original hypothesis with regard to the location of the Human/Reptilian Mutants.

However, with all said and done here about who knew what about the Human/Reptilian Mutants, Basil (The Intrepid One) would discover, on her first turn into the Reptilian Corridors, the Human/Reptilian Mutant's Chamber and she, Alice and Peter would now stand and stare agape in front of a very large window.

No, the Mutants couldn't play baseball worth a nickel but still, these bored and brilliant beings knew how to kill time and space/time for that matter or antimatter and so they designed and constructed a ship, a Living Ship that could not only create its own interdimensional wormholes but who could also question the Mission.

"But I don't want to go to Gliese 4."

Yet again, this section is about who knew what about the Human/Reptilian Mutants and so, it was at this point that Alice shyly and slyly raised her hand and sheepishly said to Peter and Basil, "I knew about the Ship."

Now Basil (the Dog who is our Co-Pilot) would be the dog that stirs the pot but not the pot of which you might think. Basil would take a turn in the Reptilian Corridors in accordance with step number twenty-one and come face to face with a herd of frozen stiff and blind mini-caribou: frozen stiff but with their noses ever so busy and then came the pause; the brief pause before the realization based on their genetic breeding; the pause before they realized genetically that any Human scent could be a hunting Human. Yes, they acted instinctually. They gathered their fellow mini-caribou for what would become the fear, joy and camaraderie that is the blind mini-caribou stampede.

Sawus got of out bed and stepped over Sawya (how did Sawya wind up on the floor?). He walked through the kitchen and opened the door to the dimly lit Corridor. He looked to the right and saw retreating mini-caribou butts. He looked to the left in time to see nothing. If he could look around corners, he would have seen the near pile-up of a dog, a Human man and a Human/Alien woman.

Sawus had given up on the idea of a good night's sleep (probably because he sensed that 'something was not right' and what could that be?) but he had still found the time; time enough to gather some blind mice from the dimly lit corridor for his favorite midnight snack – three-blind-mice-on-a-Doofus-Roll. Sawya would awaken as well, just as Sawus was about to relieve himself of his midnight hunger.

Sawya entered the kitchen and asked, "Did you make one for me?"

And most certainly, the words spoken by Sawya were heard by Peter and Alice as they pressed their curious ears against Sawus' apartment door with their mutual hope for their own time; time for them to pass safely by Sawus' apartment and down the dimly lit Corridor toward the Reptilian Baseball Training Facilities.

The burning question now for Peter and Alice was: 'did Sawus collect at least six mice for the making of two three-blind-mice-on-a-Doofus-rolls?'

And yes, he had scooped six mice and so he remained in the apartment while Peter, Alice and Basil waded through the blind rats and blind mice of the dimly lit Corridor toward the twenty-five yard Plug of mini-caribou which posed an unexpected block to the Reptilian Baseball Training Facilities and oh did I say Plug and how on Earth do they plan to get through a twenty-five yard Plug of mini-caribou who have yet to decide whether or not they want to disperse or keep up with the talk about current events?

Perhaps they even liked the Plug because the experience is new.

'This is kind of nice. Maybe we should stay Plugged.'

Alice 'saw' the problem and the solution. She rummaged through her backpack and found some Reptilian perfume. She sprayed the Team and they sat now in front of the twenty-five yard Plug of mini-caribou, which had receded a bit then a bit more and, after an hour of slow entropy, Basil saw the dim light and a hole in the Plug large enough for her to crawl through and so she did crawl through and, one hour later, the hole opened up even more – large enough for Peter and Alice to crawl through as well.

And then they passed by the Reptilian Baseball Training Facilities. They passed by labs with white coats and umpire gear on hangers. They passed by a hair salon that did scraggily hair. They passed by an Internet café, two pizza joints, an airport (curious) and a replica of the Sphinx that had used Basil for its model. They passed by all of these landmarks until they came to a narrow access tunnel and then they crawled into this tunnel; a tunnel which ascended to a secret, *Thirty-Ninth Step* look-out above the Reptilian Baseball Chamber; to a secret look-out just above the pair of Chamelea Sportscasters; Chamelea Sportscasters with their binocular eyes; binocular eyes which move in and out of their sockets such they can focus; focus on whether or not the Human umpire's calls are correct outs or safes and whether or not the Reptilian retractable six-inch switchblade may be the temptation of the moment; a temptation that would surely send an instant shiver up and down the spines of those many Extraterrestrials who have decided that War is not a good idea and that the *Universal Peacebuilding Initiative* takes precedent for conflict resolution; for self-control of the Reptilian temperament and so does baseball teach.

Episode Eight

· · · · · · · · · · · · · · · ·

GAME

· · · · · · · · · · · · · · · ·

TELEPORT

Narrator (Old Man):

You'd think me outa place – me and my accent perched high on this Victorin' porch overlookin' the Pacific but the latter is just a fancy stage for my worldly views and for my speakin' of such ponderin's. Fact is, I often stop five minutes a day and gaze and wonder if 'they' do the same. I gaze and I wonder – especially at Noon with Sun hot and small and there's only small shadows and colors are bold - artichoke greens, berme browns, white, white sands and my personal favorite: an Asilomar turquoise sea with those West Coast blues accompanin' – Janis Joplin screamin' at my bold colors.

But that was a long, long time ago.

It was a time when Dylan was at his peak and the politicians would be protested without the comedy of Elvis-lookin' Leno or the Letterman dude from Big Apple City.

It's dusk now. I'm at a loss for words again as Sun - huge and orange and on fire - rests on a heavy grey sea.

Cat's gettin' ready to pounce on an unsuspecting mouse and Dog's bein' chased by a squirrel in her dreams.

Naw, I ain't perfect neither – cigs and booze would Shirley dispose me of any Earthly political dreams or perspirations.

But that was a long, long time ago.

It was a time when Joni Mitchell worried about the ruin of Paradise from a mega-invasion of parking lots.

Yup, I'm lucky not to be in L.A.

I'm lucky to be in a place where Sun can't be stared down by a brown haze though some say everyone's neighborhood will have different weather sooner or later - blind rats and that gosh darn Climate Change.

And did I say blind rats?

I Shirley did and so Dog wakes and looks up at me with Reptilian memories and then she nose points to a dirt cloud risin' above the road to my Victorin' porch; the car comin' interrupts my rockin' chair beat to my head song of *When I'm Sixty-four*; the car comin' sends me mentally packin' and trippin' back to a time when visits by Mr. Lizard were near monthly.

Dog's sittin' up. Cat's stuck to the screen door like Velcro for the mouse that squeezed under the door and left her behind.

Again, I'm lookin' dust cloud when the Ford Falc'n stops in its dirty tracks and Mr. Lizard sits for a bit because he can sit in the driver's seat because I gene engineered a retractable tail for hisself and other Lizards so that they can drive around in Falc'ns or any other car for that matter. But even though those wheels turn on Mr. Lizard's Falc'n, especially when its tuned, it doesn't necessarily follow that Mr. Lizard's 'wheels' are turnin' in his brain and sometimes, like now, 'they' come dumb to a complete stop.

Dog looks at me. Dog node Mr. Lizard left somethin' behind because he's been unaware before and that's when any man gets that uneasy feelin' that he might have forgot to close his barn door or somethin' like it and that maybe all his studs had got out.

I see Mr. Lizard reachin' down to his pants first then reachin' over the back seat to feel for the Package that he'd forgot to bring.

Dog gets her food bowl and drops it at my feet because she node Mr. Lizard won't be back for a cupa daze and she ain't waitin' that long for her dinner. Cat's purrin' in my lap and so I put her down and watch the Lizard dust cloud as it leaves my property.

Now I rock in my Chair and I ponder night and day so I don't sleep much but 'puter sleeps frozen on occasion and now's not the desired time but it is the time anyway because 'puter, on its own terms, has locked me outa hyperspace or cyberspace or whatever the heck space it is. Heck, I node 'Sanna Spearman's 'puter aboard her ship is tryin' its best to communicate; tryin' its best to filter out all Earthly talk of War and it will clear eventually for a bit and 'Sanna's email will come through with the news that more ships are on the way and that she'll have enough Grays to perform the Task.

And Shirley it happened and in the time allotted; in the two minutes and forty-five seconds it takes for me to microwave a bag of popcorn and get me a glass of ice water for filla'.

And now I'm starin' at 'Sanna's email and so I read it to Dog.

> To: Vernon
>
> Subject: Ceremonial First Pitch
>
> Vernon:
>
> The POTUS is a good choice.
> We'll have enough Grays for the Trans-dimensional Window.
>
> Love, Rosanna Spearman.
>
> PS - Please send us the relevant specs on Air Force One.

And oh, I would have sent the specs to 'Sanna right then and there had it not been for Mr. Lizard and so I sit and rock in my Capt'in's Chair with excess popcorn in my lap but not a drop of ice water because I can manage ice water while rockin' but I have never been able to manage a bag of microwaved popcorn or stove top popcorn for that matter or antimatter whichever the case may be.

Night's wandered in with a sliver Moon and some headlights on bendy Highway 1 appear to be slowin'. Maybe Dog was wrong and Mr. Lizard had found the specs before a cupa daze. But I don't think so because the car's stoppin' before my road and someone's gettin' out on the southbound ocean side of Highway 1. Must be a hitchhiker and maybe its Chupacabra because that's what they do for us - hitchhike and perform sentry duties and what they do in their free time is their business and I wish now that I had binocular eyes like the Chamelea so that I could at least define some details of the shadow that's walkin' toward my rockin' Chair.

Dog's sleepin' and dreamin' peanut butter biscuits and Cat's spendin' the night in the field so I am currently missin' some home security but it's the durn truth that I would Shirley need security only if the shadow was Human because, aside from a ship full of twelve Ciakar, Earth is last place in the Milky Way where War is waged and my goodness, who'd think that would be the case after watchin' all those sci-fi movies?

The shadow approached with open arms but not for a hug. The Chupacabra approached with open arms because he has a solution to one of the problems.

"We'll arrange for a summer thunder and lightening show on Santa Fe Baldy and the storm will send hikers packing to the tree lines. We'll do the show shortly before the POTUS arrives."

And then the Chupacabra heads back for more hitchin' on Highway 1.

And sure, Alice and I did meet on the day before she had met with Bro Peter and we had lunch with crab sandwiches, some crunchy sand and some chowda' while sittin' in two Capt'in's Chairs on Phelan Beach in San Francisco which on that day put wet and cold sand on the feet of me and Alice and on the paws and tummies of Dog and Cat.

And yes, we did get right to the core topic of our meetin' which was about the upcomin' Summer Picnic for USDA employees at the Western Regional Lab in Albany, CA; about how we were to get them to Santa Fe Baldy Mountain and about how they were to assemble a team to play Reptilian Extraterrestrials in a pick-up and picnic game of baseball. And it was sure easier than I thought it was going to be because, after my seminar at the Lab on *Purple Lichen Beer As Picnic Food*, I simply told them the durn truth and that the POTUS would be there to throw out the first pitch.

And they said in unison, "Sure, we'll do that and so let's get on with our team picks and training."

Cat don't like the beach much - no hidin', no mousin' - so I played laser lights with her for about half hour and then she slept wind-blown on a *Beauty and the Beast* beach blanky. Dog is a Lab retriever that don't like the water. I actually had to fish her outa a holdin' pond once because she had fallen in by an act of uncoordination and so I had to haul her out by the collar and she too slept wind-blown with Cat that afternoon on the *Beauty and the Beast* beach blanky.

And then I plugged into Mozart's *Jupiter* and, while it played to me on the beach, I conjured memories of Mama's Thanksgiving birthin' Day and what a Day it truly was - what with the birthin' and teleportin' and birthin' again and teleportin' again and then birthin' the triplet on Gliese 4. Sure enough, Mama started in with the emergency birthin' of Peter in San Francisco with medical personnel who didn't node Mama's case but who had to inform Mama of twinnin' and what they didn't node is that Mama teleports herself anywhere in the Observable Universe when shocked to wits and so she was shocked with the news of a second; shocked into teleportin' herself to Jackson, Mississipa where a team of Grays helped her to birth me and then the Grays informed her of the third which shocked Mama again into goin' all the way to Gliese 4 because our triplet sibling wasn't of Human species persuasion but rather, our triplet sibling verified those little gene bytes of Reptilian that possessed Mama's and Papa's fertility make-up and, of course, Mama would have to go to Gliese 4 because they node about Reptilian birthin' which in mammal Mama's case wasn't a regular hatchin' and so they would have to grab some specialists from a game resemblin' Human golf.

And right back here in this time, Dog was right about cupa daze and so it arrives again. The dust cloud that is Mr. Lizard arrives again in his Brown Falc'n and I say Brown because it currently has the look of a UPS truck parked in front of my Victorin' porch. And so Mr. Lizard gets out and opens up the rear door where the specs are sittin' on the back seat where they should have been sittin' two days ago but Mr. Lizard assured me that the back window was closed the whole time and so the specs weren't dusty or nuttin' and that he had read them over real fast to make sure that no blackouts had occurred since.

Then Mr. Lizard told me that Carl would be flyin' the plane and that the POTUS would be joy-ridin' in the co-pilot seat and then he told me that Carl had some reservations about the POTUS thinkin' he might be the first he'd seen in the White House to be somewhat Haze resistant which means he might see the plane flyin' in the clouds one second then flyin' straight into a mountain the next second which is an event that Shirley might be a hollerin' and disconcertin' development with regards to his survival instincts and so the POTUS might feel compelled to be vociferous about the situation.

Now Carl's been in the White House from day one. Fact is, Carl spent the night before and he was the one who opened the doors for the politicians to come on in and yes, everyone asks about Carl sooner or later on what he's doin' in the White House and the politicians will say that these days, he's kind of a butler and he cooks a mean pizza and that he flies Air Force One on occasion but the Reptilians will say that he's part of a rotatin' group of Reptilian spy masters who these days, practice knuckle ball pitchin' in the backyard of the White House. It follows that these spies have also been trusted with the mission of monitorin' what the POTUS node about the existence of Extraterrestrials and that's why Carl's been reportin' his reservations about the POTUS bein' Hazed or not durin' certain times.

It's late night and the Moon's a slice. Cat is sleepin' with a nest of mice in the field like *The Lion and the Lamb* and dreamin' Dog is 'ridin' horseback on the Rings of Saturn.'

WINDOW

On a Sunday morning in June 2012, the First Lady tossed a picnic duffle bag onto the bed of our Hazed-in or Hazed-out POTUS; a duffle bag which included condiments for a hot dog, sunflower seeds, a first baseman's glove, a 33 ounce Doofus Root bat and a T. Rex kidney stone which Carl would toss up and down playfully with the added comment, "These stones stuck in their kidneys are the real reason that T. Rex roars."

And our Hazed POTUS would reply, "What did you say?"

And our Un-hazed POTUS would reply, "That's gotta hurt."

And so the POTUS now sits in the co-pilot seat while Carl warms up Air Force One and while Carl works, he sings that campfire favorite *She'll Be Coming Around the Mountain* while the Un-hazed and baffled POTUS hears, 'she'll be coming at the mountain when she comes.'

Meanwhile, one hundred and eleven spaceships, each the size of a football field and commandeered by a crew of six (do the math), pass ever so slowly over Phoenix, Arizona and, of course, the Phoenix Police give the standard reply to an excited and finger-pointing Public because spaceships the size of a football field (and much larger) pass ever so slowly over Phoenix every so often.

"Yes, we see them as well."

And then later.

"Yes, they are gone now."

And then even later at Phoenix City Counsel meetings, "No, we don't know why huge spaceships pass ever so slowly over Phoenix every so often."

But we do why a single spaceship, the Pacifier, was parked earlier Sunday over a boathouse on the shores of the Bolivian Lake Titicaca and we know that Captain James Core Halley and his crew of two were present and accounted for: the sleek, slim, well-tanned and brilliant First and Only Officer Scarlett and the Pacifier's computer Edsel who has the memory, the chips and the front grill to prove it and we do know what they did but...

Narrator (Old Man):

I ain't tellin' yet but I do node that a Santa Fe Baldy Mountain hiker by the name of Sally nodes that she ain't in Kansas but still, there's sixty-six conjurin' Chupacabras in a circle that she can see out of the corner of her eye and she can see them out of the corner of her eye no matter which way she turns and she sees that there's a storm comin' and that she had better help herself and her fellow Santa Fe Baldy hikers off the mountain in a moment's notice.

Now I node a FAA Air Traffic Controller who node Peter and on the Wednesday before, he was called into his Northern California office for an interview with a shady character which I node goes by the name of Mr. Lizard. And for sure, did he reach into his intuitive memory banks for a 'reference' to Peter because he figures and he figures right-on that Peter might be the one sendin' Mr. Lizard into his sights because Peter is always talkin' about Aliens and Mr. Lizard, now sittin' across from him in his dimly lit office, sure looks the part.

The accuracy of his memory 'resources' are further verified by Mr. Lizard's proposal to him for overtime and FAA approved work (how does the FAA know about Extraterrestrials?) that would include the monitorin' for the safe control of a configuration of one hundred and eleven spaceships hovering over Santa Fe Baldy Mountain in New Mexico and for the openin' of a Trans-dimensional Window large enough for Air

Force One to pass on through and then land with all due safety on an underground airstrip built by Extraterrestrial Reptilians and he, knowin' all too well that Peter speaks nuttin' but the truth about Extraterrestrials said, "No problem. I'll do the work from my PC at home."

Now Mr. Lizard had told him that there would be an extry perk and the perk would be dependent on the successful arrival of another spaceship; a ship tailgatin' Air Force One to the Window and so we now return to Bolivian Lake Titicaca to see if Core and Scarlett are perky and succeedin' in their mission.

Now Scarlett wasn't all that perky because she don't like bein' cold and Titicaca shore is cold and so she's huddled in some 'paca sweaters and sweat pants galore and she's got her feet in a foot warmer and the portable heater is pointed in her direction but not Core's and they are both sittin' in a row boat about two hundred yards from an old, old buoy that's red and has got a sign with some strange writin' on it.

Now the locals can't say how long the old, old buoy has been there because when you ask them about the time when the old, old buoy was not there then "no" is the common answer and then they say that ancient legend tells of particular consequence for usin' the crank handle that's attached and the consequence is bein' swallered up by the snake God Quetzalcoatl the latter of which the locals say has been layin' in wait there the whole durn time which is what we now node (because of those archeologists) is equivalent to 25,000 years.

So when Core row, row, rowed his boat close enough for Scarlett to interpret - and Scarlett interprets incredibly well - even for a lake freezin' Diva - that the sign says 'puter language was invented at the time and so was 'puter and 'puter is buried somewhere in the ruins near Macchu Piccu and straight down beneath the old, old buoy is a Titicaca Box attached to a metal line made of the same bendy metal that lined the Roswell spaceships and in the Box are some storage devices and CDs and they were to take no more than three CDs and Scarlett got all this FYI from readin' a sign with a bunch of zeroes and ones and some arrows and a pictograph of a broken CD case and aren't all CD cases in that condition?

As we all know, Carl had been suspicious of and concerned about POTUS's Hazed-in or Hazed-out condition (as are we all) and so a special lab was set up hurriedly in the Reptilian Corridors for the panicky and 24/7 research to find Haze Two and everyone knows, from watching the Movies, Two is supposed to be an improved version of One and everyone also knows, also from watching the Movies, Two doesn't always measure up and so Haze Two just might be a crap shoot as to whether or not it will work on the POTUS.

Still, Carl was left alone with the problem of the POTUS Hazing in or out during the descent of Air Force One toward the storm, the black hole and the spaceships surrounding Santa Fe Baldy.

The distractions began with the ring tone of the Presidential cell phone that, as you might suspect, is changed daily along with the dialing sequence and, of course, Carl has the White House trust for these daily tasks. The POTUS answered his cell with aplomb and a plum in his other hand and then the caller Core, whose Pacifier ship was now tailgating Air Force One, pushed the static button on his cell that prompted the POTUS to say, "The call didn't come through."

Then there was a second call with static and garbled words that the POTUS could not understand.

"Heard some words this time."

"Would you like a pen and a notebook?"

"Why would I need a pen and note...?"

The Presidential question was interrupted by another call with static, garbled words and one clearly spoken word: "POTUS." The procession of calls served the POTUS's curiosity beyond measure and Haze and, after writing down *Santa, Reptilian, Human, white coats, scraggily hair, Mutant, pizza, sports bar and Dog*, the POTUS asked two relevant questions:

"Do we have pizza aboard?"

And

"Is the Dog's name Basil?"

And Carl answered both questions in the affirmative. But Carl wasn't through with his distractions.

"Mr. POTUS, how about a free lesson in Transcendental Meditation?"

"Sure."

And Carl Cheshire-smiled because he knew that first time TMers begin to snore after about thirty seconds and so Carl sent a text with a wink and a nod to the tailgating Core.

GAME

When the hatch opened, the POTUS did not find a red carpet greeting or any waving *Yes We Can* signs. When the hatch opened, the POTUS did not even find an American flag and the Marine Band, with its fine musical Marines, was nowhere to be seen. When the hatch opened the POTUS felt the slight prick of a very fine Haze 2 dart and then he thought, 'Cool - Reptilians and Humans lined up along the sides of a purple lichen welcome mat.'

The Reptilian humming began as the POTUS stepped onto the carpet and much to the chagrin for those who know that Reptilians can carry a tune about as well as the Mutants can play baseball. Sure, thirty years from now, and after the invention of nose winds, the former POTUS and the Chicago White Sox will be greeted on Gliese 4 with a nasal Reptilian rendition of *Hail to the Chief*.

But not today.

Today, the Humans would try and help out their newly made and humming Reptilian friends but to no avail and so the POTUS said for the first time in his ongoing campaign, "No, we can't."

Carl waited at the end of the line with the POTUS 's duffle bag.

"This way, Mr. POTUS."

The POTUS entered the spacious chamber that is the Reptilian practice field.

"You're playing first base but we are going to eat first. The human food and drink are in the first base dugout and please, pay no attention to the goings-on in the Reptilian dugout. They are actually pretty good at not letting their food escape. They are also very good at not letting ground balls escape the infield and you will see this when they take infield practice. And (surprise!), I will be starting for the Reptilians so how long has it been since you tried to hit a knuckleball?"

The gong stood on the pitcher's mound 666 inches away from the home plate podium. The Reptilian who emerged from the third base dugout was a mere child. However, this mere child was of the drumming ilk and there are Human parents out there who are aware of such hammering children; give them a drumstick and, even as toddlers, they will find an erratic beat on a pot or pan or the side of crib for that matter. The mere Reptilian child took his mighty swing and the gong pealed its single note bringing to attention all Humans and Reptilians in picnic attendance and meanwhile, deep in the Reptilian Corridors, a single blind mini-caribou (the last of the Plugged and alone because of it) raised her head and pointed her curious hearing toward the unfamiliar and fading-fast sound.

The gong summoned an alignment around the podium with a Giant's broadcaster M.C. at the mike, with the Chamelea and Reptilian Baseball Commissioner Plugus and his wife Plugya on the M.C.s right and with Peter, Alice and Basil on the M.C.s left.

The POTUS had been asked to preview a brief *Declaration* before the actual reading and his preview would allow him to exercise his freedom of choice on the question of whether he wanted to read the *Declaration* and, after the preview, he said, "Sure, I will read this but who are the Blues?"

The POTUS emerged from the first base dugout and the first living being to come into his view was a Dog and he knew immediately from the only agenda item of the last POTUS's Transition Team; from CIA top secret photographs and from Carl's Daily Briefings on her movements, that sitting before him (Basil, sit!) was Basil or, better known at the highest levels of National Security as - "Stealth Dog!"

"POTUS was wrong about the Aliens," said the current POTUS about a past POTUS.

Tail wag - 'Aliens?'

The POTUS looked at Alice and shook her hand even though he felt something strange about her and then he shook hands with Peter and he thought, 'Wow, a bona-fide Human!'

"Who are you, may I ask?"

But the distracting M.C. immediately plucked the microphone like he was shooting a marble.

"And over here Mr. POTUS we have two representatives from the planet Chamelea and the Commissioner of Reptilian Baseball - Plugus and his lovely wife Plugya."

And if he felt strange upon meeting Alice then one can only imagine his thoughts when he saw one of the Chamelea's binocular eyes focused relentlessly on his chin.

"Mr. POTUS, you have a microscopic crumb of garlic fry on your chin so let me get it for..."

"No thanks. I got it."

"Ladies and gentlemen, Humans and Aliens, I present to you the

President of the United States of America."

"I want to welcome our Extraterrestrial friends to the 2012 USDA Western Regional Lab Summer Picnic and Baseball game. I have been endowed with the privilege of the ceremonial opening pitch and I have been called upon to play first base for the Humans. From what I have been told, I will be reading a customized version of the *Universal Peacebuilding Initiative* (customized by whom I wonda) and then I have been told that the hundred or so hidden construction workers have a surprise in store for us and that Coach Tubus has been informed because somebody told somebody else to tell a third party to inform Tubus."

Tubus stands up in his dugout and raises his arms with palms up.

"What surprise?"

"So please stand and remove your hats for the reading of the *Universal Peacebuilding Initiative.*

> *To all Humans, Ciakar, Reptilians, Grays, Chamelea and Blues alike:*
>
> *May we call upon the precedents and practices of the Universal Peacebuilding Initiative to guide Humans and the Ciakar to the end of their wars and avarice.*
>
> *May all of us find good health and safety in the foods we eat, the water we drink and the air we breathe.*
>
> *May all of us find security for the pursuit of our dreams and aspirations and for our agreement, implicit in Universal Peacebuilding Initiative, to live together; to live together as cooperatives in the mutual pursuit of solutions to our problems; as collaborators for the peaceful resolution of conflict and as those who hold dear the respect for Extraterrestrial and Human rights.*
>
> *May Reptilians, Grays, Chamelea and Blues replace all thoughts of violence with thoughts of kindness as if kindness was meant to be.*
>
> *May Humans and Ciakar replace all thoughts and acts of violence with thoughts and acts of kindness as if kindness was meant to be.*

And now, please remain standing for the playing of the *Carmina Burana* and the raising of the Baseball Simulator Curtain."

The Curtain rose slowly to the ceiling and so Tubus began his sweating surveillance of his Reptilian bench, his panicky search for three Reptilian outfielders and, as I have implied, three outfielders that have never played that position.
Advantage Humans.
Possibly.
I mean - do the Humans know that a fungo fly has never been sent its lofty way toward a Reptilian outfielder?

Narrator (Old Man - watchin' from home):
And no, those Humans don't node about Reptilian outfielders and Reptilians don't node about catching a knuckleball pitcher neither because Sawya was missing Carl's warm-ups and the ball was getting away even though Sawya had a catcher's mitt the size of an extra large pizza pan.
Rookya comes out to back her up but there was a pause in the proceedings due to legendary Human pitcher Michelle who was starting because she nodes a freakin' lotta pitches. Yes, Michelle node a two seamer, four seamer, curveball, slider, splitter, change-up and the Gaylord Perry spitter and she even node to deny that she throws the latter and so the ball got away because of a catcher misread and it came to rest at the POTUS's feet after his declarin'.
Now Dog's sleepin' on my feet so I ain't going nowhere and Cat's in my lap so I use Cat as a prop for my little, six inch, black and white portable television with a Tootsie Roll Pop antenna but everyone node that a Tootsie Roll Pop by itself can't get Interdimensional T.V. but this especially made and 'Sanna Pop Top Antenna can sure pull in the channels.
So the POTUS stepped up to the plate and Carl got wound up and tossed him a knuckleball down and away and the POTUS went fishin'. I mean he swung and missed the pitch by about three feet and goin' fishin' reminds me of the time Peter's cousin toke Peter fishin' and, because Peter ain't no good at fishin', his cousin took him to the Fish Market later and they bought a big ol' ling cod off the ice and then they took a picture of Peter and his fish for Family but, when takin' the trophy back to family for showin', Peter realized too late that they'd left the price tag on.

Now I'm directin' this little fish story at Humanity because I'm thinkin' it might alleviate the consternation of watchin' the first two Human hitters strike out on only six pitches thrown by Carl. But I ain't tellin' stories when Peter steps up to the plate and does his routine of practice swings, glove tamperin' and then pointin' his bat toward centerfield where he sees the Reptilian outfielder playin' too shallow for a third place hitter and so he gets a 'notion'; a 'mental picture' to hit a fly ball over his head just to see how well those Reptilians can track and run down a fly ball.

Carl gets Peter to swing and miss with his first two pitches but Peter fouls the third to the backstop meanin' he is gettin' close to hittin' Carl fair if he can just turn a Carl knuckleball back at him. Peter takes an upper cut swing for the fly ball but he gets on top of the low pitch due to his 'miscalculatin'' and so he makes contact for one of those swingin' bunts that rolls about ten feet down the third base line and then comes to a dead stop.

Now in Human baseball, the broadcaster would be callin' the play as the catcher going out and pouncin' on the ball but that wasn't the case here by any means because the Reptilian third baseman had another way of fieldin' a swinging bunt and so he sets hisself on his haunchies and then he leaps fifty feet or so and lands on the ball like he's huntin' Compys and then he digs the ball out of the depression he made and he throws out Peter by a country mile.

Rookya led off the bottom of the first with a 2-2 single into centerfield off Michelle but Michelle induced a double play ground ball and so the POTUS started the ball "around the Horn" in celebration or so said Tubus.

"What Horn?"

"Ships go around Africa's Cape Horn to get from the Atlantic to the Indian Ocean and visa versa," said Tubus.

"They ship baseballs around the...?"

But this Reptilian question was interrupted by the crack of Sawus' bat that launched a fly ball to deep centerfield. The Reptilian outfielders froze in place in the dugout and one of the Reptilian outfielders actually dropped his chocolate dipped grasshopper to the floor near the hopper cage and the kettle for dipping. The Reptilians watched as the Human outfielder turned his back to the infield and ran back to get under the ball. He was able to turn, stop and catch Sawus' fly while the Reptilians in the dugout watched agape.

"And that's how you judge a fly ball," said Tubus to the Reptilian outfielder who was chewing grasshopper and dugout dust but his mind was on other things.

The fly ball was caught by a younger version of Peter who played the position in the time of Willie Mays. As a kid, Peter played centerfield in all those pick-up games in the summer and, of course, the May's basket catch was his fond imitation. Those were confusing times for Peter. Those were times when Peter wanted to play baseball like a Negro player and when African Americans were cheered on the baseball field and yet denied a seat on a bus or counter space for lunch or a college education. For the Reptilians, baseball was still on the table for lessons learned in real life and they were attentive, focused and yet they were still untested until the arrival of the top of the seventh.

The *Wild Thing* music did not start up for the Un-plugged and blind mini-caribou as she ran out onto the field but Reptilian trepidation had risen immediately to the surface because, at the exact same time and by yet another remarkable coincidence, Peter was about to hit a high fly ball to left field, the first fly ball ever hit to a Reptilian outfielder and so the Reptilian just stood there and stuck his mitt out like a Mutant.

The outfield collision was imminent. The running scared mini-caribou, looking back from whence she came, ran straight into the legs of the outfielder and he froze in place and then he started in with the sweating of bullets because he felt the snarl form on his Reptilian lips and oh what a scene that could have been; dropping a fly ball while ripping apart a blind mini-caribou at the Company picnic.

Narrator (Old Man):
So everyone's holdin' out on breathin' while the 'bou gets even more scared and she runs and pinballs off the Reptilian centerfielder and then the whole durn Reptilian team is frozen Popsicles for the testin' of disciplines; for the holdin' back of snarly snarls while the fast thinkin' Alice is reachin' for what's left over of her Reptilian spray. And for sure, Alice sprays herself all over and then she runs out to collect the 'bou for the takin' back up the Corridor, past Air Force One and to a bowl of garlic fries and a comfort blanky that she picked from the dugout while on her way so that the 'bou might hopefully settle, feel some comfort and

maybe even sleep it off but Alice didn't figure on the Window reopenin' later and for the mini-caribou to escape into the Real World and, while this future was still in the works, Peter circled the bases for a 2-1 lead against the hazed, dazed and standin' around Reptilians.

And so the game arrived at the bottom of the ninth; 2-1 Humans with one on and Buttus up at the plate and with a Human closer with the uncommon name of Miller on the mound. He fires a fastball and with the fastball comes the television static and flicker and the Chamelea broadcaster sayin' with no picture, "He hits it high. He hits it deep."[1]

And then more flicker and then *My Friend Flicka*; my picture of a fine horse as I am sure Flicka is and so I will have to wait for a cupa daze for Mr. Lizard with the hope that he didn't forget the outcome.

BIRTH

The mini-caribou was scared, frightened to the core no doubt with the opening of the Trans dimensional Window and with the take off of Air Force One over her head. The scared mini-caribou ran blindly in no particular direction into the Real World for only about ten seconds and then she fell into a rabbit hole. But it wasn't a rabbit hole that swallowed her whole. It was a depression over a drop-then-slide feature of the Reptilian Corridors. So the mini-caribou Alice-tumbled into the Land and Lab of the Kindly Robots. The mini-caribou had found her origin.

The disconsolate and unknowing Alice sat on a first base dugout chair above a trap door which is the cause of her 'unknowing' and which opens into a Reptilian Corridor; a Reptilian Corridor that would eventually lead Basil to the Land and Lab of the Kindly Robots. Yes, Alice was blaming herself for the loss of the mini-caribou. It was, in her assessment, an egregious *faux pas* and she felt 'wasted' but no, she hadn't imbibed but one bottle of the tasty purple lichen beer.

Peter sat next to her in consolation and argument while Basil stared intently at the 'trap door' with all the dog 'insight' and 'visual acuity' that she could muster.

---

[1]   This is a trademark home run call by Giant's broadcaster Duane Kuiper.

"You can't 'see' everything that is going to happen."

"Yes, I can."

"No, you can't."

"Yes, I can."

"No, you can't."

"Yes, I can."

"Sixth Answer Rule!"

"What is the Sixth Answer Rule?"

"Well, if you ignore the Sixth Answer Rule, then the argument continues which would be boring. If you inquire about the Sixth Answer Rule then you lose the argument so why is Basil doing the G.I. crawl under your chair?"

"She's found something!"

"My goodness, it's a trap door!"

(Just as I had said previously.)

"I wonder where it leads?"

(To the Land and Lab of the Kindly Robots would be my guess.)

Narrator (Old Man):

Now I'm sittin' on a restaurant deck overlookin' the diamond sparkly tides of Elkhorn Slough. Management was kind enough to invite Dog and Cat to the deck because it's a rare warm day in Moss Landing, CA. There's a brown pelican standin' and starin' on an old wharf piling. Looks like a statue until it takes off and Dog sees it, tracks it but Cat's in my lap, her head archin', ready for the scratchin' and she's talkin'.

Cat talks all day. Dog talks in the evening like she is concluding history. I ain't sayin' nuttin' because of the Shrimp Louis but I'm ponderin' again about Reptilians because Mr. Lizard told me the score and about the trap door.

So I did some recallin' because I remember an incident regardin' info sent to Sawus' Father via periscope way back in the '60s when the risin' of social conscience and awareness was a folk singin' conversation amongst many a Hippie and, in addition to the Hippies all singin' to one another, there was this rapid proliferation of *cause célèbre* literature and so one of those brochures was picked up by a Chupacabra Sentry and sent down the pipe to Sawus' Dad who found hisself crunchin' the bones and blood of a screamin' rat while readin' the cause of the Society for the Prevention of Cruelty to Animals. And so it struck him as bein' like the totally wrong thing to be doin' and so he called for a meetin' of the Reptilian Elders so that Virgil Don Parker and his Ma and Pa could do somethin' about it and you are about to hear about Virgil comin' up shortly.

Now, as we all recall (because of our astute reading comprehension), the triplet sibling of Peter and I was born on Thanksgiving Day in the Earth year 1946 but Bro Virgil's birthin' actually took place on Gliese 4 as was told eruditely by me. In attendance for the Gliese 4 birth was a foursome of Reptilian Doctor golfers who had promptly departed the 14th Hole except for one reluctant golfer who was on course to break 100.

The birthin' of Virgil Don Parker went well. Mama did the hard pushin' to relieve herself of the thin eggshell membrane with baby encased and umbilical cord attached. Then the Reptilian Doctors began with the careful teasing apart of the said membrane followed by Virgil and, right then and there, Mama began fighting the Haze with her maternal instincts but there would be no breakthrough and Mama, exhausted from the twinin' and Virgil and from the light year travel, fell into a deep sleep.

The Human/Reptilian Hybrid Virgil was imprinted upon surrogate Reptilian parents by the name of Robotus and Robotya and they were transported back to Roswell for the raisin' of Virgil in the Reptilian ways and, along the way, Gray Captain Jane Earrie would sing lullabies to Virgil because she had mutated ear holes twice the normal size of other Grays and so, she was the only Alien in the Galaxy who could carry a tune except for the Blues, of course, and they are downright opery singers or so the rumor goes.

On the next day, Mama woke in San Francisco with one baby boy and some unanswered intuitive questions and, in her future, strange dreams that would leave behind an unresolved gut and odd feeling of disparity, the feeling that she had birthed more children then she had actually raised.

Down South, Robotus, Robotya and Virgil settled in for a life just outside Roswell and the most interesting room in their house was the garage and the elevator in the garage which led to the underground labs where Virgil was taught animatronics for all those years.

Still, on May 13th, 2012, sixty-six year old Virgil Don Parker felt enlightened to set up a lawn chair along the right field line for a Pecos League Baseball game of his home team - the Roswell Invaders. He and the old Robotus became the first of two invisible "ball dudes" to set up shop and occasionally, a foul ball would disappear down the line and then reappear in some kid's glove.

He loved the Roswell Invaders hat with the *Gray Alien* logo and, of course, he knew better. He loved baseball from the start but baseball was new to him and so he didn't know better.

Still, when I was a kid, everyone played.

LAB

Master Reptilian Spymaster Intelus set aside the upper CD case window that had come off its hinges, the window that held a little booklet that Intelus had pushed out. He turned over the little booklet to find a CIA seal on the cover (interesting - didn't know the CIA has been around for 25,000 years). He carefully pressed down on the center of the CD case bottom for the purpose of prying out the Mayan Calendar CD and this effort did not escape the attention of his supportive wife.

"You (tone) don't want to break a twenty-five thousand year old CD - do you, Dear?" inquired Intelya.

"You press down with the proper pressure and wala!"

The CD came loose and it was the only item that actually wasn't broken. He turned over the CD, held it on its edges and then he checked it for scratches or smudges. Finding none, he loaded the CD onto to his Mac and waited because the little CIA booklet, which had fallen apart into single pages, said that there would be a delay.

"Is there any pizza in the fridge?"

"You're eating dead food these days?"

"Pizza and hot dogs."

The Menu popped up twenty minutes later. At twenty-one minutes, Intelus called Alice on her cell.

Alice held onto her flashlight and flipped the switch for dim light and so the Reptilian Corridor that led to the Land and Lab of the Kindly Robots became, of course, dimly lit. The dim light reminded Peter of dusk kid baseball where he and his buds played with a new white ball until mitts were knocked off hands or, worse, some kid was black-eyed beaned with the coming darkness.

Basil had caught the scent of 'Reptilian' transferred by Alice to the running scared mini-caribou who had found her way into the expert care of the Kindly Robots and thus, Basil now led the way toward a narrow access Corridor; a Corridor which required a crawl on hands and knees for Peter and Alice but not for Basil and sure, Intelus would most certainly call the crawling Alice's cell at this time and she would have to ask (actually demand) that Peter retrieve her phone from her back pocket (Alice actually giggled a bit while Peter fumbled).

"What's so funny about the end of the Earth?" asked Intelus

"Sir?"

"Meet me in the lunchroom of the LLKR?"

"Where?"

"LLKR. Basil will take you there?"

The Kindly Robots, unaccustomed to visitors, had lavished loving care upon the mini-caribou and so Alice would eventually find an animal of a different elk (I meant 'ilk' - sorry about that). Alice would find a confident, well-groomed, well-fed mini-caribou and in fact, the Kindly Robots would have her answer the door, if need be, and so, much to the surprise of the Kindly Robots, the doorbell rang a mere three hours after the frightened mini-caribou had come into their care and yes, the confident mini-caribou ran to the door to perform her duty and so Peter, Alice and Basil were greeted by the said beast which Basil recognized spot on but it would take some time for Alice to interpret her surroundings; to recognize the mini-caribou for who she was; to absorb the warm hug of a Kindly Robot and to try and understand the meaning of the product assembly lines of this massive and yet super silly secret chamber.

Narrator (Old Man):

Now I don't node about you but I get a real hunger when revelations are heaped upon and so I'm finishin' this Shrimp Louis, sourdough and clam chowda and maybe even chocolate pie with a dollop of whip cream for dessert later because I just heard. I just heard from transient Wilfred Poindexter out in the parkin' lot who had heard from a strange lookin' and hitchin' little guy who said he had heard it from the Extraterrestrials that the name of my triplet siblin' was the one and only Virgil Don Parker of Roswell. And when I asked Wilfred about how he node that I'd be here at Elkhorn Slough at this particular time, he just said, "Alice sure can sing."

Cat's still talkin'. Dog puts her head in my lap and looks to me like she node my trepidation. And I'm quiet for a bit because I'll be packin' to be meetin' up with Virgil for the first time but heck, I won't tell him about Mama like I told Peter but he'll tell me about the Land and Lab of the Kindly Robots and the product assembly line for all those species of edible animatronics that feed the Reptilians and that he and his Dad and Mom had been inventin' all this time.

Then I opened the USDA Brown Envelope that Wilfred had bestowed and I saw the picture of a UC Davis T-shirt student pointin' his finger at fossil remains while lookin' at Peter, Alice and Basil (who was just walkin' away with a big ol' peanut butter biscuit) and so I read the date captioned on the picture as "August 28, 1859."

Then I asked for a box for my chocolate pie.

The Kindly Robots spoke very little but they remained busy both inside and outside the Conference Room during Intelus' revelations and it is common knowledge (and if it is not common knowledge then it should be) that the Kindly Robots have received permission to plant listening and recording devices on willing transients; transients like Wilfred Poindexter who roam the Earth searching for such delights as the recipe for Crab Benedict or a Dali with droopy clocks or a string quartet playing Beethoven or the fossil remains of a Reptilian death which had occurred during the Great Solar Storm of 1859.

Sure, the Kindly Robots would know some info in advance and the Conference Room was prepared with food and drink served by Robots in tuxedos; comfy chairs with headrests; top secret documents with large print and a 96" High Definition television monitor. And so Intelus began his briefing before the panel of Intelya, Peter and Alice. Basil stayed outside for the beginning of the proceedings because of the Robotic googlies ooglies and because she had already attended the meeting via time travel.

HOLOGRAM

Intelus:

"At 1:00 a.m. in the morning on August 28, 1859, a group of Colorado hikers woke up and started to cook breakfast because it was 'light outside' and it was 'light outside' due to the Aurora Borealis and not the dawn of new day which was due in about five hours. On this very same day, Baseball Manager Willy Martin was teleported from New York City to the Santa Fe Baldy Mountain Caverns. He arrived with news of the National Association of Base Ball Players and the rapid proliferation of new teams from New York to California. The offer by Willy to Sawus' great, great grandfather by the name of Sawus involved a game of catch outside and so, with the help of a grappling hook and an exposed root, Willy and Sawus climbed the slippery slope of a drop-then-slide feature of the Reptilian Corridors. Once on the surface, Willy taught Sawus how to turn his baseball glove to scoop low throws and how to protect his face from high throws and the first throw toward Sawus was high and Sawus put his glove up as told but the baseball never made it to Sawus because of a lightning strike that caused Sawus' skeleton to glow like in the cartoons and that killed him instantly along with Willy Martin. Sawus' body fell into a shallow gully and the ball rolled into his mouth before a significant mudslide. Willy Martin's body was dragged into the woods by a pack of coyotes and this event occurred August 28, 1859, under the shimmering lights of the Aurora Borealis."

"Alice, would you please fetch Basil at this time?" (interesting use of the word fetch since it is now Alice who must fetch and not the dog).

The well-groomed, well-fed and well-manicured Basil entered the Conference Room and she made her entry with a high step, with a prance of confidence. The Kindly Robots, per Intelus' instructions, had also bestowed upon Basil the ability to mentally record and project holographic movies of her past and future dreams.

"Basil, would you now project the hologram onto the table?"
'No.'
"Basil, would like a biscuit cookie?"
Tail wag - 'Like yeah.'
"Basil, would you now project the hologram on the table?"
'O.K.'

The UC Davis T-shirt student had called his Paleontology classmates over to see the skeletal claw with the old baseball glove preserved. The careful excavation of the obvious hoax would take hours and so Basil was instructed to fast forward the proceedings until Intelus spoke.

"Stop! You passed it. Basil, would you please rewind." (So, how did Intelus know the exact moment to rewind - curious - it is almost as if, as if he had seen the movie before!).

The Shadow that suddenly appeared sent a shiver down the spines of Peter and Alice and Basil was scared into shutting down the movie.

No tail wag - 'I'm scared.'

"Basil, it is o.k." (So, how did Intelus know that it was 'o.k.' uh? uh?) "Please resume."

The Shadow took the shape of a Lizard in a trench coat but Mr. Lizard had added a fedora hat with *Giants* logo because he was among the first of 20,000 fans to show up for a game against the Milwaukee Brewers. The UC Davis T-shirt student relaxed a bit at the sight of the *Giants* logo and so he inquired with regard to the possible purpose of Mr. Lizard's presence here, here at the grave site of this mysterious yet skeletal baseball player.

"I do funny facial sketches at County Fairs," said Mr. Lizard as he opened his trench coat and pulled out his precious pencil set.

"I should do an artist's rendition of this poor soul; to show what he would look like in his real life and, by the way, no one is going to believe you."

Still, Mr. Lizard did place a call to the White House shortly after he finished his sketch and shortly after he had presented it to the UC Davis T-shirt student who replied, "You have got to be kidding me!"

And, when the UC Davis T-shirt student carted in the skeleton and sketch as presentation for a grade in his Paleontology class, his Professor commented with a slight variation, "Whoa! You have got to be kidding me!"

Intelus:

"Basil, would you please show us a future? I will narrate."

"A Gray Whale will breech west of the Farallon Islands, September 2012 and when she resumes her daily swim, she will no longer possess a sense of direction. She will panic. She will swim North then East toward the shore and then she will turn South and, having calmed slightly, she will settle on this course. She will have a choice between the open ocean and the Golden Gate Bridge and so she will glide under the Bridge. She will have another choice between following an ocean going freighter back out to sea or the Oakland Ferry to the Giant's game and she will follow the Ferry to McCovey Cove. And so, on a warm September 2012 evening, the Giant's broadcaster will resume his accounts and descriptions of the Giant's game but only after a commercial break, of course."

"And so the Giants have taken the field to begin a home stand against the Diamondbacks and the Dodgers (boooooh!)."

"Tonight's pitcher for the Giants will be… and oh my goodness! It seems that we have an *Eschrichtius robustus* in the Cove. Yes folks, a Gray Whale has just set up shop in the Cove and so I must ask: is there a Marine Biologist in the House?"

And his question was followed by the voice of the Giant's Public Announcer. "Ladies and Gentlemen, there is a Gray Whale in McCovey Cove. Is there a Marine Biologist in the House?"

And so Peter, Alice and Basil stood up in the bleachers and started to wave their arms and paws frantically. They were (according to an usher who knew a Marine Biologist when he saw one) to report immediately to the broadcast booth.

"Do I know you from somewhere?" the Giant's broadcaster asked off the air.

"Yes. You did the first Reptilian intra-squad game in the history of Reptilian Baseball. You broadcasted the game via Interdimensional T.V. from underground facilities; facilities located under Santa Fe Baldy Mountain in New Mexico."

"Right. If you say so."

The Giant's broadcaster did not take the time to introduce Peter to Giant's fans because the finger-pointing Giant's fans were overwhelmed and impatiently curious about Gray Whale current events in McCovey Cove.

Peter responded thusly.

"Everyone knows that the Great Solar Storm of 1859 was a perfect geomagnetic storm that included not one but two coronal mass ejections and that the first coronal mass ejection paved the way for the second and thus, the arrival of the geomagnetic storm aligned with Earth occurred in half the normal time and everyone also knows that at least one model estimates a magnetic deflection value of -1600 nano-Tesla for the 1859 solar storm which is roughly 80 times the normal nano-Tesla level of -20 which qualifies the 1859 solar storm as a "super solar storm" and, most certainly, all of us are aware of the cancellation of Homing Pigeon races due to excessive sunspot activity and that Whales and Dolphins can lose their ability to migrate and, as we all know now, we have a Gray Whale in McCovey Cove as a result."

"Well, thank you Mister?"

"Posey."

"What?"

"Yes, our time-traveling dog Basil has suggested Posey for the Gray Whale's name and Basil says that the Gray Whale will be thrilled with her new name?"

"Your Basil talks to Gray Whales?"

"Yes. Gray Whales up and down the Pacific Coast were devastated by Buster Posey's season-ending injury last year in the collision at home plate."

"Now Panel – please subtract 2013 from 1859 and divide by 11. You get 154 years and the value 14 is a whole number which means that, if the sunspot cycle reaches a peak every 11 years, then solar storm peaks were coincidental with 1859 and late 2012 as verified by the Figure shown on our impressive 96" High Definition television (I have got to get one of those) and, of course, we all know that the Mayan Calendar chimes late 2012 – with the Long Count date of 4 Ahau or December 21, 2012."

Intelus leaned forward, Peter leaned forward and Alice leaned forward. They all leaned forward.

Basil chomped away at a peanut butter biscuit.

Intelus spoke first.

"Evacuation of the Baldy Mountain facilities must be a decision of the Elders."

"Who are the Elders?" asked Intelya.

"The question is," said Alice, "are the Elders still with us?"

"Well, just how old are they?" asked Intelus.

"They were 85 years old when they met and made the decision about the animatronic animals in the '60s so they should be around 130 years old now."

"Where are they now?"

Alice placed a finger on both sides of her temple like they were psychic antennae or something. Then she said, "Wilfred Poindexter is about to meet with Vernon. Tubus is about to tell us the whereabouts of Wilfred Perseus and Carl is in the White House."

"So, the two Wilfreds and Carl are the Elders?" asked Intelus.

'No,' thinks Basil.

"No," says Alice for Basil.

Episode Nine

. . . .

INDEPENDENCE

. . . .

ABDUCTION

Narrator (Old Man):

Now I said I'd be makin' time to meet up with Virgil in Roswell but I am still here, Victorin' house style, because I got me one of those summer colds which I fully suspect I got from the last Chupacabra visitor who sounded way too low and drawly when I asked about what happened to Bumgarner when Minnesota scored those eight runs in the first and so he says to me like Giant's Manager Bruce Bochy, "Oh yeah, Bum was up a little."

And then he says after blowin' his nostrils, "He'll be fine."

And then, "Can I go now?"

The Chupacabra left but he had also said (with his Bochy voice) that "Tubus was looking for another game and he thought that the Roswell Invaders might be a start."

So I sent one of those emails to Tubus sayin' with great coincidence that: *Virgil Don Parker is an invisible Ball Dude for the Roswell Invaders.*

And Tubus replied with: *Well how did you find out about that?*

And I replied (cc Rosanna Spearman) because I node she was listenin' anyways.

I heard it from Wilfred.

And so Tubus asked.

You mean Wilfred Poindexter?

And I replied as before.

Yes, I only know one Wilfred.

And so Tubus responded.

But I know one Wilfred Perseus and he was talking up a storm at the Little A'Le'Inn Area 51 and he said nearly the same thing.

And I replied.

What do you mean by 'nearly'?

And so Tubus responded.

Wilfred Perseus added that there's a game on July 4th so now you know what I'm thinking?

And I replied.

Well no because I got a summer cold from a Chupacabra and my intuition is down.

And so Tubus responded.

Well, I am aiming to Alien-abduct Roswell's bench play...

Then 'puter shuts down while I'm readin' Tubus and up pops the CIA Seal of disapproval and so I ready myself for another visit from the Suits and so I get the Hazer out and Dog's food bowl because they always show up at Dog's feeding time and I get them to feed Dog right away so Dog won't look at me with her big brown eyes which shows up her wills and testaments based on her daily claims of death by neglectin' dog starvation. Cat eats when she wants too and so it doesn't matter to Cat when the Suits come.

Then my cell rings and its 'Sanna on a channel from a secure dimension that the CIA don't node and she says, "Virgil heard about your summer cold and he is coming your way."

The CIA came a cupa daze later because they were slowed by those Budget cuts and now I see a big, black and shiny Ford rollin' up to my Victorin' porch and I see an automatic tinted window and a Suit head lookin' at me with the question, "How much for the Lemonade?"

And I said, "A quarter if you feed the Dog."

And then they complied with the short report for their Superiors that they "fed the Dog and everything is peachy here" and then they got back into their big Ford, drove off past an incomin' brown Ford Fal'cn and they stopped with their automatic tinted window down and they says to Mr. Lizard and Virgil while pointin' the way, "The lemonade is down there."

It's 5:00 p.m. on the beach. It's when all those beachcombers have left for dinner and so I can see whitecaps from where I'm sittin' on my Victorin' porch; whitecaps and driftwood and abandoned sand castles and I can faintly smell wood fires but children voices have gone home so I can hear Virgil a little better. I had pulled out Capt'in's Chairs for the Virgil meetin' and set out glasses of lemonade and I had put on the Sibelius Allegro from his Second because I wanted somethin' pretty but not pretty and sad like that fellow Mahler gets sometimes.

We waved goodbye to Mr. Lizard and then Virgil sat right down. Cat jumped into his lap and started talkin' and so I was wrong about the extraneous noise and Virgil had to speak up. Dog had swallowed the Chip and so she was ready for mental holographic recordin' if or when the time was right.

"Do you miss her?" asked the mind readin' Virgil.

"I keep Shirley's memory and so, are you one of those mind readers?"

"I dabble a bit. I can read only strong, emotive thoughts."

"Are you...?"

"Married? No, I am betrothed?"

"Tell me about her if you choose."

"The Hippie Rose walked into the Lab September 4, 1972, with a backpack, a guitar slung over her bare tank top shoulders and she was holding onto a fungo bat and, in her other hand, she had a baseball tucked into her mitt. We were real busy because Sawus had just sent down the order for the edible animatronic rats but the sight of Rose just stopped me in my tracks and my mind went to a place where it had never been like it was leaving Earth or something. She knew that she had Blue in her and I knew too but don't tell me how I knew and then she looked at me the same way that I was looking at her and she said, "I am looking to shag some fly balls in the 1859 Meadow." And I said "sure" but heck Brother (there's that mind readin' again), I didn't know the first thing about hittin' fly balls but she was convincing and beautiful and later she would say that I was soul searchin' for her and so we snuck out of the Corridors because she knew August 28, 1859, history. She also knew I was the calculating kind and I would get used to the fungo bat in short order and yes, she had a knee slappin' good time watching me strike out, then hit a couple of grounders and then a pop up before I hit a fly ball right to her which she caught in her tracks. Then she says "surprise me" and so I sprayed fly balls all over the 1859 Meadow so she could track them down and I even hit the last one into the tree line and so she might have even run over Willy Martin's chewed-up bones to get it. I helped her find the ball and we decided to get married in 40 years because we both had the Work ahead of us. Yes, I am a builder of edible robots and she is a Peace Builder. And the Chinese should be here in about ten minutes so thank you very much."

Dog stopped recordin' and so I had a nice wedding present for Rose and Virgil when the time comes and then Virgil and I started talkin' in code and we talked in code while chop stickin' our Chinese appetizers.

"Rosanne Rosannadanna will be sky high on 12.19.19.9.10," said Virgil into the Sender.

"And she'll be babysitting the cave bats but only those hanging under the bench," said Vernon into the Sender.

Now July Fourth in America is a red, white and blue Day. It is a hot and sweaty Day of glistening Star Spangled Bands, barbeque smoke, children's sparklers and other twirling fireworks less contained. And, most certainly, sunburn baseball games of all sorts are played all over the Country and the games proceed with little attention paid by onlookers or fans because the celebrants have much to do with the duties of fire: the attention paid to the Sun, cooking and fireworks. And so baseball is played without much notice on July Fourth but notice would be most certainly be applied if the game of baseball was omitted from the American mural. And so painted into the American mural was the scheduled July 4th, 4:00 p.m. game in Griggs Park between the White Sands Pupfish and the visiting Roswell Invaders.

In the top of the first, the starting nine of the Roswell Invaders took the hot and sweaty field leaving behind the Invaders' bench players who, at 4:01 p.m., disappeared from the full view of time-traveling, Haze-resistant, 18 year-old Franny Carpenter.

"Mom, there's a couple of old guys sitting on stools down the foul lines."

"Hold on Dear, Dad's almost finished with the hot dogs."

"Mom, I just saw a UFO!"

"Honey, I thought I heard something about a flyover."

"Mom, did you see?"

"See what?"

"We don't have any bench players. They're gone!"

"What you like on your hot dog?"

BROADCAST

The UC Davis T-shirt student settled into his Sea Cliff Motel room. He had traveled to the coastal village of Aptos, CA, on the Sunday before July 4th. He had come here to get away from the fossil with the baseball in its mouth and from the fossil's bone marrow that had stunk and skunked up the Paleontology Lab something fierce.

He had turned on the First Season X-Files. The car driven by Mulder and Scully had died and had come to rest on an Oregon highway. The static of the car radio had turned on and off as the car shook and then Mulder checked his watch. He got out of the Government car and then he spray-painted X on the pavement and then he said to Scully that it was "probably nothing."

The UC Davis T-shirt student then booted his laptop. He clicked on the August 28, 1859, folder. He scrolled to the Willy Martin file, the file sent to him as an email attachment from an unknown Lizard source (hmmm - I wonder who that could be). It seems, according to the Lizard-sent file, that New York Knickerbocker Manager Willy Martin had composed a mighty beef with the umpire about a missed tag at third base.

> *Martin charged from the dugout and he started with pointing at the bag with hand chops but the Ump held his ground and repeated the safe sign. Martin got so mad that his neck turned red like he was sprouting fish gills and then he pulled out two garden gloves from his back pocket and he waved them in the ump's face but the ump refused to budge. Martin started in with the kicking of infield dirt on the ump's shoes and the ump started returning fire at Willy because he said later that his shoes had been polished right before the game. And we all know what happened next because Willy Martin just suddenly vanished into thin air after the umpire's gesture of ejection and so, we all thought it might be a parlor trick but no, folks haven't*

seen or heard from Willy since.

Meanwhile and next door, Mr. Lizard's 'anticipation' of fish and chips and tartar was about to experience a withdrawal. Yes, the forked appetizer of breaded fish that had been summarily dipped in tartar sauce wouldn't make it to Mr. Lizard because of the sudden televised buzzer that had been so obnoxiously summoned to his room and in all the televised rooms of Monterey County for that matter:

> *This is a broadcast of the Emergency Broadcast System. Flood waters* (what? in the middle of summer?) *in Soquel Creek are expected to reach record heights by Noon tomorrow and Rosanne Rosannadanna will be sky high on 12.19.19.9.10 and she'll be babysitting the cave bats but only those hanging under the bench. This announcement will now repeat itself.*

And it did so for the next 15 minutes.

And so – what do Humans know at this time about Reptilian baseball? We know that a UC Davis T-shirt student had discovered a Reptilian fossil on Santa Fe Baldy Mountain with stinky blood, with a baseball in his mouth and with an old style baseball glove on his claw. We know from a fedora-wearing Lizard-like unknown source that Willy Martin disappeared on August 28, 1859, and that he vanished with not one but two old style baseball gloves. What we don't know or, at least, what we don't know until I tell you, is that, late Tuesday night and, while her parents slept oblivious, Haze-resistant Franny Carpenter had posted her Facebook interpretation that *cave bats hangin' under the bench* meant *They play baseball in the Caves.* And it is certainly true that Intelus, Peter's FFA contact and the POTUS would surmise the 12.19.19.9.10 date to be the Mayan Calendar Long Count equivalent of July 4th, 2012. The POTUS, in the course of human events, would then contact the National Security Agency for any further knowledge based on billions, no, trillions of cell phone intercepts. The NSA would, in turn, forward this Presidential request to "Bro" for further investigation. And who is Bro might you ask? Well, Bro is the brother of the UC Davis T-shirt student.

CONTACT

The exceedingly polite cargo crew of Roswell Invader reserves sat in two rows of six in the cargo bay of Rosanna's spaceship. The trays were in the downright position with a bag of peanuts, with a hot dog tucked into a warm Doofus Roll and with a lot of those little slippery packages of hot dog condiments all of which were placed neatly on the tray.

A Kindly Robot instructed the suspiciously polite and unusually cooperative Roswell team to eat quickly and to sit still for a brief Brainy Scope exam because it will take only six minutes and six seconds to travel from White Sands to their destination.

"Sure sir, go ahead with the exam, sir," said each member of the Team with a smile except for Bro (oooppps – let that one Wikileak); the Bro first baseman who was the only one to inquire about the function of the Brainy Scope.

"The Brainy Scope measures possible brain damage due to anti-gravity travel. The other possible side effect is an uncontrollable craving for chocolate chip cookies but we do not have time for dessert."

The Roswell Invaders disappeared shortly thereafter and reappeared in the first base dugout of the Reptilian Baseball Chamber where Bro promptly submitted a line-up card to interim Player/Manager Peter (Tubus had caught Vernon's summer cold); a line-up card which had him penciled in at first base and batting second but he would surely be like totally surprised because Basil, his dog from childhood, would be the forever happy and tail-wagging dog whenever he entered the room and she now sat, like a good dog should, between him and the on-deck circle waiting for his returned affections which is a Boy/Dog scene that would not go unnoticed by Intelus who had taken his position at second base.

Now (as we might suspect), Bro's Roswell Invader uniform literally reeked of a litany of mini-listening and video devices which had been heaped upon Bro by any number of Government agencies and I cannot begin to estimate the number of Government agents who were privy to the conversation between the Roswell players and the Kindly Robot aboard Rosanna's spaceship. Bro could actually feel his uniform move like a living cloak with the purpose of focus on the approaching Intelus; focus for official documentation of a *Close Encounter of the Fourth Kind* between Humans and Reptilians and many a Government agent would praise the encounter as the First but we all know better because of the ill-fated game of catch that took place in 1859 between Willy Martin and Sawus.

Narrator (Old Man):
Now Intelus stalled the game right then and there so he could investigate the goings-on between Bro and Basil and he started in by pickin' a Roswell player close in size and shape to Bro and he requested from Alice that she help by openin' the trap door and she did so with a smile and with a plate of chocolate chip cookies and with the followin' Intelus, Bro, a Player-To-Be-Named-Later and Basil, who just had to continue her happy greetin' to Bro all the way down those Reptilian Corridors.

Then they went into a room with a table and some small stools; stools that make their butts hang down by overlappin' and Intelus began his instructions. Intelus told Bro to strip down to his underwear and to pile his uniform onto the table and we all node what's in Bro's uniform. Intelus then told the Player-To-Be-Named-Later to strip to his privies and to hand over his uniform to Bro for his dressin' up because Intelus wanted Bro out there playin' so he could an eye on him. Intelus then put on the three hour entertainment for the underwear sittin' Roswell player and the entertainment included a Reptilian Barbie Shop Quartet humming *It's a Small World* off-key for 5 minutes followed by the Seventh Symphonies of Beethoven and that Mahler fellow and it toke about half 'n hour but the Bro uniform was able to creep itself off the table and find itself a corner of the room to hide in.

The Chamelea broadcasters came on the air.
"Well, we are here at the Reptilian Baseball Chamber under Santa Fe Baldy Mountain for a Fourth of July exhibition game between the Alien-abducted bench players of the Roswell Invaders and your Santa Fe Giants. We are certainly appreciative of the Roswell Invader's participation in this Game in spite of the total disregard of their human rights and we are somewhat surprised by their total cooperation and politeness which, at times, has bordered on annoyance. It is almost as if, as if they knew that they were going to be abducted and that they would be putting on a show for the folks back home but – who are the folks back home?"

"Well, I am only guessing mind you but I would suggest that, sooner or later, any given Government Agency in America would want credit for valid intelligence which proved the existence of Extraterrestrials and it would surely take a Baseball Insider to initiate such an operation. So, we are frankly baffled with regard to America's prowess with regard to intelligence gathering by what we just observed. I mean - why would any intelligence agency give the number 66 to a spy player and then send him to an Extraterrestrial game with the Family Dog. It is just too easy to figure and so Roswell is down a player but the Giants still have their own problems and so, have the Giants made any progress on their out-field play?"

"Well, it seems that Tubus found out that Virgil Don Parker knew about hitting fungo flies to his fiancee' and so the said object was "located" by a Chupacabra and sent down the pipe to Tubus. Tubus said that it's taken a couple of weeks but a fly ball was actually tracked down and caught last Friday by the centerfielder. Tubus said that the outfielders move out of their "cement boots" now to try and get under the fly ball but that's all the progress they have made. It looks like Intelus has returned to his position at second base and we are ready for the gong and the reading of the *Universal Peacebuilding Initiative*. Oh Baseball on the Fourth of July – ya gotta love it."

ARRIVAL

Rosanna Spearman's spaceship arrived at the Area 51 Landing Pad at around noon on July 4th and, of course, the landing took place within the binocular and camera clicking view of three or four hundred dedicated Ufologists who had been invited to a newly-constructed, Government picnic playground on Freedom Ridge for a July 4th celebration which, according to the official Government invitation signed by the POTUS, included food, a softball game and a fireworks show over Groom Lake.

The UFO celebrants were most certainly taken aback by the Government's newly-found transparency which involved verbal and visual confirmation that Area 51 is now and always has been a landing site and maintenance bay for UFOs and sure, all camera and video equipment were activated for the ramp descent of Carl (yes, the White House Carl) and two Wilfred transients from the ship.

The Ufologist's laptops quickly identified Carl which was a development that sent a Tweety stir through the hot dog and apple pie encampment. The names of the two homeless transients remained a mystery. Carl and the two transients were downloaded into the back seat of a Ford Falcon Station Wagon driven by a shadowy figure and accompanied by another old man in the passenger seat who nobuddy node. A Dog and a Cat slept unseen in an incredibly cute Dog/Cat pile in the rear of the station wagon. The Ford Falcon then promptly disappeared and reappeared six minutes and six seconds later in a reserved, handicap parking space at the Little A'Le'Inn in Rachel, NV.

The July 4th UFO celebrants on Freedom Ridge had just completed the last of their Twitters, texts, Facebook OMGs, emails, cell phone calls and they had settled down to picking teams for softball when, as part of the Government's attempt to unveil the secrecy of Extraterrestrials, the huge door of one of Area 51's old hangars began to slowly rise and it rose slowly with the screech of a metal door that had not been WD40ed for a long, long time and so the Ufologists were treated to both the sights and sounds of this revelation. Most prepared for documentation but for some this July 4th spectacle was too much and so a small crowd gathered at the two *Porta Potties* provided (due to a clerical error, the other eighteen were on route) and yes, there was some nausea but no one barfed due to any terrified anticipation of what might be behind 'Hangar Door Number One.'

Narrator (Old Man):
There was this delay, you see, while the three old, old Reptilian Elders were loaded into the waitin' Black Limo in the Hangar and the delay was due to the inexorable and turtle speeds of anything the Elders tried to do. There was the complainin' about this and that and the canes were bumpin' the Limo driver's legs like he was the one slowin' them down. And for sure, there were ice tinklin' whiskey shots and warm tingly footbaths provided by the Las Vegas Limousine Service in the back seat and so the tips and toes of the Elders were currently nuttin' they could complain about and so it was a kind of motivator for them to perk up and question the Limo driver regardin' their destination and they did question the Limo driver and he said they were limo-driving to the Little A'Le'Inn on the newly-paved Groom Lake Road and that they would be takin' the *Extraterrestrial Highway* to Rachel for meetin' up with informants Carl, Wilfred Poindexter and Wilfred Perseus. Then he said to

buckle seat belts and enjoy the ride and to ignore the parade of those Ufologists who'd break away from July 4th picnicin' and decide to follow the Black Limo with the tinty windows up Highway 375.

The Black Limo pulled into handicapped parkin' at the Little A'Le'Inn and Mr. Lizard opened the Limo door and began the unloadin' of the Reptilian Elders who had managed to get back into their shiny black Sunday shoes and so they got out all bent over and dressed in black suits and ties and they were lookin' like *Men in Black* but we all node that the *Men in Black* and the Black Helicopter Pilots have this Federal Holiday off and that's why the Black Limo was allowed to proceed to Rachel with the Ufologists followin' close in their SUV's.

The Elders did have the time to shuffle their slow, slow way past Pam at the counter and towards the Government and secure Conference Room built yesterday for this Meetin' and yes, the lead Elder did say somethin' about their passin' by, "Watch out! Comin' through!"

And then the middle Elder asks Pam for a slow dance to Elvis later and he started in singin' off key: *Wise men say, only fools rush in.*

And so Pam was kind enough to oblige his request and she said the dance floor would be cleared out for later.

The slow, cane clickin' and pokin' procession entered the Men's Restroom because the Government figured and they figured right-on that the Elders might need to relieve themselves before their Meetin' and, just in case you are interested, the Elders were relievin' at the exact same time that the eighteen *Porta Potties* were pullin' into Freedom Ridge and so the July 4th party up there was turnin' back on. So after their relief, the Elders stepped into an elevator by the stalls and they were sent down to the waitin' Wilfreds, Carl, Dog, Cat and the facilitator of the Meetin' who was yours in Truth.

Now I had put on Beethoven's Fourth Piano Concerto to make the Elders feel intelligent and intellectual. Mr. Lizard had called in Elder orders for root beer floats, fries and *Alien Burgers* made by special design while we had ordered from the counter and so food was on the table along with three documents in large bold print for the Elders to see but they were just interested in our verbal summaries of salient information.

So the Wilfreds talked Mayan Calendar and the Great Solar Storm of 1859 and how the Sun's stormin' would be at its peak at the end of 2012 like hurricane season and then they showed a 2012 picture of Posey the Gray Whale in McCovey Cove and then a picture of the 1859 Sawus fossil with the baseball in its mouth. And then Carl spoke about War on Earth and how Humans hadn't found a way to end War and how the POTUS had read and understood how the *Universal Peacebuilding Initiative* might provide the precedents and practices as progress toward the end of Human War and the beginning of World Peace.

Carl had told the POTUS all this because he suspected, by all accounts and by what the POTUS had remembered recently about likin' the purple beer and about likin' the read of the *Universal Peacebuilding Initiative*, that he was somewhat resistant to Haze 2 and thus, he now node more about Reptilians than ever before. The POTUS did initiate, based on his suspicions, the fact findin' intelligence which led to the Presidential conclusion that Reptilians were obviously here from Gliese 4 to learn the game of baseball and that someday real soon, he would address the Nation and talk about Basil's doin's and about Haze-resistant Franny Carpenter of Roswell, New Mexico.

The thirty minute meeting of the Elders ended with the red button pushing by Elder number two and with Elvis coming on in the Main Dining Room of the Little A'Le'Inn as a result and there waiting was Pam and a couple of girlfriends that she had quickly called up.

CHOCOLATE

The game between the Roswell Invaders and the Santa Fe Giants had reached the top of the fourth with Roswell holding on to a 3-2 lead. Roswell had scored all three runs in the first as a result of Rookus' rough start which included walking the first three hitters. With the bases loaded, the Roswell cleanup hitter then pulled a low line drive down the third base line which was so close to the chalk line that the Reptilian left fielder thought it might be foul and so, instead of chasing it down right away, he stood and looked to the umpire for help. Well, all the Reptilians in the Chamber started yelling at the Reptilian to go get it and that reminds me of my Little League days when they had to put me in for the required six outs and so I was put in right field at sunset and so all I ever heard was the crack of the bat and the ball hitting the fence behind me and people yelling at me like they were yelling now at the Reptilian outfielder and, if it weren't for his panic and leaping ability, the Roswell hitter would have had an inside-the-park homerun. It was just so bad for Rookus because Rookya was catching him and so she went out to the mound after the bases-clearing triple to have a little chat with the hubby.

Rookus had started in with his warm-ups before the top of the fourth but then, to everyone's surprise (including mine), both dugout phones started in ringing and everyone was surprised as I said because dugout phones do not ring and, not only did the dugout phones ring, but they pealed a ring-tone with panache' which included the crescendo and canons of Tchaikovsky's *1812 Overture* and you might think that fireworks might have been added especially on July 4th but no one (me included) would have slightest inclination that a dugout phone could ring in the first place because all it is there for is calling one way to the bullpen for pizza orders or pitcher relief.

Peter and Tubus dared to answer and so Peter called his hitter back to the dugout. The Roswell Invaders' bench players, the Player-to-be-Named-Later and Bro's uniform (minus the pile of espionage devices) then disappeared and reappeared in the cargo bay of Rosanna's ship for the six minute and six second, fast eating, get it down, peanut, hot dog and chocolate chip cookie ride back to Roswell where Franny saw them reappear in the dugout but this time, Franny would keep this FYI from Mom and Dad and just tell her text friends now and her Facebook friends later that these current events were a matter of some serious evidence for the existence of Extraterrestrials on Earth.

Back at the Chamber, Peter, after some head-nodding talk on the dugout phone, called Alice over for ear whispers but he wasn't tickling and titilating her ear bones with sweet nothings and that's for sure. It was something else said and so Alice, Basil and a big plate of chocolate chip cookies promptly left the scene.

Narrator (Old Man):

Now Alice stood before the Living Ship and the Ship says "no" again for leavin' to Gliese 4 and so she starts in with her convincin' and convincin' not by askin' 'why questions' because 'why questions' would help Ship's cause and resolve so she tried the 'back door' strategy to get Ship into a frame of mind for her suggestions regardin' the matter at hand but Ship stayed firm from the get go.

"Hello, my name is Alice."

"But I don't want to go Gliese 4."

Alice ignores.

"Do you have a name?"

"No."

"Well, would you like a name?"

"Maybe."

"Maybe is not a name. How about Voyager or Gliese?"

"Uh?"

"A name can make you famous you know. You could say, 'I rescued the Reptilians from the War Planet Earth and then I became the hero ship Gliese!"

"But I don't want to go Gliese 4."

Alice didn't miss a beat.

"Are you a male ship or a female ship?"

"Male."

"Well, I hear that the Yucatan Ship is female and she is hot and she wants to go to Gliese 4."

"No she doesn't."

"Yes she does."

"No she doesn't."

"Yes she does."

Alice interrupts.

"Sixth Answer Rule!"

"What?"

"You answered. You lose. You go to Gliese 4."

"But I don't want to go Gliese 4."

Now Alice's convincin' really didn't mean to do the job right away. It was one of those stallin' tactics and so it made some time for Peter to follow her down to the Mutant's Chamber and for hisself to go to the room next door and warm up a big plate of those chocolate chip cookies that Alice was to use as a secret weapon because she node about chocolate chip cookies and endorphins and how endorphins can be addictin' so that her convincin' could ring true to the Ship and so Peter brought in the hormone stimulatin', harmonic and happy cookies and Alice started wavin' the odiferous essence of the chocolate chip cookies in the direction of Ship and it worked almost instantly along with Alice's sexy suggestion, "You can have some of these cookies on your way to Gliese 4."

PASSAGE

Basil circled three times then she settled into her bed.

She could hear voices from the front seat but she didn't recognize any of her favorite words like 'walk' or 'biscuit.' The human voices were, nonetheless, very comforting as was the hum of Alice's VW.

Basil's eyes twitched, her legs stiffened and an interdimensional window opened up on the Pacifier where she was welcomed with googly and oogly greetings by Core, Scarlett and Edsel.

Edsel had just prepared the little focaccia bread sandwiches which had been warmed in a microwave on high-power for exactly ten seconds per Alice's instructions.

Basil was aboard the Pacifier as a witness to the passage of two Living Ships as they left Earth orbit and it sure was a scene with the window-sitting Reptilians; the window-sitting Reptilians who waved their Doofus Bats in the air and then they pointed them, Babe Ruth style, toward the Gliese Star System.

The game of baseball was leaving Earth.

And yet below (yes, on Earth) did the red lights begin to flash off and on again within a dimly lit, supercilious and possibility deadly missile silo in Utah.

Episode Ten

. . . .

DUGWAY

. . . .

Imagine all the people living life in peace
- John Lennon

Narrator(Old Man):

Now it was high noon in Dugway on July 4, 2012. It was high noon and Sun was burnin' so all the Carpenters were inside. They were inside their cool settlement homes with each family buildin' their own rocket fireworks for their annual contest.

I node where I was at the time. I was in the Little A'le'Inn in Rachel, Nevada. I was entertainin' those old and cranky Reptilian Elders. And yeah, they did just a little more than call for the Reptilian evacuation of Earth due the possibility of a 2012 Solar Storm. They did a tad more because they had also produced an Interdimensional Television broadcast that would stop the Carpenters in their 2012 rocket fireworks tracks.

Yup, the Carpenters stopped what they were doing because all their televisions came on loud and clear at once and there were three old guys on their televisions that sure looked like spittin' images of ol' Julius and Julia Irving right before they passed. The Carpenters were naturally curious about the contents of this stellar and tellin' broadcast (as we are all) and a few Carpenters might have some intuitive specula- tions because of some previous hints with regard to a fellow named Core Halley; that Core Halley might have been the source of the harmonic revelations that these old, old and strange lookin' folks were preachin' about; all this Reptilian and Elder preachin' about the demise of Earth's Second Moon. Maybe speculatin' Carpenters had huddled and cuddled around a campfire somewhere between Dugway and Boston, sometime between 1784 and 2012. Maybe they had compared such notations as the capitalization of *Core* in the 1777 communication from the USPS's future.

The broadcast showed all those details that Peter and Alice could not have seen or imagined because they were removed as a matter of history and technology but not so for present Carpenters. It was no longer a remote possibility that Extraterrestrials in a spaceship with nukes could be the cause of the heinous, heinous crime that is the destruction of Earth's Second Moon simply because human science fiction has traversed a violent path and so the Carpenters agreed with eyes wide open and so later that evening, they ran out their front doors into a warm summer night to see what the broadcast had promised.

Sure enough, there were two pesky missiles and you could see them in the distance. They were Gray prepared and had emerged into the two Eyes of the Smiley Face. The countdown was for a 9:30 p.m. launch and the red Core lights on top of the missiles were flashing on and off just as they had done in 1776.

Now the Carpenter settlement was a wide semicircle of homes and in the middle was a recreation room, a park and a playing field with lights and sure, the smoking barbeques by the recreation room on this July 4th evening were blasting out burgers and hot dogs while the teams were assembling for an evening softball game under the lights and so the Carpenters and the Goshutes were warming up for their annual game and the game would be followed, of course, by the biggest display of illegal fireworks in Utah's history.

The Goshutes were naturally curious about the two missiles standing out in the desert in the Eyes of the Smiley Face and Sally Carpenter answered the Goshutes but, while talking about this Carpenter sensitive subject matter, she started to dig her fingers into her husband Charles' shoulder blades and she kept repeating like she was in a trance or something that "Core Halley was going to get his" and the pain got to be so bad for Charles that the Goshutes stopped their inquiry right then and there.

Yes, the Pacifier had been to Lake Titicaca to pick up the Mayan

Calendar CDs. Yes, the Pacifier had tailgated Air Force One to the Trans-dimensional Window.

However, what I neglected to add (until right now - I mean - how convenient is that?) is that Scarlett had received an email from Rosanna Spearman (cc Rose, the Blue) which had included the sexy suggestion that they all fly to Utah on July 4th "for like the best fireworks show ever." Rosanna also said they would beam the Transdimensional Lens over so that they could see the Smiley Face and the fireworks show up close.

And so it happened that Scarlett forgot to inform Core until the eleventh hour meaning 9:30 p.m. and so Core asked, "What is that?"

And Scarlett replies, "It is a Transdimensional Lens. Want a lookie-poo?"

"Sure."

Core Halley focused down on Utah and we sure know what he saw and what he saw was that two missiles had been launched from the Eyes of a Smiley Face and one of the missiles with flashing red lights quickly filled up the Lens leaving Core to thinking and concluding that maybe, just maybe, these two missiles had the Pacifier in mind as a target and so he says, "Whoa Boss, missiles have been launched!"

And so Scarlett asks, "What missiles?"

And so Core looks away from the Transdimensional Lens because it is no longer useful and he says, "Look out the window!"

And so Scarlett looks out the window and she says, "Wow! The Smiley Face! You can see it from Space!"

And Core reminds her about the missiles and she says, "You mean the two missiles that are headed right at us?"

And Core says empathically, "Yes, those missiles!"

And Scarlett suggests, "We need to jump the ship."

And Core says, "I agree. Let's jump the ship."

And so Core adds, "Edsel, jump the ship."

And Edsel says, "I am not talking to you anymore."

And so Scarlett says, "Ten seconds to impact."

And so Core repeats, "Edsel, jump the ship."

"No."

The End (just kidding)

As we recall (because we are all so darn smart), the Warring Winged

Reptilian Faction referred to as the Ciakar were subjected to a stasis field and were only allowed to make very, very slow progress toward their kick butt ship. The creator of these stasis fields is none other than Rose, the Blue; Rose the Peacebuilder and Rose, the expert on the humane concept of totally defensive weaponry. And so Rose quickly and expertly established a stasis field between the incoming missiles and the Pacifier.

The missiles stopped dead in their tracks and then they began their descent back down toward the Carpenter's Smiley Face and so now it was the Carpenter's turn to sweat bullets and they did so as the missiles reentered with a flaming trajectory aimed right toward the Carpenter's settlement.

The Carpenters and the attending Goshutes did "duck and cover" (as if duck and cover might actually work as a response to two nuclear bombs dropped on their little village).

And so the missiles fell from the sky.

The End (but wait, there's more).

And so the missiles fell from the sky but they did not fall all way to Earth and no, they were not armed at all with nuclear blasts but rather they were filled with the most remarkable fireworks imaginable and so duck and cover was changed immediately to Carpenter and Goshute amazement as Smiley Faces, Flowers, Peace Signs, Fish and John Lennon's image filled the night and July 4th, 2012, sky.

Episode Eleven

BIPOLAR

VERNON

The old man stood on the beach.

His crushing toes curled over and over again as he established a foothold in the wet sand.

His pale and thin lumber for legs shook violently with the wind and the cold gave him an unsteady appearance; a weakness which mocked strength; a weakness which conveyed the shaky service of water with the rattle of ice.

His butt faced the beach road.

The woman pointed her cell phone and he hadn't seen her and so he didn't know when the police would arrive.

He did not hide from the wind.

He did not fold arms to warm his bare chest nor did he lower his face to retreat from blown sand.

He had thoughts, mostly of his wife and his sons.

For him, moments of reason were transitory.

Sure, it was December 20, 2012, and he was here at dawn and he was here all day for the sunset.

He would tell the police that the Extraterrestrials had abducted him and they had forgot to return his clothes.

Truth is, he didn't know.

He simply woke and he made serious and determined tracks onto the beach.

Dog and Cat had died a month ago, both on the same night, and so he woke every morning since in a 'place' unknown and with no one to feed or care for.

Rose and Virgil had come to town.

Rose and Virgil stayed at the house.

Rose would come with Captain's Chairs for all of them.

She would come before the police and she would bring him a robe.

They would sit all day on the beach waiting for the Sun to set; for the Sun to set as a reminder that the world as he knows it still exists.

The old man woke in his skivvies.

His knees were locked.

Someone slid arms under his knees.

Someone lifted his knees.

Someone rotated his legs for his release from bed.

He couldn't remember that he had actually gotten up on his own.

His numb feet landed on Dog's bed.

Dog hadn't circled her bed three times.

She hadn't even circled it once.

She had curled into a ball and went to sleep for the last time and Cat followed later in the space between Dog's dying legs.

The plane's flight was in the hands of a small child.

It dipped and rose again with the random flight plan of a child's whim and fancy.

It fell from the sky when the child dropped it for another toy.

The plane with the screamers crashed on his beach.

There was a ball of fire.

He saw little fires beneath broken fuselage windows.

He saw the trackless trails of ghosts as they marched toward the pillars and the rectangular plane of brilliant light.

He had walked naked onto the beach - pale as the ghosts who had passed before him.

The woman held up her phone again for the SWAT.

Rose placed the robe gently around his shoulders and she guided him into his Captain's Chair.

She brought coffee and Dog news.

Molly is twelve.

She is blind.

She has liver cancer and she has, at the most, six months of life.

A friend for six months is better than no friend at all.

The old man walked slowly down the hallway.

The house was cold; freezing cold and the ice pack had stopped the bleeding.

His good arm; his right arm; dangled on his side as a matter of some incomplete and amateur dismemberment.

His left arm did a Nazi salute - if not for cause then perhaps merely for balance.

He must have been waiting for a heart transplant.

There was a cavity in his chest with ripped arteries and veins.

He walked on, zombie-like, toward his garage.

He picked up his sand wedge.

He walked onto the beach in search of a golf ball.

He tried to hit the ball out of the sand with the wrong side of the club.

He tried again and again and sand flew in all directions but the ball wouldn't budge and Dog and Cat were watching.

He knew Dog and Cat were watching.

Dog and Cat were the first witnesses of Zombie Beach Golf.

So he smiled inside.

He nearly laughed as a transitory escape from his grief.

Rose said that we would retrieve; that we would rescue Molly when the Day comes, when December 21, 2012, comes.

Rose said to the old man that he would have to wear clothes for the rescue of Molly because they just might turn him away.

The old man warmed.

He recalled life and its struggles.

The sea gull with the broken wing screams.

The sea gull makes circles in the sand as it crawls nowhere with its broken rudder.

The screams became desperation lost.

The screams become muffled as it tires and as it becomes weary of life and its struggles.

A beach towel is laid across it then wrapped around it with hands and with the beach towel comes renewed strength; enough strength to peck and jab without gratitude at the hands; at the hands which have no ill intentions.

The sea gull finds itself in a splint.

The sea gull finds itself returned to the exact location of its putative demise.

The sea gull lifts its wings and struts down the beach to a dead sand crab.

The sea gull grabs it and flies away.

It flies away to become an anonymous storyteller amongst his fellow sea gulls.

Not true.

Rose says that no other sea gull will know its story because the sea gulls in its flock are preoccupied with life's struggles.

Rose says that we help those who want help.

Rose says that we, the Peacebuilders, help those who want to help themselves.

Rose says that the few on Mount St Helens who wanted to stay; who chose to die in their homes or on their front porch should not be questioned; that a search and rescue; that a savior intervention was too much help.

"I brought you a robe and some coffee. Virgil will bring your waffles, butter, maple syrup and eggs. I saw a video of Molly. She wants to live. She gives you hope on the day when the world may cease to exist."

The old man sat at the foot of his bed.

Someone had rolled up his underwear.

Someone had lifted his legs and had placed his underwear over one ankle and then the other.

Someone had instructed him to raise his knees.

Someone had pushed and pulled his underwear over his knees.

Someone had instructed him to raise his butt.

Someone had pushed and pulled his underwear around his waist.

Someone ran a thumb around the waistband for the proper fit.

He could hear the screams and laugher of children playing on the beach.

156

The little girl played in the sand with her red shovel and her green pail and her idea for a simple sand castle.

She felt the burst of her brother's water balloon on her back.

She screamed.

The little girl ran after her brother.

She stopped and stared as the little wave tumbled toward her feet.

She stopped and stared at the heart as the little wave rolled the heart into her cupped hands.

She lowered the heart to the beach.

She put sand on it as a matter of some unexplained ritual.

She ran with the sandy heart to her Mom and Dad.

She gave the sandy heart to her Mom and Mom quickly passed the icky heart to Dad.

The heart pumped once in Dad's hand.

It sucked in a little wet sand.

The heart pumped a second time and blew out air because the wet sand had stuck to the inside of its chamber.

On its way from Japan, the bobbing and drifting heart would suck in seawater and then spurt pathetic little whale spouts.

Dad dropped the heart on the sand with the second pump.

Rose was there.

Rose picked up the heart and said, "I know the recipient. He is waiting in the Dentist's chair."

Rose and Virgil gave him sunglasses for the overhead light.

Rose opened his robe and saw his underwear and so she was relieved for a few seconds.

Virgil said this wouldn't take long.

Virgil said it was a simple procedure.

Virgil said that he would give him something for the pain.

Rose threaded the needle with one eye looking.

She threaded the needle on the first try.

Rose threaded the needle so Virgil could sew his right arm.

"Got to seal the leaks before we start the pump."

Rose and Virgil talked of Baseball and wedding plans.

They would wed today, on December 20, 2012.

He would sit in his chair and listen to the words spoken; the words spoken and the Bach played for the true and soulful love; for the hope that is Rose and Virgil.

He would sit in his chair on the beach with Dog and Cat and witness this marriage.

But that vision was a month old so, at noon today, he would witness the wedding of Rose and Virgil in his chair; in a chair sunk a little deeper into the sand; sunk a little deeper from a heavy heart restored.

But it was Rose's and Virgil's day – wasn't it?

And thankfully, he wouldn't be the only one.

Peter would drive down from Pacifica.

Alice would beam down from Rosanna Spearman's spaceship.

Rose would request two more Captain's Chairs and more coffee.

The old man stood in his underwear.

He stood in front of a mirror.

Someone had told him to look into a mirror.

He looked into the mirror in his Funny Farm room.

The white orderlies, dressed in white, drove the van.

They drove the unmarked and white van.

The only color on the white van was a red light flashing.

They drove to the crash site.

The Grays were dizzy from the concussions.

They wandered aimlessly about the beach.

It was easy for the white orderlies to load them into the back of the van.

He was guided into the van.

He huddled shoulder to shoulder with the Grays in the van; his shoulder touching a Gray shoulder, his waist touching a Gray waist.

They couldn't cuff the Grays because their wrists were too thin so they used duct tape.

They cuffed him.

The Grays disappeared.

He slid on his butt to the front.

He knocked.

The van pulled over and stopped.

The white orderlies opened the door.

He asked for more clothes.

He asked for sweat pants and his *Giants World Champions* T-Shirt.

Rose was there.

Rose went to the house for his pants and the T-shirt.

Rose told him to raise his arms like he was under arrest.

Rose rolled his T-shirt, stretched it and then placed it over his arms.

Rose tossed him his pants.

"You do the rest. I will ask you to wear a shirt and a tie. I will ask you to give me away."

The old man heard the creak of a chair.

They were in his kitchen.

The three Galactic Elders had opened his hallway closet.

They had found three chairs.

They sat around his kitchen table.

The *Book of Humanity* was still open.

The *Book of Humanity* was open to the last page.

They had brought their drinking glasses.

They had each brought a small drinking glass with a round bottom and a wide mouth.

He would provide the "right kind of Oreo cookies."

He would provide the milk.

He opened his pantry and reached for the package of Double Stuff Oreo Cookies.

He opened his refrigerator.

He said that he had milked a cow named Bessie.

He said the milk was as fresh as it could get.

He lied to the Elders but he was wearing clothes.

No one believes a naked man.

Watch this procedure carefully.

He poured the milk to the "line"; to the "line" which made full immersion possible; possible based on the eyed circumference of an Oreo cookie.

He had stacked six Oreos on four small plates.

You slide your Oreo cookie off the stack.

You use two fingers to gently pinch your Oreo cookie.

You lift your Oreo cookie over the glass.

You slowly lower your Oreo cookie into the milk for full immersion.

Yes, you will get cold milk on your fingers.

You watch for the bubbles.

You wait for the bubbles to stop and then you quickly lift your Oreo cookie out of the milk.

If you wait too long, your Oreo cookie gets too soggy.

It might break apart.

If you panic and let go, your Oreo cookie will either float to the top or sink to the bottom.

No one knows for sure.

You allow the excess milk to drip from your Oreo cookie.

You are now ready for consumption.

The Galactic Elders, with fingers made for spiders, picked and dipped Oreo cookies for fifteen minutes or so and then they returned to thoughts for the last page - for the last page in the *Book of Humanity*.

Rose tells him that Einstein said that World War IV will be fought with sticks and stones.

Rose asks him to preside.

Rose asks him to write a speech.

Rose tells him that someone else would be in attendance.

PETER

He had left the button bandages on.

It was cold so he had put on his sweater.

He had pulled his sweater over the three dot bandages.

Two were for the shots and the other was for the drawn blood.

They talked about Santa Claus while they drew his blood.

And that was 'o.k.' with him.

They said his arm would ache for a day or so.

They said his left arm; his bad arm; would be useless for a while.

Alice told him to try childbirth.

He would remember that day very clearly; that day when his son was born blue. The day they took his son away for the time it takes to wrap a Christmas gift.

Press here so I can finish the bow.

And wala! You have a healthy baby boy.

Don't worry.

The collarbone will heal.

The missing patch of hair torn from your beard by your innocent wife will grow back in no time.

The stars and planets were hidden this early morning.

He wouldn't be able to aim his telescope at Saturn's Rings.

His telescope was not powerful enough.

He could not focus on Dog, the Dog who rides horseback on the Rings of Saturn.

He stands in front of his bathroom mirror.

He snatches the bandages and quickly tears them off.

He tosses them into the trash.

He throws away the dot bandages with the little spots of dried blood.

Plans change.

Alice would not beam down.

She would pick him up at 6:00 a.m. for the drive to Santa Cruz.

There would be an extra stop.

He sits on a beach towel.

He sits with his chin on his knees.

She walks on the beach in front of him.

He can see her from Space.

He can see her walking on a tiny beach from Space.

He suggests to the Elders that love is the art of detail.

He suggests to the Elders that love is the attention paid to details.

Alice is here.

He opens the car door.

He sits on a cold seat and listens to her breathe.

She says the heater is broken.

She says the drive to Santa Cruz will be cold.

He has stopped his thoughts about the Big Picture.

He says he is 'good' but he misses Dog.

They both look to the back seat.

Dog slept there on the way back from New Mexico.

The Reptilian Baseball Teams are gone.

Dog is gone.

She felt her pang again.

She aimed the VW at Highway 1.

Living room furniture looks better.

He says the older he gets, the better his recliner looks.

Both arms were locked and loaded.

He reclined.

He saw it falling from the sky.

The fireball broke into pieces; the fireball with the bodies and the sadness.

One of the burning pieces was heading right towards him.

Forty thousand fans at AT&T and the foul ball was coming right at him or maybe at the woman with the baby next to him.

It was a line drive.

It was coming fast.

He could actually hear its hiss.

He turned his mitt for a backhand catch.

He turned to protect the baby.

The baseball struck his wrist.

The hot chunk of Columbia crashed down on the roof of the VW Bus.

He covered her up with his arms.

Maybe his fragile bones could save her.

The baseball rolled under the seat.

The baby cries.

The smoking VW rolls toward the cliff at Dead Man's Curve.

She says she needs to make a stop.

She says she has a craving for donuts.

She says she wants to stop in Half Moon Bay for coffee and a chocolate French cruller.

He was sugar high.

He was caffeine blasted.

The three Galactic Elders sat in the back.

The wide-eyed Elders wiped their chins with their spidery fingers.

They tossed the napkins over their shoulders.

The box of thin cardboard with the broad rings of soaked fat caught the donut dirty napkins.

He turned his head quickly; like an owl, only faster.

His bloodshot eyes were open; open wider than ever before.

His vision was blurry.

The Highway Patrol had done their job.

The Highway Patrol had pulled them over by Pescadero.

They had decided to drive the speed limit.

It was a consensus.

She would use discipline.

She would not yield to the donut and coffee buzz.

The Galactic Elders pulled out their notepads, for their research on the last page of the *Book of Humanity*.

The Highway Patrol rolled its ticket pad to a blank form.

The Highway Patrol wrote a traffic ticket for driving the speed limit.

No one drives the speed limit.

You will explain your actions to a Judge on this date.

And they said 'o.k.'

We have had our coffee and our crullers.

We must be on our way to Davenport.

See you in Court.

Mr. Lizard is a hang glider.

He hangs over Davenport and then he descends.

He lands by the Gift Shop.

He unfolds his *Lemonade Stand*.

Free Lemonade and Psychic Readings.

He sets up before Peter arrives with his traffic ticket.

No, Peter is not naked and wrapped in Saran with holes cut open around his mouth and nose.

No, he is not in the fetal position poised for a rebirth, for a reawakening.

He is on the Funny Farm.

He slides down the Funny Farm wall in despair.

His back is against the wall.

His head is between his knees and his catharsis begins.

Perhaps it was for his benefit. He gave up the charade and he threw away the drugs.

He wanted to go home early but they made him stay longer.

They drove him across the Bay Bridge and he wanted to jump.

He wanted to jump into the alligator pond at the California Academy of Sciences but a child walked by.

The child leaned over the railing and he worried about the child.

Perhaps the child has better balance.

Perhaps he wasn't thinking about me; me and forever me.

It was temporary.

The child ran off.

No need to talk to Alice about suicide.

He is older now and she can sing.

She can play her guitar and sing all day if she wants.

He drinks his free Lemonade without a straw.

'Thank you very much,' says Elvis.

Mr. Lizard kicks the file box under his stand.

Mr. Lizard loosens the files.

Mr. Lizard finds the red, white and blue envelope with the pretty stripes.

It has his name on it.

To: Peter

Subject: Proposal

Date: December 20, 2012

Oh Peter, Peter, Peter. What are you waiting for? Put down that glass of free Lemonade. The Gift Shop is right in front of you. The little bell will ring when the door opens. The little bell will ring twice. Ring, ring. Two gold bands wait for purchase on the jewelry stand. Charge them. By tomorrow, all the computers in the Land will be toast. There won't even be a record of your purchase. The only mail will be future mail sent to Mr. Lizard. What else can I say?

Love, the United States Postal Service.

P.S. You can also purchase stamps in the Gift Shop.

She played her guitar.

She sang about crying and Argentina.

He wasn't quite sure.

He was too 'far away.'

Was Alice crying for Argentina?

Was Argentina crying for Alice?

He couldn't tell.

They drove south.

They drove past *REPENT!*

They drove past *JESUS IS COMING!*

They drove past *MAYAN CALENDER BRUNCH AT ALDOS. SOME ITEMS ARE HALF OFF. CHOCOLATE CHIP COOKIES ARE FREE BUT LIMITED TWO TO A CUSTOMER!*

She lies with her chin on the floor of her kennel.

She lies with her chin down, a sad Sphinx of a Dog.

She cannot see.

She can hear.

She is a top contestant for *Who's That Smell?*

'Doberman Pincher,' she thinks while on her daily beach walk.

'Black Labrador retriever,' she thinks as if she might think in English. 'Young.' 'Maybe a year old.' 'Catcher of Frisbees.'

This is her last day on Earth.

They will take the young ones.

I'm not cute anymore.

She hears voices.

'Who's That Smell?'

'Human.'

'Don't know that smell.'

She hears voices.

'What's a flower girl?'

The Captain had lost control.

The Captain held hands with his crew.

They bungee-jumped the ship without a bungee cord.

The wake of the oily ship was aimed at the jetty, at Aldo's dock.

Peter and Alice sat at a table under a gas lamp, under warmth.

Molly was under the table.

Peanut butter biscuits had been smuggled.

They ate their free chocolate chip cookies.

He slid the little box across the table.

He did not get down on bended knee.

He was old.

He might not be able to get up.

Sometimes, he even shuffled a bit when he was tired.

The oil tanker was close.

It crashed into the jetty.

It tilted on its side and rolled toward Aldo's dock.
Aldo's boat was crushed.
The wave spilled onto to the deck.
The oily sheen ran toward Molly and their feet.
'He reached for life jackets.'
'He reached for Alice and Molly.'
"Oh Peter, Peter, Peter. What have you been waiting for?"
She had read his mind.
Maybe she had even read his mail from the future.
But he was 'o.k.' with that.

WEDDING

Will you still love me, will you still need me, when I'm sixty-four.
- Paul McCartney

I'm sitting in my Captain's Chair on a windy beach.
I'm sitting with the waves pounding.
I'm sitting under a black sky at sunset.
Dog is lying on my feet so I am not going anywhere.
Still, I have a new Dog for a foot warmer and I hope folks are right.
I hope folks are right about the journey of soul, about how animal spirits leave the body for a new host.
Maybe Dog is still alive somewhere.
Maybe she has found a sad child.
Maybe she is resting her head in the lap of a small child.
I suggest to the Elders that the journey of soul might be veracity.
I suggest to the Elders that the soul might be the continuation of life or at least the perception thereof.
I talk to Molly.
I tell Molly that we will see the Vet tomorrow.
I tell Molly that we will see the Vet about those six months.

I had me one of those bipolar days.
I got up cold and mournful.
By Noon, I was dressed in slacks, a shirt and a tie.
By Noon, I was walking arm and arm with Rose in her dress and

Alice in her Buster Posey jersey.

By Noon, I was giving Rose and Alice away.

I got to preside over the marriages of my best friends.

I met a flower girl with the flowers taped to her collar because she kept shaking them off.

I had to ask Alice if she wanted to marry Peter or Buster Posey.

They played baseball on the beach all afternoon.

They played baseball on the beach on their honeymoon.

Sure, it could happen.

It could happen tomorrow for real.

The sun could erupt on schedule.

The Galactic Elders would certainly know.

The Galactic Elders have most certainly seen it happen on other Worlds.

The solar storm collapses the Earth's magnetic field.

The lights go out.

The lights go out all over Earth.

The lights go out like the Wave at a baseball game.

And the Humans would kill each other with the guns and ammo left behind.

And when they run out of ammo, the Humans would gather sticks and stones just like what that fellow Einstein predicted.

But heck, we are sitting in our Captain's Chairs on the beach.

We have lit a beach fire.

We're showing the three Galactic Elders about roasting marsh mellows; about how to roast them brown; about how to hold them high enough above the fire so that they don't get burnt black.

We tell the Elders about Hershey Bars and Graham Crackers.

We tell the Elders about "Some Mores."

The Galactic Elders leave Earth for the *Book of Humanity*.

The Galactic Elders leave Earth for the last page.

Episode Twelve

· · · · · · · · · · · · · · · ·

GIANTS

· · · · · · · · · · · · · · · ·

MESSAGE

The old man woke to an empty sky.

He surveyed the carnage in his living room.

He slowly rose from his Chair and, prodded onward by the cold and wet nose of a Labrador retriever, he shuffled through the debris to his telescope platform.

He suspected, based on Basil's wild gesticulations, that he ought to check on the plateau and so he said "O.k., o.k." to the excited Basil.

He sat in his planetarium bucket seat and started to operate the levers - pushing and pulling on the levers until he rose high enough to see the big Child's etching of Mommy and Daddy's huge spaceship - an etching so detailed as to reveal the *Earth or Bust* plot.

He had finally connected all dots and felt suddenly both alarmed and obligated - seriously obligated to immediately report to Earth that a spaceship the size of Earth's Moon was heading its way.

I mean - it makes sense.

He is totally an active member (former President actually) of the Society for the Prevention of the Exposure of Alien Existence.

It is his sworn duty to report any relevant observations.

But he was hungry.

Starving in fact.

Basil was hungry too.

So he would eat second (after feeding Basil first, of course).

He gathered his pots and pans for a dinner of crab raviolis in Alfredo Sauce; brilliant green spears of microwaved asparagus dipped in mayonnaise and an ice cold Coca Cola in a frosty bottle.

But he did manage to send a little message through The Cube to all SPEAE members: *Jupiter's Sixty-eighth Moon is back.*

He sent this message before his dessert of apple pie *ale mode* with a scoop of French Vanilla ice cream.

CROWS

The all-black bird (crow-sized) used his grabby crow-like talons to attach himself; to hold himself tightly and precariously onto the hooked tip of a tall, tapering Italian Juniper the scene of which, by all accounts, resembled the picture and context of a true crow's-like nest. The all-black bird was blown around like a paper bag; its crow-like wings flapping at random or when he felt the need to compensate for variations in the speed and direction of the wind. He would puff out and his crow-like neck feathers would rise and he would 'caw' much as would an actual crow 'caw' and 'screech' in defense of his territory.

It was dusk and there were two other all-black birds swinging around and puffing out as the wind blew through two other Italian Junipers. But no, these three crow-like birds were not defending their territory but rather, in a kind of scary and prophetic moment, did these three communicate and then they took wing to join ten of their buds who were flying overhead and so the gang of thirteen flew off but soon, they would land and they would begin to strut in someone's backyard and they would literally threatened the neighbor's cats, dogs and children and I mean - it was a 'group threat'; like a 'group threat' in such a way that Mom or Dad would feel compelled to gather the pride of their genetic make-up and haul them into the house.

The 'Gang of Thirteen,' the 'Alfred Hitchcock Gang of Thirteen' however, did not haunt the sleepy and coastal town of Bodega Bay, CA, at this time. No, they haunted San Ramon, CA, (my hometown) in the winter of 2012 just hours before the tic-tock turning of the Mayan Calendar and I just think that it would be really creepy if the gathering of these thirteen all-black birds in San Ramon and the prophecy of the Mayan Calendar were somehow related.

Just a thought and yes, the all-black birds were actually crows as you hopefully have surmised but no, they weren't talking crow on Draconis Prime. They weren't talking crow when the twelve Ciakar were released from the stasis field established by the peacebuilding and Blue Alien Rose; a stasis field, which had been overseen by Dorian Gray who was tickled pink but who could not actually be tickled pink because he was a Gray.

Still, Dorian Gray's amusement was ended abruptly because something had gone seriously wrong with the stasis field and the Ciakar crew of twelve was released prematurely and it was at the very same moment that the 'Gang of Thirteen' had taken crow flight over San Ramon (wow - pretty creepy uh? - like Stephen King creepy).

EXTRICATION

It happened on Draconis Prime.

Yes, one by one, did the small-armed, punching bag Ciakar; one by one (until it added up to twelve) did the cigar-smoking Ciakar fall into the frickin' muddy marsh of the mighty muddy planet of Draconis Prime.

No one knows what went wrong with Rose's stasis field. No one knows the precise detail although it might have been the palindrome Bob. It might have been Bob the Rock Star who had accidently tuned in the exact U2 frequency. Yes, this is the same Bob who lives in an impenetrable hut on Draconis Prime, who had witnessed the Brad the Brahma Bull accident at Fatima and who loves extremely loud Rock 'n Roll and I mean like the loudest ever due to his construction of high rise amplifiers the latter of which provides the surround sound for to keep the Ciakar away. But alas, it was on this fateful day that Bob's rock and roll had literally amped out the stasis field and (as I had said before) the Ciakar then plunged hence into the slick, glossy and marshy mud.

And oh, it was indeed lucky for the Ciakar that Draconis Prime mud is slick and glossy. Had it been thick and sticky, the Ciakar would have actually fallen from one stasis field into another and eventually, they would have become fossils for the space-faring, time-traveling UC Davis T-Shirt student to discover but no, the Ciakar found that they could move their limbs somewhat.

Be as it may, the twelve Ciakar (with violent brains the size of a walnut) proceeded with various experimentations with regard to the proper mud extricating postures. Pushing down into the mud with their small arms (inherited from T. Rex) only left the Ciakar with muddy and sunken small arms and with faces that were perilously close to mud immersion. Rising on their haunches left a face of mud. However, after a few hours of face painting, one Ciakar realized (finally - geez) that pushing from the Pterodactyl pose, that pushing on the pointy shoulder prop of his wing provided the needed lift and so one Ciakar at least rose slowly above the rest.

The muddy-dripping and shaky-legged Ciakar made their way to their bicycle rack - the bicycles lined up in a neat row in front of their cigar-shaped, spiky-hair ship. They rode their bikes with determination and serious faces like Auntie Em in the black and white of *The Wizard of Oz* but without Toto in the back seat basket. They rode to the Palace. They rode to their Queen with a plot in mind, a plot which had been so slowly and insidiously planned and communicated during their long stay in the mud (a plot which neither Dorian or the rest of the non-smoking Grays would discover until it was too late!).

The Ciakar began to warm. They warmed as they rode. They warmed and then they snarled and smiled shortly before they settled down in front of the Palace doors; shortly before their furious knocking, shouting and bell-rocking announcement of their arrival, of their obnoxious and overbearing demand for the Queen to stop whatever it was that she was doing and to open the darn door right now so that they could come in and maybe take some warm showers and wash off the cold mud. You know - kind of clean up and kick back a little before they reveal their plot which involved "sticking it to Humanity."

PLOT

"Pass some intestine," said one Ciakar to another as they have gathered for live breakfast.

The twelve disciples and the 'starving to death' Stealth Dog Basil had gathered before the entry of the Queen for morning breakfast; the light-sleeping Queen who wakes before and then eats after the twelve and impulsive Ciakar disciples who could attack her at any moment but who are not likely to attack at this time because nothing calms a Ciakar like a warm shower, a breakfast of live food and a chair-comfy cigar and, of course, today would be especially calming because of the sudden, surprising (and calming) influence of like one of the cutest dogs that the Ciakar have ever seen.

The Queen entered. She picked up Basil's food bowl. She took Basil's bowl to the front; to her high chair and then she opened the bag of dog food and poured it out but then she also included some chicken breast, green beans and a peanut butter biscuit for dessert and then she got up and took the offering to the tail wagging Basil.

The huge gavel came crashing down (the Queen loved this part of her day) and then she said, "Let's do our business. Any ideas?"

"Hah, hah, hah."

"How about a rogue asteroid?"

"Hah, hah, hah."

"How about a gamma ray burst or we could cook them with microwaves?"

Buzzer!

"Disqualified. Please, one idea per person."

"Hah, hah, hah" (forgot his idea).

"Hah, hah, hah" (somebody rang first).

"How about nukes?"

Buzzer!

"Disqualified."

"Forgot 'hah, hah, hah' even though you rang first."

"Hah, hah, hah."

"How about a…"

Buzzer!

"Time for second breakfast!"

"Blind rats! Said the Queen."

"Where did the dog go?"

A clear yellow puddle was left in the space vacated by Basil; in the place occupied by Basil's empty food bowl and oh she felt so terribly guilty even though it wasn't her fault because the Ciakar Queen just didn't know that "doing her business" meant quickly finding a spot for a 'number one' or 'two' and so did Basil just feel so bad about doing her business on the Palace floor.

BOOTS

Narrator (Old Man):

Woke up at dawn; a December dawn on the Pacific coast; the beach with its high tide pushin' and pullin'; three or four foot waves poundin' the shore and a surfer floatin' out there on his cold board amongst the kelp waiting for the six foot wave; might be the "seventh wave" or so I've heard.

It was a clear mornin' with pelicans fishin' the schools; wings tucked; crashin' jumbo jets; hooked, tipped and long beaks capturin' a fish almost every time and you wonder how they see their little fish targets from so high above; fishin' pelicans with eagle eyes.

But my eyes this mornin' were blurry like half the beach had settled in and so I rubbed out the sand and that worked fine but when I went on to try the hallway light, the socket just sparkled pretty; the electricity flickered with a little smoke and smell and the light buzzed over my head like it was killin' bugs and so I thought for a moment that I might be at the movies; capricious, incorporeal beings playin' ghosts; ghouls playin' around with the World Grid which would be my guess and sure, I node why it was happening right here and now.

It happened late at night. December 20, 2012, became December 21, 2012, just like skeptical folks predicted but It came in the night and It scared Molly into jumping up and crawling into bed with the old man.

Alice was stirring around the kitchen when it happened, Alice in her Buster Posey jersey making coffee. Peter was asleep on 'Mt. Olympus' - ninety thousand feet above the Martian landscape. Rose was twirling her wedding ring around. She held it up to the light for to see every nook and cranny and Virgil had gone for a night walk alone on the beach and that's when it happened.

He looked back, searching for the comfort of the lights along the Wharf and the Boardwalk but all those lights had suddenly vanished and from above, the Aurora Borealis had descended like a curtain call. Six coronal mass ejections instead of the 1859 two were aligned with Earth

174

and Earth was being tested before dawn in Santa Cruz, CA, and all over the World for that matter but oh no; this solar storm wasn't the Ciakar's or the Giant Family's doing at all. They had just caught an extra bonus: the Great Solar Storm of 2012.

Narrator (Old Man):
We had assembled on the deck; every one of us nervy and stirrin' coffee even if we had nothin' in the coffee to stir and the trepidation was palpable; something to behold because of the talk on the Basil's Stealth Dog video.
"Hah, hah, hah."
"How about a rogue asteroid?"
"Hah, hah, hah."
"How about a gamma ray burst or we could cook 'em with microwaves?"
Buzzer!
"Disqualified. Please, one idea per person."
"Hah, hah, hah" (forgot his idea).
"Hah, hah, hah" (somebody rang first).
"How about nukes?"
Buzzer!
"Disqualified."
"Forgot 'hah, hah, hah' even though you rang first."
Hah, hah, hah
"How about a…"
Buzzer!
"Time for second breakfast!"
"Blind rats! Said the Queen."
"Where did the dog go?"

And so it followed, and in an event unrelated to the Great Solar Storm of 2012, that a rainbow rim would be following the rising sun; a rim that looks first like a black and bold line along the curvature of the horizon. And sure, it was seen as a shimmering rainbow like a child's bubble blown with delight as it came overhead.
It was an advancing rainbow because Mommy's and Daddy's huge ship had stopped at a far out Hippie's place for lunch on Alpha Centauri; for a lunch of live, wavin' and squirmin' plants and also there had been

some rainbow-color input from the high Hippies on what the Sphere should look like when the Establishment was lookin' up and so we were left to figurin' like in the Steinbeck book about the angry grapes except we had Transdimensional Cell Phones instead of sticks and dirt but we were still left to figurin' anyway and so Molly thinks for all of us but we didn't node what she was thinkin' 'cause she's a dog but she sure was intrepretin' anyway.

'It's a Dyson Sphere,' thinks Molly.
"It's a Dyson Sphere!" said Virgil in his calm Spock voice.
"A what?"
"A Dyson Sphere."
"Who's Dyson?"
"Better ask what the Sphere would be doing to our Space."
"Do you know, Virgil?"
"Yup."
"Well, what should we be doing, Virgil?"
"We might want to ask Rosanna Spearman to beam us down some of those fashionable gravity boots. You know - they come in all colors and sizes so I'm sure she'll find some to fit us all."

FAMILY

The Giant Egyptian and 'Other Side' Family (actually, they have never been to Egypt) sat around their big table for a Giant Family daily dinner. Osiris and Isis focused their big eyes on Horus, the big Child who had etched the huge ship on the plateau of the old man's planet near the Edge of the Observable Universe.

Now we all know that Humans choose to wage war and yet they also choose to help their middle school students with their science fair projects if need be.

Well, the same is true with the huge Family who, after lunch with the high Alpha Centauri Hippies, had suggested to Horus that his Earthly Dyson Sphere might stand for color and hence, Horus' scale model was so rainbow rendered.

Glowing yellow was the Giant Family, glowing and fading in and

176

out of unknown dimensions.

Osiris lowered his huge San Francisco Giant's root beer and foamy mug and it was followed by many foamy mugs until, at last, all of the many foamy mugs rested - merged as a single mug - on the huge dinner table (how do They do that?).

The same could be said for words spoken – whole sentences were lost in the echoes of the ship's humongous Chamber but they seemed to merge as a single voice, which emanated from a single speaker.

Osiris rose to his full height and began his speech (found only as a commercial interruption of the Food Channel), which, of course, sent words careening off the walls of the humungous Chamber, the mess of words of which can only be interpreted by Isis and so she began to translate Osiris' speech (how the translated closed-captions appeared on the Food Channel is a mystery unsolved to this day).

"I am Osiris. My wife is Isis. And our son is named Horus."

"We are a Giant Family from the Other Side and we mean no harm. We have come to Earth for two purposes. One, Horus is about to activate the Dyson Sphere and, if you don't mind, we would like Google-driving instructions from here (where?) to the Giza Plateau in Egypt. Lastly, we sincerely apologize for the scotch tape damage to your Moon and for the extraction of your Moon from its orbit and for the sticking of it to the wall of the Dyson Sphere."

"So, which way to Egypt? We wish to visit our own Great Pyramid of Giza."

But now it is time and so Horus stepped up to the big red button and so Molly (having heard of Basil's previous actions with to regard to red buttons and the Big Bang) cringed and prepared herself for Interdimensional travel but no, Horus' pushing of the big red button did not cause a second Big Bang but the effect was impressive to say the least.

There was a pause.

Everything and everyone stood still as did the Earth below like in the movie.

And then there was this contraction of everything and everyone accompanied by a low hum in C major which was sung by the ghost of Elvis and then the Light burst forth as the Gravity Generator started up with such vibration that the Moon was released from the inner shell of the Dyson Sphere and actually, the Moon was helped along. It was torn off by some unknown suction much the way a child sucks in pasta noodles. Still, the Moon was given the proper push toward its old orbit.

And so down on Earth did the wide-eyed and enraptured Humans begin to slowly descend and pile up on the ground but no, they could not keep their eyes off the glowing huge ship and the Dyson Sphere which now encased their wars. They found it hard to believe that they were touching the ground again; that Humanity had two feet solidly on the ground.

They looked up and saw the rainbow veil and then the Dyson Sphere began to fade. And yes, probes and ships sent subsequently barely traveled beyond Earth's Moon before they disappeared and astronauts were returned to their families.

HAVANA

Meanwhile (and in Havana and within the sight of an illegally parked, spiky-haired, cigar-shaped spaceship) did a Ciakar say (with his eyes all squinty from rising cigar smoke); did a Ciakar casually say to a smug Castro (who was sitting across the way with his arms folded and with that 'dictator' look on his face); did a Ciakar say, "Hah, hah, hah. The Giant Family. Hah, hah, hah."

Episode Thirteen

. . . .

SOLO

. . . .

66,043,000 B.C. (OR THEREABOUTS)

CONVENTION

Peter Carpenter was there.

Ancient - millions of years ago - Peter was privy to the then and there.

It wasn't clear at all.

Ancient muddies - it does not equate that antiquity necessarily means primitive.

Deep Throat turns to Mulder and he says, "They have been here for a long, long, time."

Revelation - we are "prisoners of mystery" - or says Bob Dylan.

Erudite and so why Earth?

This after all is the Einstein question - why did the Galactic Federation choose prehistoric Earth for the Declaration?

Oh sure, there was the Dome - the Dome constructed to keep the Dinosaurs out - the frustrated Tyrannosaurus Rex roaring and clawing at the Dome - the pondering herd of Brachiosaurs that refused to go around - the Compsognathi skittering to the top - looking for a way in.

Peter had found the way in.

He had found the hatch in space/time right before it closed.

Serendipity - Peter had found the hatch on one of his solo journeys.

He has begged modern Humanity for the end of War and for the beginning of World Peace.

Contemporary - war - the absurdity, the atrocities, the redundancy sold by monger propaganda - prospectors - businessmen parcel Humanity into who shall die or who shall live.

Narcissism - the death knell of Human rights for everyone.

Peter had left Earth in disgust and never looked back and he brought Basil, Pulitzer books, Beethoven Masterworks, Elder Scrolls video games, Bob Dylan, the Beatles Anthology and a foreign policy never tested on modern Earth - the first policies to World Peace.

Peter wasn't invited.

He hovered inside the Dome waiting for an invitation to a Conference that had been convened millions of years before Humans destroyed the Trees.

Anger - Indonesia burns carbon-rich peat and gasping monkeys fall from the smoke-filled Trees just for the palm oil to flavor and texture Peter's beloved candy and he didn't know then but he does know now; not in Space - no palm oil will he take into Space on his solo journeys.

Peter will take his stand whilst on the Convention floor.

They move about and then they all come to an abrupt stop as though a single thought had crossed their minds.

Discovery - they look at Peter (for answers or lessons learned?) and he said out loud enough for all to hear, "End war rhetoric."

They had invited Basil and Peter down to the Convention floor, had given him a number, a bag of chocolate chip cookies, some peanut butter biscuits and then they told him to wait in line for disinfection.

Remember - Peter's college days as a Baby Boomer - waiting in line for classes with Bob Dylan erasing his numb conscience and replacing it with, "there must be way out of here said the joker to the thief."

The wait was brief.

The multi-tasking Octopoid from the planet Octopus, the lovely Octopoid with the big eyelashes and with the eight waving and wet tentacles could really speed things up; eye scan, fingerprints, swab cheek for DNA, body scan for pathogens and toxins, a cold tentacle wrapped around Peter's leg then into his rectum for fecal analysis, a badge, a slap on the buttocks and finally a big smile and a sucker-lips kiss on the cheek - all done within one motion - all done within seconds.

She handed Peter a cherry Tootsie Roll and said, "Welcome to the Conference, Human and Dog. Please step forward into Light."

"I see the Light," responded Peter.

Love - he turned and looked back and blew the Octopoid a kiss in return - a kiss for her good nature, charm and speedy bureaucracy (the cold and wet tentacle up the butt was, as anyone can imagine, the worst part).

Love her still - 'No paperwork,' Peter surmised with relief and so he stood upon the disinfection conveyer as instructed but sad - the lovely Octopoid had turned around quickly to process another and had missed his blown kiss.

Celebration - the disinfection conveyer moved him along with lights and more body scans and then the unexpected - Extraterrestrials celebrate - goggles were slapped on and a bucket of champagne was poured over Peter's head - rinsed off and then he was blown dry like a car at the end of a wash.

Peter Carpenter then stepped off the conveyer and into a Cretaceous garden.

Pastoral - Beethoven's Sixth - some of the Extraterrestrials strolled under the tall conifers; some congregated by the lush ferns; some stood by the pier - the Dome stretched out to an inland sea, to accommodate the Dolphinoids - their golden ship glowing under the dock.

Basil ran up and down the pier barking and chasing after the Dolphinoids. Occasionally, she would stop and a Dolphinoid would rise up to the pier's edge. The thrilled Basil would smile and bark and the Dolphin would sing.

Who knows what was sung but she ran to me.

Happy - the Dolphinoid had brought Basil a measure of happiness.

Communication - Peter walked amongst the Extraterrestrials in a Convention about Peacebuilding.

Contradiction - the Convention floor was noisy and silent - a complication for the Fermi-Hart Paradox, for *silentium universi*.

There were Humans talking; Grays composing "thought balls,"[2] Blues singing improvised operettas and Reptilians playing baseball.

Unconditional love - Dogs and Dolphins would have to be here and then the Convention stopped again - all eyes and ears on Peter and he said, "Precedent and practice. Talk the talk and walk the walk. An Einstein thought experiment - end war rhetoric and replace it with peace-building chosen words. The solution to climate change is not a fight. It is an adaptation. The solution to cancer is not a war. It is the cure."

Fate - Peter saw her again later in another capacity.

He saw her behind the counter - the Octopoid whose pearl necklace flopped this way and that while she served root beer floats and *Alien Burgers* - eight orders at a time and she got them all right.

Four floats and four burgers were waved about as she filled the orders for Peter and the three Reptilian Elders - each served with a wide and infectious smile.

Love - Peter sent another blown kiss and this time, the lovely Octopoid saw it coming and so she wrapped a cold and wet tendril around Peter's neck and drew him to her for a closer look.

Nonsense - the three Reptilian Elders picked up their floats and burgers and walked toward the edge of the Dome.

The Dinosaurs had calmed down - the napping T. Rex, the grazing Brachiosauri milled about and the Compys had settled, as an incredibly cute pile, into their nest.

Genetics - the Dinosaurs and the Reptilian Elders share ninety-nine percent of DNA and yet the T. Rex hunts while the Reptilian Elders order over the counter.

Behavior - oh that one percent that seems to determine the ratio of instinct to choice and commitment but still this ratio becomes the moot point at a Convention of Peacebuilders.

Rights - and the convention stops again in unison and listens to the Reptilian Elders who have the made the time.

They stood by the Dome's window holding onto their floats and burgers and paused for reflection. They watched the Dinosaurs and thought of their rights and passed along their thoughts while the Convention stopped and listened. "Respect and support the rights of others," said

---

2   Prudence Calabrese, *Intentions: The Intergalactic Bathroom Enlightenment Guide* (Imprint Books, 2002)

the Reptilian Elder after sipping his root beer through a rather big straw.

The Octopoid with the luscious red lips pulled Peter to her and changed her colors as Octopi do.

She changed to red polka dots

Telepathy - she read Peter's thoughts as they bumped heads and she quite agreed that all should live in a World of choice and commitment to the rights of others and so she blushed red and the polka dots turned white.

Love - what can one say?

"My name is Alice," she said.

Peter and Alice walked hand-in-hand on a Cretaceous promenade.

Alice levitated and moved along at Peter's side as if she was a hovercraft churning up a water swirl on a mountain lake.

Peter walked with his right hand clasped in hers but I cannot say which particular tentacle (no numbering system as far as I know) was in play for Alice (use of one of the four on her left side would be my guess).

But what does it matter?

Yes, there was scattered applause as Peter escorted Alice along and the Blues actually stopped their operetta to applaud the strange but love-struck couple.

Cooperation - Peter escorted Alice to her next Octopoid assignment - setting the stage for the precedents and practice of cooperative prosperity, which the Blues would propose and the delegates engage. The Blues rolled out the large round table on wheels - the table with the foot-brakes used to stop it in its tracks in the middle of the Convention floor.

"Technology cannot hold back the rise in sea levels nor can it tow back the melted icebergs," so said a soprano Blue in a voice of crystal clarity; in a clear voice as she dined on the vegetable appetizers, the vegetable burgers and the vegetable cupcakes served with Alice's waving arms.

"Humanity can choose and commit; choose and commit to adapt to what cannot change."

Silence - the convention became quiet again as the soprano Blue clinked on her glass of vegetable juice and simply said for all to hear, "Cooperative prosperity - the profit sharing, the salary sharing, full employment and renewable energy - all for a lasting civilization."

Exhaustion - Peter fell asleep along the edge of a bed; the bed next to the large and bubbling salt water tank; the tank with the colorful fish and waving kelp; a resting place for the Dolphinoids and Octopoids. Alice propelled about the tank and she would check on Peter every time she passed.

Peter teetered on the edge.

He wasn't paying attention and so he rolled the wrong way.

He fell out of bed.

His head hit the floor and so he fell amongst a galaxy of stars.

He fell into the many discoveries of Earth's wondrous telescopes: the X-Ray flare from the Milky Way's Black Hole for one; an asteroid perhaps swirling down the Black Hole's drainpipe.

Alarmed - Alice crawled out of her tank and down its large window to Peter's bed below. She peered over the edge of his bed only to find him *Lost in Space*.

She could read his mind now without bumping heads - such was her newly found love.

Kiss - Peter woke to a kiss.

No, it wasn't the familiar dog kiss of Basil.

It was the kiss of his new friend; Alice the shape-shifting Octopoid, Alice now the woman of Peter's dreams.

But business is business and so Alice said pragmatically and with authority, "Get dressed Peter - we need to get out of here."

The steam rose off the backs of the mud-caked Ciakar.

The Ciakar emerged as quickly as they could.

They responded as quickly as they could to the red light blinking, to the obnoxious bell ringing that is the wholesome clack of their Emergency Broadcast System.

They did not bother to towel down nor would they run to their bicycle rack.

No, it is time for the Ciakar to fly.

They opened their wings and flew - twelve mud dripping Ciakar toke flight for their cigar-shaped, spiky-haired ship.

They did not bother with the traditional bicycle pump start-up.

They just rushed to their stations and within seconds, their ship rose above the might muddy planet of Draconis Prime.

The smiling buggers had recently learned to hitchhike on the six-minute-six-second technology of the Grays. The Ciakar had learned this technology very recently (in their very last mud bath, in fact) and so they arrived rapidly at the Dome sight of the Universal Peacebuilding Convention.

They had arrived to crash the party but, no, the Dome had just faded out before they arrived and so they stood oh so briefly on Earth.

They looked up at the sky only to see the fiery and molten rock - the spewing trail of a five-mile asteroid as it entered Earth's atmosphere - the proverbial overkill scene - the bazooka aimed at twelve fruit flies.

Communications - both spoken and visual - went dead on Draconis Prime and so the oviparous Queen sighed and started her work all over again - the eggshell formation and the pushing of twelve new eggs into their incubation chambers.

The Ciakar Wars would continue for millions of years and Humanity would join the war *esprit de corps* much to the chagrin of the Human Peter Carpenter and his former Octopoid but now Human wife, Alice.

Episode Fourteen

. . . .

MALFUNCTION³

. . . .

2015

The old man slept on the Moon.

    Sleeping in sadness was the old man - Molly, his old black Lab - the flower girl at Peter and Alice's wedding - had just passed away. The vet had given Molly six months but she lived two more years - slow years but two years nonetheless. Then, there was that inevitable night when Molly could not get up and the old man had to carry her inside from the rain.

    So the old man went to the Moon shortly thereafter - to sleep in the Moon's silence - to ponder Molly, the Moon's craters and the cavity left behind in his chest. The old man woke to the reminder that Molly would want him to move on - she was the happy dog and so, why not him?

    The old man collected himself from his morning dizziness. He stretched and flexed muscles (but not to the point of cramps) and then he rose and balanced himself (some days are better than others). He dressed in his traditional blue jeans and his *Giants World Champions* sweater. He grabbed his cane and walked carefully hence from his sleeping pod into The Pizza Parlay. He was here for the comfort of the early morning

---

³ Opening story for *Malfunction: The Misadventures of a Childish Living Ship*

breakfast crowd and the coffee cup noise. Molly would have him order from the top of menu for to bolster his spirits and so he scanned for his favorite Dungeness Crab Benedict.

He was served - not in six minutes and six seconds by the Grays via the Cube - but by a lovely Octopoid with ruby red lips and a large purple Kentucky Derby hat with a heavy purple rose on its side. Her smile, the coffee and the Crab Benedict was a definitive revival for the old man's circulation - the blood flow to his head - and perhaps it helped deal with what happened next.

There are secret passageways within the Dyson Sphere - the transparent Sphere that surrounds Earth. Meteorites strike it often and so from the Earth or the Moon, one can see flashes of light - flashes of light that were once seen as meteor showers on Earth. The borders of the Dyson Sphere - the encasement of the war planet Earth by the Giant Family - are clearly defined as sparkles but still, only the very few know the locations of the secret passageways and they aren't spilling the beans (or any other vegetable for that matter).

Peter and Alice Carpenter and their new dog Fulton had already bounded out of bed, had eaten breakfast, had taken a joyride around the Solar System and had found a secret passage through the Sphere but it was time to get serious now and so they materialized hence in a booth of four at The Pizza Parlay.

They were here to tell the old man of the adventures (or misadventures) of a Living Ship - of a childish Living Ship.

CALLING

Twelve is the number of red roses that he bought for her on Christmas Eve. He bought twelve red roses for her and, on Christmas Day, she divided the bouquet into four each. She put the red roses into three vases and placed them on the tables for the Christmas Day panoply: the rose decor was part of that Christmas Day expression of the chaos theory, which is called "family" on Earth.

Peter, the husband who had bought the flowers for his wife, and Alice, the wife who had set the tables for Christmas Day, had answered the call and no, it wasn't a blinking phone message or text gibberish or even the real Calling - you know, those intransigent and imperative thoughts; that drumbeat conclusion in one's mind that blasts, 'She is the one and only!'

No, it wasn't that kind of call at all.

It was an email sent from a Living Ship.

Now everyone who has experienced The Calling are rarely given caveats or prior warnings of either Beethoven's Ninth joy or Mahler's Fifth Adagio of deep sorrow. No, this seemingly innocuous Calling sent from the Living Ship was simply the affirmation that they had been "hired" and that Peter, Alice and their dog Fulton were to "report for work" on "January 2, 2015, at 10:00 a.m." or "whenever." Peter, Alice and their yellow Labrador retriever cheerfully accepted the job as "the cleaning crew of a sterile Ship." And yes, this incongruity; this eyebrow-raising contradiction was indeed picked out from the trillions of email messages by the ever vigilant NSA.

"Hey Bro, this does not make sense - a cleaning crew for a sterile Ship."

"Well, spending redundancies really piss off the Republicans."

"Got it, let's report this information to the President - Democrat eyes-only."

Eleven is the number of senses programmed into the Living Ship. The Mutants added pain, movement, balance, speech, complaining and revelation to the traditional five senses. The Mutants living under Santa Fe Baldy in New Mexico had essentially created a moody, paranoid and wuss of a Living Ship and, even though it was a moody, paranoid and wuss of a Living Ship, it was still our "moody, paranoid and wuss of a Living Ship" or so said the Mutant supervisor in charge of the Living Ship's senses and emotions.

The Living Ship, complaining previously of rope burns, had fallen asleep while moored to stanchions and looked every bit the pirate ship docked and tied down with heavy ropes. The ropes actually swung about as the Living Ship tossed and rolled; dreaming possibly of a painful and vicious attack by those unwanted peckers; those nasty, flying and pecking Ciakar. And oh the serious pain caused by a door-jam or worse - a hull breach. These dreams gave the Living Ship the creeps but life wasn't so bad - not with revelations like *all in green did my love go riding* and yes he did know green and, on occasion, he did know love and friendship. And he was sterile or so claimed the email to Peter, Alice and Fulton.

They knew the drill. Stand in an athletic position with knees bent and elbows raised so as to stabilize your center of gravity and then wait for dematerialization, the beam and then self-assembly aboard Captain Barbosa's spaceship.

Just everyday stuff for Peter, Alice and Fulton - the Gray Captain Barbosa and his crew of six taking them for a six minute and six second ride to Baldy Mountain followed by dematerialization, the beam and then self-assembly into the Mutant's huge chamber where they would cast eyes upon what is the sleeping stud and spoiled child that defines our Living Ship.

The tail-wagging Fulton was the first to approach and, not realizing that the Living Ship was napping (it is kind of hard to tell), greeted the Ship with a loud and friendly bark and a raised paw for the handshake (the proper protocol according to dogs everywhere). The bark echoed throughout the chamber and everyone was startled and so the Ship suddenly rose and lurched back on its tethered moors so as to test their strength. The ropes lost so the Ship ascended with ropes dangling down on an unscheduled flight to the top of the chamber where it bumped its whittle head and, after the long pause of a wide-eyed and startled baby, did the Ship begin to cry.

Ten is the number of seconds that it took for the baby blubbering Ship to descend from the mean ceiling ('bad ceiling' - we used to say this to our kids). And, while descending, while accompanied by the familiar '10... 9... 8... *etcetera*' countdown, did Peter comment, "What a wuss of a Ship!" and, speaking off the top of his head because his mouth is located on the top of his head, did a Mutant say, "He is going to have a puffy lip. We should put some ice on it right away."

Yes, no one can read the lips of the Mutants unless they are looking over the top and the 'food-for-thought' joke has been whispered way too many times whilst dinning formally with the Mutants. The Mutants refused anatomical prevarication and so, after the initial evolutionary shock, they exhibited an attitude of nonchalance. They actually found delight in catching raindrops or talking up to trees without having to move their heads. Pride and their positive attitude lead to some features of Ship design in their likeness and hence the bruised and baby bloody lip of the blubbering child of a Ship.

A bucket of ice was tilted over and ice fell as an icy rain aimed at the Living's Ship mouth so as to hopefully numb the lips and perhaps stop the crying. It worked to a certain extent and so the Living Ship sat back on its moors and simply sniffled as the pain receded and self-repair began. Within seconds, the lip was healed but the Ship still whimpered on for the social media drama of it all.

Fulton approached the Ship again and this time offered a paw for a handshake but without the welcoming bark and this gesture seemed to help calm the Ship but still the welcoming doors of the Living Ship remained steadfastly closed.

"Would you please open your doors and welcome the new cleaning crew."

"No."

The head Mutant (get it?) then spoke to the ceiling while looking directly at Peter, Alice and Fulton.

"These Living Ships can be quite stubborn."

And so, just like Picard on the Enterprise did the head Mutant say to the roof, "Meet me in my Ready Room."

Nine is the number of conferees present in the Ready Room - six Mutants, Peter, Alice and Fulton. The Mutants have had plenty of practice with mixed company namely the Reptilians and so six small and soft pillows had been placed on the table. The Mutants, for the love of transparency, would lean over the table's edge and carefully place their foreheads on the pillow such that their spoken words could be heard directly. Still, missing are the telltale eye movements - the furrowing of a brow for instance - but the lateral voice was preferred to the vertical voice and the effort was much appreciated by Peter and Alice. Fulton had jumped into his chair and he sat with ears erect and, as for the talking mouths, he didn't seem to mind (although I personally find the whole scene a bit creepy).

Mouth Number Three started the proceedings with, "We have had this problem before with this particular Ship."

Now it sounds fortuitous and it actually is like totally fortuitous that Alice has had some real time experience with coaxing Living Ships into the participation of assigned tasks. She had indeed convinced a Living Ship of its job description - the transport of a Reptilian baseball team back to its home on Gliese 4. Her secret weapon was, of course, the irresistible endorphins released from a warm and freshly baked batch of chocolate chip cookies and hence her jump-the-gun question, "Have you tried chocolate chip cookies?"

"Of course," said Mouth Number One.

"No go," said Mouth Number Six.

Now I was frankly surprised and so was Peter that Alice was not surprised when the famed and dependable cookies did not work on this particular Ship and actually, no one in this room would be surprised if they knew what Alice knew about variations in chocolate chip cookie recipes and so Alice sat for awhile with like her index fingers pressed against her temples as if she was trying to make some kind of like psychic retrieval of relevant data which may apply scientifically the appropriate variant and no one knows how (not even Alice) but she spoke out-of-turn as if inspired and so, while the Mouths mumbled on the table, did Alice abruptly question, "Did you try the oatmeal variant?"

There was this collective gasp in the Ready Room as if the purpose here was to suck all the air out of the room. The six Mutant Mouths gasped with Alice's revelation and so did Peter gasp while Fulton chewed vigorously on a "peanut butter bone" (a little bit of peanut butter smeared on a chew toy for to keep Mr. Fulton out of trouble).

Eight is the number of extra large chocolate chunk oatmeal cookies baked in the Mutant's Chamber and seven is the number of seconds it took for the Living Ship to release its doors and lower its loading ramp for formal greeting and entry. Six is the number of Mutants - three on either side - who cheered upward because they could cheer upward at the lifting of the crane, which held fast to the plate of eight cookies that were unceremoniously dropped into the eager mouth of the Living Ship followed by eight gallons of whole and warm milk.

Peter and Alice pushed their rattling and raucous cleaning carts with the jangling mops and the splashy solutions and they paraded past the applauding Mutants toward the welcome ramp. Fulton pranced behind but passed them up on the ramp and so he was the first to enter the spacious chamber that was the single living room for occupancy aboard the Living Ship. The ramp closed quickly behind Peter and Alice

- so quickly in fact that one of the Mutants was knocked to the floor and so five is the number of baffled and concerned Mutants standing before what could be, in their estimation, either a puerile prank or an actual kidnapping!

The ramp closed behind Peter, Alice and Fulton and four is now the number of sentient beings aboard and, "three... two... one..." bellowed the Living Ship as the ceiling of the Mutant's huge chamber began to open to the outside. The Living Ship initiated its launch sequence and, once again, the rope bindings are ripped from their moors as the Ship slowly rose toward the big ass hole in the ceiling above.

"No, this wasn't supposed to happen," said one Mutant to another.

"Must be a malfunction," said the other Mutant in reply.

www.ingramcontent.com/pod-product-compliance
Lightning Source LLC
Chambersburg PA
CBHW071717140626
46557CB00012B/909